Look and Tremble

Ocheesee Oaks,
Apalachicola
River

EERLE
BOWDEN
'94

Also by Jesse Earle Bowden

Earle Bowden: Drawing From an Editor's Life. More than Forty Three Years of Cartoons, Caricatures and Illustrations, Pensacola News Journal, 1950s-1990s, 1996.

Gulf Islands: The Sands of All Time, Preserving America's Largest National Seashore, 1994.

When You Reach September: An Editor's West Florida Essays and Other Episodic Echoes, 1990.

The Write Way: Editor's Guidebook for Students of Writing, 1990.

Pensacola: Florida's First Place City (Photographs by Gordon Norman Simons and Sandra L. Johnson), 1989.

Iron Horse in the Pinelands: Building West Florida's Railroad: 1881-1883, Virginia Parks, Editor, 1982.

Always the Rivers Flow: Deliberately a Memoir, Essays on West Florida Heritage by a Pensacola Newspaper Editor, 1979.

Florida in the Civil War: 1860 Through Reconstruction. With Alan Rick and other members of the Civil War Round Table of Pensacola, 1961.

Emerald Coast Review. The Fifth Annual Collection: West Florida Authors and Artists. Co-Editor with Donna Freckmann, 1993.

Emerald Coast Review. The Sixth Collection: West Florida Authors and Artists. Co-editor with Seldon Pierce, 1995.

Emerald Coast Review, The Seventh Collection: West Florida Authors and Artists. Co-editor with Bonnye Stuart, 1997.

Emerald Coast Review, The Ninth Collection, West Florida Authors and Artists. Co-editor with Margret Hildreth, 1999.

JESSE EARLE BOWDEN

Look and Tremble

A Novel of
West Florida

Portions of this novel were published originally as short stories in another form in *Emerald Coast Review*, Volumes II, III, IV, VI, VII, West Florida Literary Federation, Pensacola, Florida.

06 05 04 03 02 01 00 / 10 9 8 7 6 5 4 3 2 1

Manufactured in the United States of America by

FATHER & SON
PUBLISHING, INC.
4909 North Monroe Street
Tallahassee, Florida 32303
800-741-2712
http://www.fatherson.com
e-mail lance@fatherson.com

For my loving family—wife Mary Louise,
sons Steve and Randy,
granddaughter Jessica,
and the good people of a small place I call Ring Jaw.

Contents

Look and Tremble

Ochlopee Oak,
Apalachicola
River

'94

Prologue

The knife.

The knife cut.

Grandpa's old pocket knife.

Worn and thinned, honed by whetstone, the Barlow blade of tempered steel tightly hinged between brown bone.

The knife has not been used in thirty years.

Now an artifact of remembrance, the knife of the strong Old Man who became legend.

My fingers feel the knife's heft—as if fitted for Grandpa's strong fingers. I feel the cutting edge—once sharp as Grandpa's old straight razor ... sharp enough to slice sheets of paper or whittle persimmon wood into honest, primitive artistry ... or cut open the belly of a scalded shoat suspended from gallows on a frostbitten, hog-killing morning.

A man could carve a country boy's slingshot from a pinewood board or a forked limb sheared from a sweet gum. Or slice a chewer's jaw of tobacco from a store-bought plug of Brown Mule as if it were cow butter. Or castrate male pigs with surgical swiftness amid squealed raw pain and blind loss.

The knife is much on my mind now.

Long time ago the knife became my sentimental symbol of the Old Man.

The knife's ancient endurance bespeaks a man's survival in an age and a small place: the Old Man's time of hateful hardship and—as Grandma bemoaned—his hell with the heathen.

Sharpness of the blade and the chipped bone handle resurrect fear and courage and vengeance and inner soul of the Old Man calling the Barlow his tater blade and frog sticker.

The antique whispers episodes of the now far distant West Florida pineywoods—raw violence and bloodshed and blind courage in Grandpa's wilderness of the heathen.

Holding Grandpa's knife, remembering a life, reflecting on stories and legends of distant time, I hear words of the Prophet Isaiah from Grandma's Good Book:

And thou shalt be brought down, and shalt speak out of the ground, and thy speech shall be low out of the dust, and thy voice shall be, as of one that hath a familiar spirit, out of the ground, and thy speech shall whisper out of the dust.

—dust of a far distant river valley, phantoms brooding, mourning.

I hear them still in a thin summery wind, sweeping sun-parched sandbed streets of a small crossroads settlement of boyhood; green fields of corn and sugarcane and peanut vines; live oaks bearded with Spanish moss and casting aged gray silhouettes on the rim of ivory-blue skies; thickets of slender longleaf yellow pine—tall and lean and soldierly ranked, speared by slanting shafts of sun; and vine-tangled sand banks of a narrow, crystal river flowing cool dark water through time and memory.

—a river haunted, whispering ghostly laments.

The Old Man fixes his eyes on the dark green foliage fencing the river. "Hear it?"

"What is it?"

"Hear the wind, the river"—

"What?"

—*"Sometimes rain. Sometimes storm brews. Sometimes strange torment"*—

"The river?"

"Yes. River meanness"—
"I still don't hear."
—*"Sometimes just a cool breeze. Sometimes a whisper. Sometimes damnation."*
"I don't hear at all."
"You will, boy. Someday you will."

I hear now by the river, skeletal oak shadows shrouding eternal currents. Dark moody water frames mirrors of yesterdays, animates old legends, resurrects fragments of cursed reality.

—a river day and night cool and sweet, fusing me with fresh pulsating vitality of nature's soul and man's unrelenting spirit—webbed and reborn in the gold of sun and the silver of moon. Old phantoms moan and whisper, stirring the dust of ancestors with muted terror of old bleeding wounds.

Grandpa's old Barlow.

Just a rusting relic: keepsake of my yearning; of the mainstream of remembrance—flowing hauntingly as a dark brooding river I knew in innocence.

In a time of harsh discovery.

And an awakening.

The knife cut.

The knife.

And whisper out of the dust.

Why do the heathen rage?

Somewhere down the endlessly winding tunnel of pine, wading cypress and white flowering magnolia runs the river.

Who owns the river?

Wind, rain, creatures then—now, time timeless.

Time of earthly sweep, of unending ages—fusing past with tomorrow; of soul, sorrow, shadows, eternity, now.

The Old Man and the river speak, an echo drenching my soul:

"Remember, you make your own memories.

"Don't run with the heathen."

Part One
The Journey

EARLE BOWDEN '95

1

Ring Jaw

"Look'n Tremble, huh?" The gasoline pump operator giggles. He flicks cold dead ash from a cigarette, and curls pale lips into a crinkled grin. Redundant words worm through smoke in the dewy haze of sunshot dawn. "Down yonder on the ol Chapully, eh?"

Hunky Hoggen sees a husky stranger with rust-red hair and freckled arms driving the weathered gray Ford sedan, suddenly in morning stillness, asking about the river shoal. Echoes of the chugging engine fall to silence.

"Yessir, Rivah Road's blacktopped all the way cross the Chipola...folks in olden times said *Chapully*. Just turn down yonder at Willis Bridge. Foller the sand trail long the rivah. You'll see white water. Hear it, too. Purty place."

Gasoline gushes into the tank, and Hunky tightens his knotted, sun-bitten jaws. Gnats about his face whine like tiny saws. He squints brown bloodshot eyes shadowed by a greasy sweat-ridged red visor of a frayed Rebel Oil cap patched with a Saint Andrew's Cross flag starred with the galaxy of the Confederate States of America. "Say, Mistah—you from roun heah somers?"

"No sir. I live in New Orleans." The driver's eyes sweep the crossroads of the West Florida town. He

9

squints, looking through the open window, then the insect-pocked windshield. "But I know this place. Born here. Spent my boyhood here, and along the banks of the Chipola—"

"Hell, you say!" Hunky speaks hoarsely. "I thought I knowed most folk roun heah."

Hunky stoops, casting a reed-thin shadow on the car. He stares at the driver. The Rebel Oil cap partially obscures a bony, hatchet face; yet the dinged colors spill onto long, knotted arms—embroidered with blue and red veins of the tattoo artist from wrists to biceps: an American flag and eagle, an oriental dragon spitting flames, a U.S. Navy anchor; bosomy nude female figure. "What's yo name?"

"Cahoon. Chance Cahoon."

"Cahoon, huh? Heared that name. Any your folks live roun heah?"

"Oh, no. My folks long gone." Chance glances at the gasman, exposing liquid brown eyes and more of his strong square leathery face measled with freckles. "In the dust of Chipola Cemetery." He nervously taps a plastic charge plate on the door panel with his red-knuckled left hand. "In the dust ... long gone."

"Last of a breed, eh?" Hunky mutters, the pale wings of his nose aflicker. He giggles and squeezes the pump nozzle trigger, draining fuel into the tank. He shifts his gangling legs sheathed in faded denim pants, tight at a flat waist with a brown leather belt and an oversized circular brass buckle sculpted as a coiled rattlesnake. Hunky scrapes leather soles and tapered heels of scuffed oxblood-and-tan cowboy boots over the sand-gritted, oil-stained pavement. The gasman persists: "Who was yo pa?"

"Lived with my grandfather down on River Road," Chance says. "Called him Uncle Sol. Solomon Cahoon's been dead thirty years." Chance gazes at dully weathered buildings clustered at the crossroads.

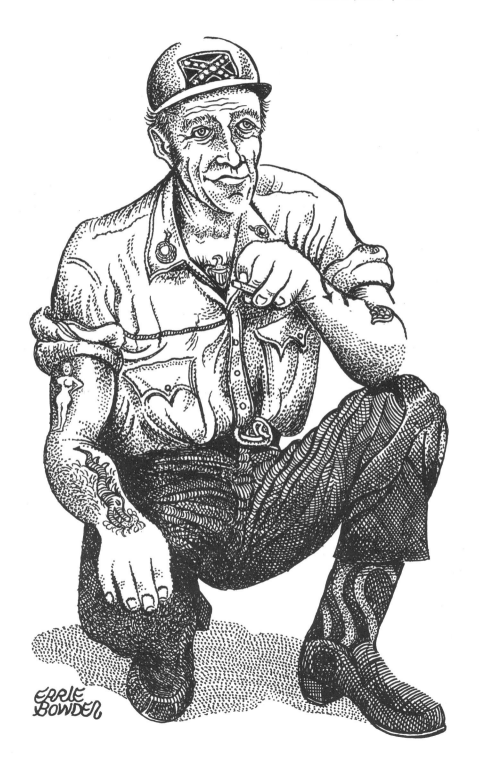

"*Yeah*, I heared of him! Uncle Sol! Ol man of Ring Jaw." Hunky wheezes words in a suppressed cough, spitting a ghostly residue of smoke. "*Yessir!* Helluva legend roun these rivah woods. Real much of a man, I'm told. Folks still talk about how damned tough he was—tougher'n whiteleather. Afeared of nawbody. Yessir, folks roun heah say they don't make men like Uncle Sol no more."

Chance nods. "So they say. He taught me about life. Taught me about growing up."

"Yessir, taught lots of folks lots of thangs in his time." The tattooed man's eyes remain on Chance. The driver's vision is a clot of roadside buildings, wood porched houses, leafy yards and live oak, pecan and pine trees shaping the small town of Ring Jaw.

Hefty feller under broad shoulders, Hunky figures, gazing at the silhouetted back of Chance in a blue chambray shirt. *Maybe forty-five*—thick neck, flecks of gray peppering a wiry pelt of red hair, freckled brow, sharply chiseled coppery face.

The July sun smothers morning mist, hurrying humidity thickening still stale air embracing the Ring Jaw Rebel Oil Service Station and Garage. Oily metallic odors of the auto-repair shed waft over stained pavement, rising from dismantled bowels of a pulpwood truck suspended on a hydraulic lift ... as if the garage were a surgical ward awaiting a doctor's return.

Chance waits. The pump groans; electronic numbers speed gallons and price. The gas station hugs the crossroads corner in the shadow of a two-story, whitewashed masonry building with red-trimmed letters spaced below the roof line: Chipola Hardware and Lumber Company.

Next door, squeezed between the hardware store and gas station, remnants of what he remembered as the picture show and sweet shop are partially hidden by plywood boards and two-by-fours caked with mildewed, peeling white paint. Above the boarded-up front, a vertical signboard with washed-out letters and fringed with worms of lifeless neon juts up from a rotted marquee sagging over a concrete porch. The letters, now faint outlines, once stood shadowed in red and flashing neon, telling Ring Jaw moviegoers this is the Tupelo Theatre. A wall of plywood hides the sweet shop, where Ring Jaw teenagers once sipped cherry cokes and chocolate milkshakes and gobbled down fifteen-cent hamburgers and stringy french fries.

South of the gas station, across the asphalt river road on the parallel corner, ruptured neon winks Catfish Corner. A porchless, unpainted relic of a building sags with age on the opposite intersection corner. A faded Coca-Cola sign nailed above the screened door announces Apalach Oyster Bar and Pool Room. On the opposite corner, across from the gas station, a clock tower and small asphalted parking lot leads to a glass-fronted, yellow-brick building shaded by a clump of ancient live oaks. Metallic letters on the clock tower sharply contrast the grayed surroundings: First Fayette Bank & Trust, Ring Jaw Branch.

"Sho purty stretch of rivah down yondah," Hunky says, replacing the gas tank cap. He hangs the nozzle on the pump, and writes license plate numbers and totals on the credit-card receipt. "Folks roun heah been tryin to git the state to make Look'n Tremble a park."

The gasman hands the clipboard to Chance. The man from New Orleans writes *Solomon Chance Cahoon* in swirling ballpoint ink with his left hand—a hand scarred between the thumb and forefinger like some cattle brand: a mosaic of seared skin indented and twisted, and zigzagging like a crudely scrawled letter S.

"Look'n Tremble's a popular place these days. Them canoe paddlers run the shoal," Hunky says, his red-rimmed dark eyes fixed on Chance's left hand.

"Pardon me, sir," Chance says, "did you remember the man they're burying here? Roscoe Ransum. Called him Rattler when I was a boy here."

"Yeah, I heared of Rattler Ransum," Hunky says. "Yore kin?"

"My grandfather's friend."

Hunky jerks away his cap, and combs his fingers through sandy tufts of hair stringing thinly over his balding pate. He sweeps sweat from his furrowed brow, coughs deeply, and heaves beads of ropy spittle on the pavement. "Some folks say he was lot like your grandpa. Ol Rattler, they tell me, left this country long time ago. He got cut-up and shot many times. Couldn't kill him with a fat-lighterd knot. He just might been the toughest man evah come outta Chipola Country. Besides your grandpa, cose. Woun up ovah yondah roun the Mississippi line, near Mobile somers. Raisin goats, of all thangs. Folks say ol Rattler got religion—"

"Would you know, sir, how he died?"

"Tragic, really. It was Mistah Elleck Dunkane—that feller up the road yonder usta run that old grocery store—one cross from the schoolhouse—he got word Rattler was dead ovah there in Mobile somers. Somebody musta kilt him."

"Too bad. Sad ending."

"Yessir. Somebody cut his throat; opened his stummick with a knife. Foun Rattler bleedin to death—guts in his fingers—in a trashpile backuh ol jookjoint. Rattler purty old. You know him?"

"No. Not really." Chance looks away. "I remember him when I was a boy. But I won't forget Rattler Ransum. Especially *that* summer—"

"How's that?"

Chance turns away.

"Well, suh, Mistah Cahoon, must know this town. Had real meanuns back'n old days."

"Yes, I know. I know—"

"Why, quieter a graveyard now. Folks livin right. Fishin the rivahs. Huntin birds, chasin widderwomen. Still grow groundpeas and soybeans. Raise cattle. Cut paperwood.

"Shoot, policeman sleeps most time yondah in shade them oaks. Got ourselves a branch bank ovah there."

"I see," Chance says. "Ring Jaw's different. This corner used to be Silas Haymoor's garage—"

"Oil company bought it after ol man Haymoor died. Tore down his garage shed. Hell, this place up an died— closed the picture show yonder. Hasty Ponds who ran the pool room uppen died last year."

"And the post office?"

"Feller heah built the government a fine new brick building up the road north of the old Dunkane store. Ruby Barefoot moved her café there—that ol greasy spoon yonder called Catfish Corner now.

"Shoot, these dirt farmers roun heah walkin in high cotton these days." Hunky laughs. "Buyin condos down on Panama City Beach. Got airplanes, dustin they own peanuts and soybeans. Some hunt deer and elk in Wyomin. Even cruisin down yondah in the islands. Real dirt-road sports these days."

Chance smiles. "No more grunting fish bait, pulling gophers, and making whiskey for a living, eh?"

Hunky giggles, lowers his head, bobbing it repeatedly. "Hell, man—" He looks up, grinning broadly, nicotine teeth yellow as his shirt embroidered with twirling lariats on the dingy collar. The gasman punctuates words with tattooed arms and meaty hands, denimed legs shuffling cowboy boots over the oil-darkened concrete. "Now, suh, wouldn't go that far. Some of them still do. But for some like me it's probably like you member—root hawg or die pore. Yessir, feller can still find a drank of good stumphead likker roun heah if carryin a thirst."

Chance smells sour liquored breath. "And what about those hot-to-trot cross the river girls?"

Hunky snickers. "Shoot, man, you know bout these backwoods!"

"Ought to—"

"Hell, them ol gals still ready to jook evah Saturday night. Say, wanna lil toddy?"

"No—no, thank you," Chance says, laughing. "Never touch it. But I remember. Lord, do I remember smelling that old rotgut. What's the condition of the river?"

"Folks roun heah love that rivah more'n ever. Got some pollution, they say. Hell, still eat them Chipola bass and shellcrackers and stumpknockers if I can get em. Say, heah, feller, Mistah Cahoon—bad scar on your hand. Burnt or somethun? Wounded in the war?"

"No, sir—just a little scratch." Chance smiles, rubbing the scar. "Something I'd rather forget."

"Back fer the funeral, are yuh?"

"Yes—and other reasons. I'm interested in the river," Chance says. He looks south, viewing the wooden stoblike spire of the Chipola Primitive Baptist Church a block away. "I've read the Chipola remains one of the most picturesque and pristine in Florida, but endangered. Shame. The Chipola I remember was wild, always fresh and cool in summer. Always strangely and hauntingly beautiful." Chance hesitates, glancing toward the River Road. "Besides, Chipola Country's important to me."

"You right bout the rivah," Hunky says. "Something's killin it. Aint nothun like she used to be. Somebody upstream's dumpin poison in the water. Some folks say it's pesticide squirted on fields from airplanes."

"Like many of our waterways—used for garbage disposal," Chance says. "Price we pay for our planned obsolescent society—"

"What's that?"

"—or what we Americans like to call progress."

"Hell, aint much heah."

"More than you realize," Chance says. "I'm pleased the road's paved—all I remember was a long winding sandbed road falling off into a valley with an old steel bridge over the river."

"Suppose you know, Mistah Cahoon, lotta strange things happen down roun Look'n Tremble in olden days. Yeah, these ol boys roun heah still scare younguns with that old, old story about the ghost of the peglegged, headless murdered man a'prowlin the woods at night. Evah heared the story of ol Whiskey George Gillwater? Shot off his leg, then cut off his head. Some called him Pegleg George, buried down yonder in three graves."

Chance laughs. "Yes, I've heard the story many times. I suppose many unpleasant stories haunt us. But lots of happy, memorable moments, too, even though the past was never as good as it looks from a distance. The shoal means a great deal to me. You know—when you pass forty, you have an urge to go back, trying to find where you came from—"

"Yessir, already happen to me," Hunky says. "I'm nearly fifty. Been right heah most my damn life, except pullin a hitch in the Navy over'n in Pensacola and few years dredge boatin down roun Apalachicola."

Chance nods. "Sir, are there any descendants of the old black families still here?"

"Few. Most been gone long time—hell, since turpentine played out. They scattered. One time lotta niggers lived down yonder in Shantytown on the old Major MacNab place folks used to call Mulehead Pond Plantation. And that's bout gone now. Colored folks left, they tell me, after one of Major MacNab's turpentine niggers died mysteriously one night in that old calaboose yonder by Mulejaw Branch.

"Folks still talk bout the time somebody give a nigger a drank of whiskey through the bars one night. Town marshal, ol Moses Trottah, foun him cold dead next mornin. Course, later on, suppose you know, we had bad nigger trouble up yondah in Redlands County. Strung up a young buck fer rapin and killin a young white girl. Back'n the thirties."

Chance turns to Hunky. "Yes. I've heard the story."

"Now there's ol Uncle Charley—Charley Crowe, livin down yonder in the edge of Bearthick Swamp. Up'n age, been heah forever, usta dig graves. Hell, saw him last Sunday, walking the highway, going to look after Aunt Hattie—Hattie Santee."

"Aunt Hattie still living?"

"Oh yeah, she's ageless," Hunky says. "Her grandson a hard-workin colored feller livin up river yondah at Ring Jaw Island, name of Willy Buck—"

"*Willy Buck?*"

"He's the grandson of ol Niggertoe Willy Santee and Aunt Hattie. Ever heared of ol Niggertoe?"

"Yes, I have—"

"Call him that cause he had this heah little extra thumb on his left hand. Said it look like them niggertoes we used to get at Christmastime, member?"

Chance frowns.

"Hell," Hunky says, "the law tracked that old rummaker deep in Bearthick Swamp with bloodhounds. Tore open his backside with buckshot."

"My grandfather told me about Willy Santee," Chance says. "And his grandson—Willy Buck and I played together as boys. I remember the old calaboose—"

"*Yeah?*" Hunky rushes his words. "Called that black boy Dink, or Nig. His pa Willy Frank Santee killed in the war. Uncle Charley mostly raised him. Boys roun heah used say, 'Nig dance a jig!' Couldn't say that now— Willy Buck's a man of means, now—fine feller. He enlisted in the Army and was in a lotta that hard fightin in Korea. He went up yonder to that Chipola Springs

College, then went in bidness haulin pulpwood for the Port St. Joe mill. He's gotta crew cuttin cross the river now. Ol jail you mentioned still yonder up from the branch, back'un the pool room."

Chance sighs. "Aw, memories, so fleeting. Thomas Wolfe said you can't go home again. But I suppose, as we know the long years, we are driven inwardly, desperately searching our true self."

"Thomas who?"

Chance pauses. "Wolfe, Thomas Wolfe. North Carolina writer."

"You a writer?"

"Of sorts. Hardly in the big leagues with Wolfe. He wrote *Look Homeward, Angel*."

Hunky's back straightens. He tosses the burned-out cigarette to the pavement, and mashes the damp butt with a boot heel. "Hell, man, sholly aint nothun to write bout roun heah. Aint no angels neither. Just us po raggedy-ass country folks workin our fingers to the bone. Like Pa used to say, he was a patch-seated son of a dirt farmer with mean poor land and six-cent cotton. Only view was the daily look at a mule's bunghole slowly movin down a plowed furrow—"

Chance turns, curls his lips into a smile.

"—and drankin good beaded white whiskey, and chasin them hongry widderwomen Saturday night."

Chance jerks with laughter.

"Hell, man, folks roun heah too poor to paint and too proud to whitewash. Folks with shoes look at us like we aint got none—"

Chance still laughs.

"—and us ol heathen and them saved and sanctified Holiness churchfolks payin the preacherman for our sins on Sunday mawnin. That's bout all, except for pool hustlin, cooter-giggin, and whiskey drankin. Sure you don't wanna join me for a little mawnin nip?"

Chance chuckles. He turns the ignition key. A glint of sunlight strikes the gasman's red-veined eyes. "*Heathen? Holiness?* Ring Jaw's not changed. Still the good life—"

"Say, capm, preciate yo bidness. Yessir. And hurry back, Mistah Cahoon. Hope you find what you lookin for."

"Thank you. Good place to begin is the river and Look and Tremble."

Hunky Hoggen giggles, lighting another cigarette. "Good place for ghosts."

"Yes, ghosts."

The Ford engine hums in the morning stillness as Chance pulls away from the gas pump. He brakes momentarily, parking on the edge of the River Road. His eyes hurriedly search:

Ring Jaw, then:

a smear of squatting, porched storefronts: Chipola Drugs and Sundries, Dixie Bus Stop, Ruby's Café, Hasty's Pool Hall, Silas Haymoor's garage, Tupelo Theatre, the one-chair barber shop; and a long shadowy porch a smudge of Oakwood benches, rocking chairs and rosiny overalled old codgers with lipped snuff and corroded black-briar pipes. And jabbering and laughter of rhythmic whittlers comparing wood artistry and whispering gossipy embellishments in the lonesome heat of the day.

Yes, Ring Jaw, back then:

as it must be still—a small ageless place hard by the road now grayed and patched with inky pancakes of asphalt, between spreading fields, sleepily clinging to vanished night, washed by the dew of darkness; yet stolidly alive awakening another day like all days.

A small spot at a crossroads with cool running creeks and deep-sand pigtrails hot to a barefooted boy's feet—feet festered with unseen sandspurs; a town transformed from decay of withered years, refocused with unfamiliar landmarks now strangely obscuring images plucked from boyhood memory; a town grasping for notice and purpose in West Florida backcountry and bypassed in fleeting mobility of asphalt-swept haste—its yawning desire now signaled ironically by a red-and-yellow light suspended over the intersection, winking traffic warnings ceaselessly.

Ring Jaw, remember:
the unpainted pinewood post office squatting on the crossroads nook, now winking broken-neon Catfish Corner. A treasurehouse of hardware and store-bought novelties lining shelves of a mercantile store across the road—now a porchless, unkempt pine-planked antique reduced to oyster-shucking and pool hustling.

Always the pool room—
Back then, there were two—one a dusty corner of Ruby's Café; the other Hasty Ponds', reeking with sour stale bottled beer and smoky stink of whiskey drinkers and rum runners animating the place with chattering voices and robust laughter and hard striking numbered balls over the green felt of two tables. The noise and the voices mix with lonesome lyrical phrasings of nasally country singers lamenting hard-luck times and blues of faded and fractured love from a three-for-a-quarter Wurlitzer jukebox.

Yonder, the cemetery:
There, unseen: on the grassy slope up from Mulejaw Creek, graves of my forebears in shadows of the granite tomb of Major Malcolm Grant MacNab etched with the Southern Confederacy motto, *Deo Vindice,* and capped with spreading wings of an American eagle in bronzed flight. There still, beneath the old gray stones: the major's daughter, Savannah, next to her husband of fifty years, Jeremiah Jackson Cahoon, who helped the one-armed major defend Chipola Springs against Yankee invaders. And in the deep clay beside them, my grandparents,

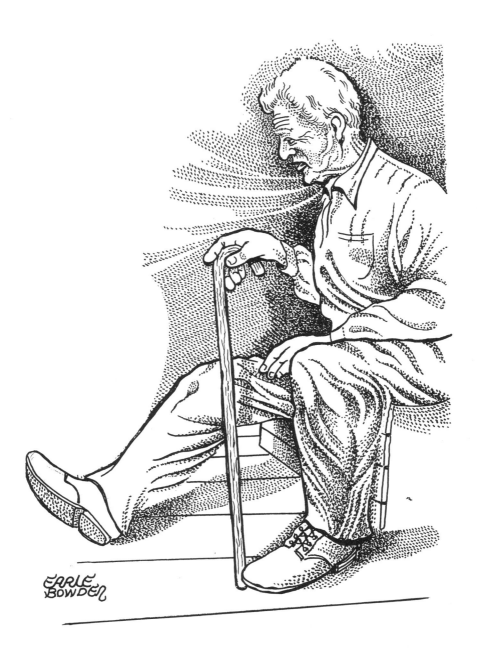

Solomon Jackson Cahoon and Sarah Rachel Dunkane Cahoon. Many are the graves, sloping down to Mulejaw Creek, including Grandpa's only son, Uncle Adam Amos Cahoon. And Grandpa's two brothers Paul Zachary Cahoon and Silas Simon Cahoon. *Whispers out of the dust of the cemetery spreading a bone orchard beneath the sun, mossy oaks and glossy magnolias—granite stones, wooden markers, and rowed seashells bleached ivory white, decorating mounds of red clay. Whispers I hear seeking the spirit of the singing shoal, which long ago washed to the sea the dust and bones of Shawn Solomon Cahoon—long-forgotten redheaded Irishman and American Army scout for General Andrew Jackson, and his Creek Indian princess with dark dancing eyes he first saw in the light of a campfire at Look and Tremble. And now, going into the red clay, as if the family graveyard ghosts drew him to their bosom—Rattler Ransum.*

South, beyond the church and the cemetery, the road to Estiffanulga fades into a pine-green horizon, hiding wet flatwoods of slim limbless saplings and a moist underworld populated with Chipola Crawlers, most desired earthworms of South Alabama fishermen harvesting rivers, sloughs and limestone-sink lakes veining the broad wedge between the Chipola and Apalachicola rivers.

Grandpa grunted fishbait in the dark moist bogs of what he calls River Styx south of the old plantation fields; yes, remember: rotting bones of a turpentine distillery bleaching beside the tracks of the Red Level Railroad line near the old cypresshead pond. And Mulehead Plantation, owned by Major MacNab, Great Grandma Savannah's Alabama-born Scotsman father who rode with Nathan Bedford Forrest, led militia at the Battle of Chipola Springs and built the railroad; a shingle-roofed family house with broad verandas shaded by canopies of pecan trees; nearby a string of clapboard, open-windowed cabins ringing the root-tangled banks of a limestone-sink lake shaped like the head of a beast of burden ... a beast working and sweating with white and black men in pineywoods during Hard Times, which Grandpa said hung misery on folks like beggar's lice. Yes, misery in Shantytown, on the edge of a pond where turpentine black folks hooked catfish from dark waters...sometimes red with blood of black bodies slashed with pocket knives and straight razors, and fished from its boggy shallows amid cries of sorrowful women and before stark hollow frightened eyes of barefooted children.

Chance turns onto the River Road bordered by weedy vegetable gardens, chinaberry trees, crape myrtles, and flowering Althea hibiscus.

Yonder, a two-story limestone building, vivid in his memory as the Ring Jaw Mercantile Company, stands ghostly decadence: dilapidated, abandoned, its once cool shaded porch a junkheap of castoff washing machines, refrigerators, and rusting stoves; rock walls chipped and pocked; window glass shattered; scabs of paint peeled from a bay-window facade; sheets of tin on the angled porch roof curled and twisted and rusted. *Strange. Once throbbing heart of country-town trading and bartering now stilled. Store skeleton eroded by age; frayed and tortured by sun and wind and storm: remnant of another age, bypassed in haste of generations, now an ancient artifact—harboring phantoms from the silent seeping old dead time.*

Chance looks beyond the store to cracked crossties and rusting steel rails—the weedy, tie-gapped roadbed of the Red Level Railroad Company's short freight line. *We younguns called it the Red Devil*, hooting through flat fields and pine thickets of the Red Level farming plateau, along twenty-seven track miles joining Ring Jaw on the north with Chipola Springs, the region's major

WILLY BUCK
SANTEE

agricultural-market-city and Redlands County seat, and on the south with Estiffanugla, Fayette County seat with sawmills along the Apalachicola River on ground where the last Seminole Indians claimed valley swamps bordering Florida's largest river.

Sad. The decaying debris of a railroad. Grandpa loved the soft, hoarse song of steam like an old Jimmie Rodgers lonesome blue-yodel tune: creaking, rhythmic iron wheeling over trembling earth—propelled by an inferno leaping flames and bowels snorting hissing power; voice clanging brass-bell echoes of lonesome, laboring journeys through wilderness with endless thickets of verdant pine and cypress.

There are no automobiles on the roads; Chance moves under the winking traffic light and pulls to the edge of the River Road.

Three pickup trucks are on the curb at Catfish Corner. A middle-aged man stands in the poolroom door, a shadowy speck of grayed beard and khaki grasping a straw broom. The July morning awakens; soon so will Ring Jaw.

Trees and tangled summer foliage of Mulejaw Branch partially obscure the town's brown-rock calaboose. The single-cell jail was, even in Chance's boyhood, a legendary landmark—ominous, dark mysterious Florida frontier relic of hardcase turpentine-era justice when the twentieth century awakened.

Chance remembers: *Willy Buck—barefooted black boy with happy eyes and white-toothed, twisted grin and two insulting names—Dink and Nig. Here he goes, brown spindly-legged caboose of a ragtag clot of summertime adventuring younguns on hot, deep-rutted sand streets in the small world of Ring Jaw. There's Ben Henry Swinnard, nicknamed Pigpen—his father Shadrack raised and butchered hogs—and R.C. Hickery called Hickernut, playing in the*

Pine Thicket, whirling on the long pine log atop a stumptop Flying Jenny; darting through pines with cap pistols and clothespin rubber guns; all four of us making up our summer adventure even as the world far from Ring Jaw fractured into war.

Chance hurries by green yaupon hedges, fig trees with swollen ripe fruit, and grassy lawns with crape myrtle and oleander rioting over gardens of wooden and brick houses bordering the River Road.

He passes the white-walled Pentecostal Holiness Church, standing where he remembered a rough-hewn pinewood tabernacle squatting on the edge of a thicket watered by Mulejaw Branch. *Mulejaw, winding snakily through the valley, spilling into the river at Cooter Landing. Yes, remember: naked as a jaybird, sailing off a live-oak limb—bellybuster! And the tabernacle: hot July nights and hellfire sermons burning heathen ears, and sawdust stirring and hot rattling breaths and emotions and rhythmic contortions of worshipers thoating Hal-lay-lew-yah!*

He speeds by a Florida Forestry Service observation tower, following the serpentine River Road, moving into the edge of a valley patched with sloping red fields, leaving Ring Jaw—awakening its morning—in the distance.

Ring Jaw. And down this road, the river.

On the grassy edge of the roadway, a gathering of buzzards peck reddened beaks at fragments of flesh on the ribs of the shoat carcass.

In a corn patch spilling over the valley, a crow caws a gravelly protest and wings away.

Hunky stands by the pump, greasy fingers sweeping sweat from his brow. He squints tight eyes in sunlight, searching the River Road long after the Ford with the Louisiana license plate moves away. Now, the car's gone—vanishing into the valley with sloping pinewoods spreading to banks of a narrow river.

The Chipola
flowing yonder:
south from Alabama creek-trough headwaters through limestone depressions of Redlands and Fayette counties, slithering a narrow spout of dark brooding water over the valley floor into the densely forested alluvial plain with creek-riddled fingers watering cypress-rooted swamps, and bleeding into the wide brown Apalachicola, snaking seaward to the Gulf of Mexico.

And Look'n Tremble.
Chance Cahoon asked; now he's gone.
Cahoon. Ol mossback riverrat, Uncle Solomon. And Rattler Ransum, Chipola country's biggest hellraiser—real bull of the woods.
Sheeit, shoulda knowed that man. No wondah I was puzzled about his scarred hand. Suppose he was that snotnose youngun didn't have no daddy? Hell, musta been that boy wild and restless Rebecca Rachel Cahoon had heah long time ago after runnin roun with ol Rattler Ransum. Sholly ol Rattler was the nigger in that woodpile. Evahbody called him Lil Sol. Hell, nevah thought he'd mount to nothun. Aint thought about him in a coon's age.

Hunky turns nervously. The smell of breakfast at Catfish Corner fills his nostrils. Across the street, the screened door of the pool room whines. The day's first shooters arrive.

Another gawddam scorcher. Hotter'n hell's half acre. Hotter'n them biscuits and coffee I swallered before daybreak yondah cross the road. Damn place gonna come alive again, them dirt farmers and widderwomen sweatin and yappin bout heat. And them loafin old good-fer-nothing boys ovah yondah at th pool hall smart-mouthin and swiggin beer like a pig suckin an ol sow's tit.

*That redheaded feller had to be old Rattler's bastard.
Wait'll Rooster Reddoake hears who's done come back....*

"Mawnin, Hunky."

Hunky turns quickly, watching mechanic R.C. Hickery
in grease-smeared overalls wobble across the road from
Catfish Corner. The moon-faced, round-shouldered,
heavy-hipped man with tight brown eyes and
salt-and-pepper hair grins as he walks into the shadows
of the cluttered garage. A toothpick moves with his lips:
"How's your hammer hanging?"

Hunky's eyes turn back to the River Road,
momentarily ignoring the burly mechanic who learned
his trade working on jalopies under Ring Jaw shadetrees.
*Grease monkey R.C., lardass, living with the crazy name,
Hickernut.*

"Oh, howdy, Hickernut," Hunky says through a puff
of smoke. "Willy Buck wants the truck today."

"Hell, I know that, Hunky. What's the matter? Looks
like you've seen a friggin ghost."

"Yeah, man. Ghost. That what it was. You see
Rooster?"

"That sonofabitch Nub Reddoake still feeding his face
over yondah. And a'braggin like always. Never knew a
bastard hated the world more."

Rufus Reddoake, known in Ring Jaw for most of his
forty eight years as simply Rooster, tugs at the curled
brim of a straw cattleman's hat. He pulls a paunchy body
through the doorway of Catfish Corner into morning sun.
He belches. A khaki shirt salted with sweat rings girds
his protruding belly, now swollen with fried eggs, grits,
ham, buttermilk biscuits and black coffee. Aged denim
jeans, grayed by time and wear, hang on broad hips and
curve around a thick midsection and loosely sheath stumpy
legs and scuffed woodland boots. Sprigs of gray line his

bushy brown sideburns, framing a sun-bronzed jowly face with tight hazel eyes and hawk-like nose. Rooster tugs at the elastic band holding the folded portion of his left sleeve, ever conscious of the stump severed above the elbow.

Rooster seems always seething with nervous anger. He never lets folks in Ring Jaw forget how his father, Elijah (Lige) Reddoake, was wrongly convicted of murder. He's quieter now, but no one really knows when he may unleash into another temper spasm.

Poolroom loafers, beer drinkers and eight-ball shooters whisper other descriptive sobriquets for Rooster behind his back: Dominecker, Hacker, Machete, Nub. Mostly Nub.

Nicknames Hacker and Machete really fuel his rage. He still feels the machete blade butchering his arm, severing a mass of meat hanging from bloodied tatters of skin. He tries to forget the rainy chilled night he felt the fever of death, looking up into a deputy sheriff's flashlight from the muddy ditch on the Estiffanulga highway after he'd been tossed from the cab of his pickup trunk. In a frenzied, painful flight, racing from the Buttermilk Hill jookjoint, he had lost control of the steering wheel; the tires had skidded on the wet pavement and the truck had swerved off the asphalt, severing two pine trees and bucking to a steaming halt with him mired in mud and oozing blood. And, awakening on the surgeon's table, crying out in a drunken lament that the arm was gone.

At first, when the amputation healed, he'd strap a steel hook on the stump, heightening fear he wanted to leave in his path. But the angered county judge ordered the hook confiscated after Rooster punctured a pool shooter's neck in a fight at the Silver Dollar Bar south of Estiffanulga. Now Rooster never steps into his jeans without a pearl-handled switchblade knife he bought in a

Chipola Springs pawn shop. The knife bulges in his back pocket.

Sometimes gawkers stare at his empty sleeve. He caresses the rounded nub, saying he still feels stubby fingers on the hand maimed by a machete and removed by an Estiffanulga surgeon. He calls the stump a nub with a wink and a snicker. Others using the nickname risk triggering Rooster's temper and flashing switchblade.

Rooster pushes the hat back on a balding head, and relights a half-smoked cheroot cigar. Through the smoke he sees the slender man by the gas pump across the road.

The one-armed man steps into the cab of a black Ford pickup, slams the door, hesitates, belches again and turns, suddenly grinning in self-amusement: The long drink-of-water with tattooed arms stands alone with sun radiating blue and red of the Southern emblem of his oil-darkened cap. *Haywood Hunky Hoggen. Haywood, hell! He's just plain old Hunky, best known for hunkerin down to most anythang—specially hongry widderwomen and rotgut drinkin whiskey. Ol Hunky, wakin up in a Pensacola whorehouse bed with a woman weighin two hundred pounds, black as midnight. And him scamperin out a window with his Navy uniform and shoes in his hands as police raided the place. Musta been a helluva sight—barenekkid as the day borned. Tattoos everywhere but his pecker, and I aint too sure bout that. Ol Hunky Hoggen, you redneck pissant peckerwood. Been a pain in the ass all my natural life.*

Rooster wheels the truck across the road and pulls alongside the gas pumps. He clears his throat in a small cloud of cigar smoke, and steps from the cab. He yanks the moist cigar from his teeth, yawns lazily, and pushes a arm and nub in a long stretch. "Hunky, who was that feller?"

Hunky giggles. "Solomon Chance Cahoon." He reads the name slowly. "Remember long time ago—that snotnose boy they called Lil Sol?"

"I'm be goddamn. Uncle Sol's boy, huh?"

"Yeah, he mention that old coot."

"Hell, Hunky, he looked like he'd been eatin high on the hawg for a po-ass country boy with such a goddam mean old heathen for a grandpa."

"Said he was a writer. Lives in New Orleans."

"Back for Rattler's funeral, huh?"

"Yeah, wanted to know bout Rattler."

"Where he headed?"

"River. Look'n Tremble."

"Figgers."

"*Huh?*"

"Dammit, Hunky, can't you member nothing? You probably too goddamn drunk that night. You bout half tight now, aint you?"

"Hell no, Rooster, aint drankin. Had a few snorts last night, a lil toddy this mawnin—sheeit, if I member right you was the basturd who was high as a kite that night by the rivah."

Rooster laughs. "Recognize you?"

"Naw, hell, been a long, long time. Sheeit, Rooster, we was shirttail younguns back then."

Rooster snickers, spitting a brown tobacco patch on the concrete. He relights the cigar with a silver Zippo lighter, then drapes his arm stump on Hunky's thin shoulder. "You pissant. If that's Lil Sol, he goddamn shore goin back to the place where he got his baptism—down yondah at the shoal."

"Hell yeah, Rooster," Hunky says, grinning. "He aint forgot that night him and them three other lil peckers met up with Rufus Rooster Reddoake—"

"You held him, Hunky—member? Haywood Hunky Hoggen, scarin that lil youngun out of a year's growth!"

"Me, hell! You did it. Found courage in that pint of likker."

"Naw, come right outta Mason fruitjar."

They laugh.

Rooster turns, looking toward the River Road. "Maybe we just better foller him down yondah. Give him company."

"Yeah, yeah, Rooster. Maybe so."

"Gimme ten dollars' worth regular, Hunky. Put it on Willy Buck's account."

"*Willy Buck?* Now aint that funnier'n hell. Told him he might find Willy Buck down on the river."

"You what?"

"Yeah, he membered Willy Buck. Didn't mention nawbody else but Rattler Ransum."

"Well, Rattler was his pa. And like his sorry old grandpa, that boy always was a nigger lover."

"Yeah, his eyes lit up when I mention Willy Buck."

"Hunky, tell Hickernut to watch the pumps til you get back."

"Sheeit, Rooster," Hunky moans. "Might lose my damn job."

"Go tell him, *dammit!* I'll gas up when we get back. Hell, man, this is an emergency. Might have ourselves a lil reunion at Look'n Tremble. Get'n the cab!"

Hunky removes his cap and sweeps beads of sweat from his brow.

"What's the matter, old buddy?" Rooster says. "You sweatin like a nigger on election day."

"Thinkin about Rattler's funeral. One's enough for such a hot summer day."

Rooster's eyes tighten. "Hell, that sorry old Roscoe Ransum, he never done us no favors. Member that time he called the law on us?"

"Yeah and him goin after you with that machete."

"Bastard finally got what he deserved," Rooster says, spitting cigar smoke. "Get'n the truck. Don't call the undertaker yet."

They laugh.

Hunky jerks his head back, coughs and yells, "Hey, *Hickernut!* Got an emergency. Watch them pumps!"

"Your job, dammit!" R.C. Hickery yells, sweat beading his round face, grease steaking his hands. The mechanic doesn't look up from the bowels of the truck, hearing the shrill voice. Then he straightens, walking into the sunlight. The pickup truck owned by Willy Buck Santee and driven by Rooster Reddoake turns on the River Road, disappearing in the morning quiet.

"*Damn em!*" R.C. Hickery mutters. "Useless as tits on a boar hog."

The clock on the bank tower reads ten minutes to seven o'clock as the green-and-white Fayette County Sheriff's cruiser car slowly approaches the Ring Jaw winking light. Sheriff Ben Henry Swinnard straightens his back and jerks away his smoke-lensed sunglasses. He pushes back his tan Southern cattleman's hat. His blue-green eyes search on both sides of the highway. The driver, Deputy Wiley Widderson, holds a boot on the brake. The sheriff glances toward the garage where a school classmate, R.C. Hickery, changes sparkplugs on the paperwood truck. He lifts his hand, pointing. "Pull in, Wiley. He's usually somers roun heah. Ol Hickernut might know."

The deputy turns off the highway, and drives slowly toward the live oak shadetree behind the garage. He cuts the motor, gliding to a stop in the rear of the Rebel Oil Service Station.

Sheriff Swinnard's not a tall man, but sturdy; the low-crowned hat makes him appear stocky. Graying sandy hair is close-cropped—a crewcut he's worn since he quarterbacked the Ring Jaw High School Wildcats to nine victories, including the much-heralded 36-0 stomping of the Estiffanulga Seminoles. His skin's a shade redder than most men. He usually looks sternly serious behind smoky sunglasses worn winter and summer, but can smile, tell ribald stories and entertain womenfolk. He grew up in Ring Jaw, son of Shadrack Swinnard, who raised and butchered hogs at Cowpen Curve on the river, south of Look and Tremble.

His mother named him Ben Henry, but for boys of Ring Jaw it was first Pig Ben, then Pigpen until the tenth grade. He'd fought many schoolyard battles over the pride-hurting nickname. But when he entered politics, running as a wounded Korean War veteran, everybody came to know him as Ben Henry. The former U.S. Army corporal succeeded in wrestling the sheriff's office from the aging Cicero Turnbull, who had held office since 1936.

He never talks about Korea and his ordeal on the Yalu River, trading gunshots with Chinese troops—that frigid November day when the whole mountainside turned out to be Chinese: some 300,000 Communist troops swarming United Nations positions, swallowing up entire regiments. He had tried to forget the long retreat in the arctic cold of early winter, men bloodied, dying in a nowhere icebox of snow-crusted hills. Then the bullet that shattered his leg bone came as the Chinese advance was finally halted near the 38th parallel, along a rim of low-lying peaks later known as Heartbreak Ridge and Pork Chop Hill.

By the time the U.S. Army surgeon had reconstructed Corporal Swinnard's knee, and he was back in a San Antonio Army hospital, walking the hot parched grounds on crutches, President Harry Truman had fired General Douglas MacArthur for insubordinate lobbying for an all-out war against China. The war had sputtered on for two more years. By then Ben Henry was campaigning across Fayette County, nailing Ben Henry Swinnard election posters to pine trees and fence posts, and reading in the newspapers about the armistice signed at Panmunjom, in the no-man's land between the two front lines.

He never takes chances. The sheriff limps slightly from the stiff knee, stepping softly along the side of the garage. Standing quietly in the garage doorway, the sheriff sees R.C. Hickery's broad rear and stubby legs and the rest of him shadowed by the uplifted truck hood. Ben Henry muffles a weak laugh—*Rupert Calvin Hickery, too overweight to pass an Army physical but a wizard niggerrigging automobiles with haywire, axle grease and socket wrenches. Ol R.C. Hickernut—I'd know that fat ass anywhere.* He exhales a puff of cigar smoke, and pulls the hat brim nearer his eyes. "Morning, R.C."

The mechanic slowly withdraws from the hood. "Why, howdy, Sheriff. What brings you up heah from Estiffanulga? Ol Pigpen homesick?"

Sheriff Swinnard pulls the cigar from his teeth and grins. "Lookin for Rooster, Hickernut."

"Just missed him. Drove off with Hunky somers."

"Know where?"

"Nossir. Didn't say. Took the River Road. Probably going down yonder where Willy Buck's cutting pulpwood. Shouldn't be gone long. Hunky's supposed to be running the gas station. But he loafed off somers. What you want with Rooster? In trouble agin?"

"Just wanna talk with him."

"Guess you going to Rattler's funeral?"

"I'm a pallbearer. He's getting military honors, you know. Bout time he was recognized for serving his country—"

"Helluva thang, Ol Rattler cut to pieces. Man, he was uppen age."

Sheriff Swinnard looks into the sunshine. "Throat cut. Stabbed seventeen times. Face, back, belly. Helluva way to die. Found him in a trashpile at a jookjoint just outside Mobile. I gotta call from the sheriff of Mobile County. Coulda been a fight with another drunk. Coulda been murder—"

"Murder?"

Sheriff Swinnard pauses. "R.C., now don't jump to conclusions. The Mobile sheriff's just exploring possibilities."

R.C. steps slowly to the garage door, his eyes on the gasoline pumps. "Damn that Hunky Hoggen. He knows better'n loaf off. Ben Henry, Mistah Elleck Dunkane told me that Rattler had cleaned up his life these last few years. Didn't drank no more. Nobody'd heard much from him since he left. They must know who did it."

Sheriff Swinnard hesitates. "Don't know. You say Rooster just left?"

"Yeah. You know he works for Willy Buck."

"Behaving himself?"

"Far's I know, Sheriff. But I heard him and Hunky talking about something. You never know about them. Seemed mighty interested in that Ford with the Louisiana tag that pulled onto the River Road a few minutes ago. I did overhear Hunky say something about an emergency."

Sheriff Swinnard laughs. "Hell, the only emergency Rooster and Hunky ever had was chasing meanness."

"Reckon so, Ben Henry. We oughta know—"

"Yeah, I still think about that night."

R.C. nods, frowns and removes the toothpick with oily fingers. "Me too. But aint chasing ghosts any more. Bet you'll find him down yonder at the river woods. Willy Buck's gotta crew cutting paperwood near Willis Bridge."

"Take care, R.C.," the sheriff says.

"See you at the funeral, Ben Henry."

Hickernut Hickery snatches a paper towel from the wall dispenser and wipes oil from his hands. He hears the car door shut, and the Sheriff's cruiser engine ignite. He pokes the toothpick back into his teeth, and walks out of the garage into sunlight. He throws up a hand at Sheriff Swinnard as Deputy Widderson steers the cruiser under the winking caution light onto River Road.

There's no air moving. R.C. Hickery stands with aching feet on the sun-parched pavement, digging his gums with the toothpick. He turns, facing the truck with hood up and wires worming across the fenders like black snakes. *Can't let Willy Buck down. Hard day's work ahead. And ol Hunky's done run off with that no'count bastard Rooster on some damn foolishness.*

Who'd ever want to talk to that one-armed sonofabitch, out of the Atlanta pen again? Too bad that machete didn't knock some that hate out of his swole up head. Shoulda gone to the gang for trying to shoot Rattler Ransum long time ago. No, Rooster had to go slapdab crazy and rob the Scotts Ferry post office for forty seven dollars—pocket change—with a twelve-gauge shotgun, shooting up the place and scaring that postmistress half to death. He shoulda been kept in Atlanta, doing hard time. But he got out somehow. Caught peddling likker for Hasty Ponds cross the Georgia line. Got out agin. Probably Willie Buck helped him like he does lotta folks. Shoulda locked up the ol one-armed skirtlifter fer life. Rooster and Hunky been chasing meanness and poontang all these years.

Never forgive em for that crazy night down yonder on the river. Long, long time ago but still get scared, seeing em come outta the dark, grinning in the firelight.

Just like Rooster and Hunky, step ahead of the law.

And everybody talking about Ol Rattler, going in the ground yonder. Sad turn of luck.

Wonder why ol Pigpen Swinnard who could throw a football like a bullet wants to talk with Rooster Reddoake? What the hell....

NATHAN
BEDFORD
FORREST

2

The River

Mists of rain pepper the gray shadowed streets as
Chance Cahoon drives through pea soup fog. Cottony
swirls, rolling up from the Mississippi River, shroud the
ancient French Quarter and the concrete, steel and glass
skylines of New Orleans. Chance turns onto Canal Street
from the Garden District. A tugboat horn groans
mournfully through the hovering fog. Lights bloom
vaguely and scrawls of neon wink in the approaching
dawn.

His Ford sedan moves away from the river along Canal,
walled by older brick buildings and high-rise towers
jutting up along the broad traffic spine dividing Creole
New Orleans and the leafy Garden District. Shadows and
darkness silhouette the streetscape against the slowly
spreading orange glow of the sun hurrying the morning.
Street lamps spray ghostly light on the wet sidewalks and
pavement.

Chance hears the muted whine of car tires splattering
damp surface. Now on the edge of daybreak, he's part of
the silence of the sleeping city. Somewhere on the dark
river behind him a freighter's whistle bellows shrilly. For
an instance Chance feels the loneliness of spirit which is
an occupational disease of a writer fighting a war with
himself to gain a toehold on destiny.

In the rearview mirror, he sees only blurred fragments of the skyline of the river port: here he lives, teaches Southern history at the University of New Orleans and— true to a historian's instincts—chases old ghosts for academic journal articles and book themes.

Before him, the sun crescent edges the horizon, slowly advancing dawn, spearing light on trees and rooftops of the Southern city sleeping beside the Fathers of Waters.

Behind him, in the lengthening distance, the giant brown river flows a sweeping crescent by the city. The Mississippi moves moodily south, watering Louisiana swamps and bayous for one hundred miles more, seeping into the salt of the Gulf of Mexico.

The river.

Another river.

Another place, another time.

Toward the morning sun.

The yearning has been there a long time. Yearning for the places of boyhood.

Ring Jaw. And the river.

—Thirty years since the chilly gray December morning when a life ended and another began. When Rachel Rebecca Cahoon and her teenaged son began a journey northward from the sleepy West Florida crossroads town between two rivers. Etched in memory, the day of leaving now seems ancient: time of innocent youth—innocent fruit of old passion.

Yet now still, a hunger.

Ring Jaw and the river.

Yonder, toward the sun.

Suddenly, beyond the city, fog and rain are behind him; Chance watches the sun wiping away darkness.

The highway will take him to Florida—concrete and asphalt threading the sweeping Gulf Coast shoreline crescent from Texas to the Florida peninsula, bridging

Lake Pontchartrain and the Louisiana, Mississippi and Alabama sloughs, river bottoms and deltas; then splitting the Florida pine-green roof in a four-hundred-mile line from Pensacola to Jacksonville on the Atlantic coast.

In Mississippi cool coastal breezes waft inland from the Mississippi Sound beaches of Pass Christian, Gulfport, Biloxi and Pascagoula. Coolness collides with steamy air of the cypress heads, salt marshes and pinewoods bordering the interior expressway. Vistas of Southern Mississippi enliven memories of water-veined Chipola Country.

Enduring images return more. Now, in mists of memory, a blend of pained lonesomeness and mellowed heartache.

On the day of leaving, Ring Jaw of boyhood shrank abruptly in the narrow framed haziness of the rear window of Momma's sputtering old Chevrolet gaining speed: images captured indelibly by watery innocent eyes harboring sadness and emptiness. Fading in the distance, landmarks of a pineywoods town: a cluster of bunched-together buildings wreathed by pine and oak and pecan along sand-rutted streets, there still, somewhere hidden in Florida's Panhandle.

I see it still, suddenly swallowed by the brown autumnal horizon and the curvature of the blacktopped highway as I then faced the unknown.

Another time and place.

Yet the ache of my past remains.

Now the death of Roscoe Ransum.

For years he had vowed bitterly never to return—*never.* The jarring ring of the telephone and a voice from the past on a rainy New Orleans night came as if a ghost, reawakening the urge for a journey he knew he must make.

"This Mister Chance Cahoon?"

"Yes, may I help you?"

"You may not remember. I'm Moss Musing. Knew

your Grandpa, Sol Cahoon, long time ago. You were just a boy."

"Of course, the editor and publisher of the *Chipola Springs Courier*—"

"Yes, but I'm an old man now myself, mostly retired. I called because I thought you'd like to know the death of Roscoe Ransum. They're burying him next Saturday at Ring Jaw."

"Yes, the one called Rattler. I didn't know—"

"Died over'n Mobile. Didn't have any family left. Thought you might want to be at the funeral."

"Mister Musing, I've been intending to go back—"

"Funeral's Saturday."

"I'll be there."

"Before Rattler left Ring Jaw, more'n thirty years ago, he told me about you. Said if anything ever happened to him, I was to let you know. He didn't have much—small bank account, mustering out pay from the Army, few medals brought home from the war—but my name's on a piece of paper that says you inherit all he's got."

"I'll be there."

"Stop by the newspaper office. I'll explain."

"Mister Musing, I read your book, *The Lynching of Buck Santee*."

"Did you, now?"

"Mister Musing, I even remember the article you wrote for that detective magazine—"

"Look and Tremble Murder Case?"

"Yes. Grandpa had a copy til the day he died."

"Look time ago, Chance. My first published article. Your Grandpa, ol Sol, helped set me straight before he passed on."

"The book's fine work. I'm pleased the university press published it."

"Took some doing. Spent most of my prime years pecking at a dog-eared manuscript. Couldn't find a publisher. So I just bundled it up and sent it to Gainesville."

Moss Musing laughs. "To my surprise, the editors saw the story with a damning social message. The book upset lots of folks here in Chipola Country. Thought they might string me up on that courthouse oak."

"Grandpa always said you knew where the bodies were buried."

"Sol Cahoon surely knew. Have to go for the truth, even if I'm just an old worn-out country editor running a newspaper with an old broken-down flatbed press and a shirttail of type—"

"Yes sir, you have been at it long time—"

"Fifty years this spring."

"Mister Musing, remember teaching us eighth graders at Ring Jaw School?"

"Yeah, Spanish, believe it was—

"We had a study hall period, and you as principal of Ring Jaw School put us in the room with four seniors."

"They needed a credit to graduate, best I remember. That was after I returned from the war, trying to be schoolmaster in Ring Jaw and a jackleg newspaperman in Chipola Springs at the same time. Feller's got to make a living somehow."

"You sure turned me on to reading good literature."

"Well, I suppose I did spend more time on Hemingway and Wolfe and Faulkner than I did the Spanish language."

"You did that. Talked about the novels you were reading. I'm a writer because of it."

"Chance, I sure enjoyed reading your fine book on Nathan Bedford Forrest. You captured his spirit as the warrior. I liked your subtitle, *Southern Lightning in the Saddle*. Specially the part about your great-grandfather riding with Old Bedford across North Alabama—"

"Major MacNab was at General Forrest's side until he lost his arm."

"Folks here know him for leading the militia during the Battle of Chipola Springs, and then building to railroad to Estiffanulga. He cast a big shadow when the century was young—running that big turpentine operation and owning the Ring Jaw Mercantile Store. We'll talk when you get here. I'm glad to learn I helped you in school, Chance. Your Grandpa had high hopes for you. So did Roscoe. I helped get him transferred to my Army unit just before we went into Normandy. Fine soldier, he was—"

"I'll be there. Need to look around that country—"

"This river country's changed, but Ring Jaw's still about the same. But I'm still at the same place, across from the courthouse square. You can't miss it. You're only about six hours driving from New Orleans."

"I'll be there, Mister Musing."

"Still got that flaming red hair?"

"Yes sir. Some gray."

"Roscoe surely loved that woman—"

"Momma died a few years ago in Memphis."

"Sorry, I didn't know—

"She said she'd never go back to Ring Jaw, not even in a pine box. She's buried in Memphis."

"Tragic. Such a beautiful woman. I wonder if Roscoe knew?"

"I'll be there, Mister Musing."

The sun moves into midmorning as Chances drives through Mobile, Alabama's sister to his adopted seaport city, French in origin, similar with an urban skyline and metallic fingers and port wharves spreading over the riverfront and jutting into Mobile Bay.

He speeds along the curving interstate bridge over the mud-brown waters of broad, river-fed Mobile Bay reaching for the Gulf. Chance tries to visualize Admiral David Glasgow Farragut in the rigging of his flagship

USS *Hartford* steaming past the Confederate mortars of Fort Morgan into legend: *"Damn the torpedoes, full speed ahead!"* But in the momentary historic blur, as if deeper memory intrudes, vivid as the midmorning sun sparkling on the slow river current feeding the bay, *there's Rattler Ransum, standing in Elleck Dunkane's Ring Jaw store, his dark brown eyes on a small timid boy, his own blood staining the tail of his dingy white shirt. Here, somewhere near Mobile, Roscoe Ransum's life ended; they're returning the corpse to Ring Jaw—*

He moves through flat sweeping South Alabama fields green with corn and potato vines and laced with pine thickets and farmsteads and barns on the sunshot horizon. Chance nears the Perdido River, once the water line on colonial maps as Spanish, French and English struggled to control the Floridas and coastal provinces. Beyond, he will be in Florida.

During my teen years in Memphis, I remembered the Florida that Momma and I had left on the sad December day following Grandpa's funeral. I often thought of Grandpa's backwoods Florida when I grew up the son of a woman who worked her fingers to the bone as a restaurant waitress and a department store clerk, putting me through Memphis schools; during studies at the University of Mississippi, walking with the ghosts of William Faulkner's fictional Jefferson and Yoknapatawpha County around the Oxford court house and at his home he called Rowan Oak; when I wore U.S. Air Force blue and gold lieutenant's bars during the Korean War. And now, as a teaching historian trying to write a book gnawing at my soul.

More I sense my own mortality.

Bittersweet memories of boyhood are now earnest yearning, possessing my inner self. I hunger for answers I feel await me on the back roads and riverbanks of that isolated town of West Florida. If not discernible answers, at least the elusive truisms I know instinctively yet suppress subconsciously; at least an intelligent assessment of my troubled ancestral lineage; at least some clarity of a turbulent, abstractly perceptible past; maybe even erasure of bittersweet scars.

Now, Momma, a voice still speaking: Chance, you must study hard—they can't take away a good education. You're the first Cahoon ever to finish high school. And now my pride soars—an honors graduate of a university, a teacher, a writer of books. Go, my son, my only son, on into the world making your own way, never, never looking back on that tormented beginning, that evil and soulless land of your Grandpa's bunch of heathen....

In five years, Chance Cahoon will be fifty: half a century; and with his second book in preparation, he struggles on those long nights, layering his narrative with human essences of a time in the rural South now mostly lost and forgotten in the haste of the Twentieth century. He spends afternoons reading Florida history and folklore in the university library and studying maps of the state. He tries to visualize the state's verdant roof atop the long peninsula jutting west of Tallahassee two hundred miles, shaped like a panhandle, bordering Alabama's southern boundary, and wetting its sugary white quartz-sand coastline in the northern Gulf of Mexico. But now the geography shrinks to a black dot and a small-type name he circles on a Florida highway map: *Ring Jaw*. In spirit, the troublesome manuscript is turning autobiographical; its working title, *Biography of a Southern Boyhood*, foretells his hunger as he searches archives of memory to portray slices of life crying out of the far distant past.

His wife, Katherine Ann, understands his troubled searching. She and Solomon Chance Cahoon II, their fifteen-year-old son, share his uneasiness. They feel his incompleteness, twisting now into an obsession. In the long night, staring at an empty computer screen, Chance's words bleeding in the frustration so far blur into tormented formlessness, souring into disappointing say-nothingness.

"You've changed," Katy says, suddenly standing in the doorway. A sea of papers clutter the desk of the small room walled with shelves jammed with books.

"Not really." Chance says, jerkily snapping the computer screen black.

"You sit here, staring at the old pictures of your Confederate ancestors and that shadowbox of Civil War relics. You conversing with ghosts now?"

"Flesh and blood. They help me think."

She laughs. "You used to say you'd not go back to that hellhole."

"I know. 'Land of the Heathen,' Momma used to say. Hell, that ought to be my title."

"Yes, maybe simply 'The Heathen.'"

Chance grins. "That says it all. But first I've got to write the damn book. Just won't jell."

"It will. Give it time. Chance, go back. Go alone. You'll not finish the book until you live it all again."

"Yes, I have to go back—"

"Chance, you're a sentimentalist with an autumnal heart. Your work reminds me of the themes of Thomas Wolfe."

"Wolfe? That mountain of a man poured out an ocean of words about his own life, his eccentric family, his town," Chance says. "Faulkner said he was the best writer of his time—better than Hemingway because his failings were of such splendor. Wolfe was brave enough to experiment and avoid the expected conventional story telling, while Hemingway never veered from the path of convention. Wolfe evoked emotion, his work epic, oceanic. He intoxicated southern writers like no other, despite the critics' harsh view of his flaws of form and his work merely autobiographical. But what do critics know? Blood's thicker than water."

"Yes, you're ever drawn to the past, seeing everything in historical perspective, even the land, the rivers, the South you love so."

Chance snaps off the desk lamp, and pushes away from the desk. "Faulkner said it: the past is not past. There is no such thing as *was*—only *is*. So what is past exists only in a present state of human consciousness. One has to know where one came from before facing the future—"

"Yes, Chance, I've heard your speeches, your lectures—history is not a chain of things done, but a continuance of things been."

Chance laughs. "All experience exists only in a moment of present consciousness. Katy, seamless continuity, in present tense."

"Remember when you were writing the biography of Nathan Bedford Forrest? You spent weeks tracing his footsteps in Tennessee, Mississippi and Alabama. Said you wanted to know what it was like to ride in war, smelling his sweat, gunpowder and horse poot."

"A writer must live his characters, snapping them to life. Yes, growing up in Memphis I became fascinated by ol Bedford, sitting up there in bronze on his old warhorse King Philip and his remains buried right in the heart of the throbbing city on the Mississippi River bluffs. He was an unlettered genius of cavalry—"

"Forrest became your obsession then. Now, this going back to your own past, not sure whether reality can be fiction or fiction reality—"

"This will be different, Katy. Nonfiction written like fiction. We write best what we know."

"You didn't know much about Forrest."

"But I began by knowing that my great-grandfather, Malcolm Grant MacNab, rode with Forrest in North

Alabama. I still see his tomb, standing against time in Chipola Cemetery."

"With a name like Grant?"

"They shoulda put his middle name on the tombstone that I played around back then with Willie Buck, Ben Henry and ol Hickernut Hickery in Ring Jaw. Wonder what life brought them?"

Katy walks to the window, looking into the night. "And all those other heathen fighting and cutting and killing that you talk about. You talk about your grandfather and that man you call Rattler as if they were heroic—"

"They frame a typical southern boyhood, as bizarre as these characters appear—trapped in their own time in a small country town. And the heart of goodness of those who survived. I'd like to put it all on paper."

"Yes, Chance, go back—"

"I must. Must try to recapture my soul."

"Go back—"

And the river.
The Chipola, now my private river of remembrance. I will go—or as Florida's once proud, intrepid and arrogant aboriginal Chatots pictured the white dancing waters of their sacred stream—Look and Tremble.

He crosses the narrow, tree-shrouded Perdido River separating Alabama and the panhandle-shaped finger of West Florida, once a Spanish and British province before Florida became a state.

The highway runs across the northern fringes of the old colonial capital of Pensacola. The city edges the broad blue bay and beyond, like a rope, the sugary white quartz sand of Santa Rosa Island shapes the harbor—landmarks of ancient beauty charted by Spaniards who struggled in wilderness to earn a footnote in history with the first settlement on the Gulf Coast.

Chance speeds across the concrete ribbon, seeing the bay coveted by Europeans, Englishmen and Americans during more than four centuries. Here West Florida began, in the westernmost corner hugging Alabama, threshold to the long finger of Florida.

He feels mystical, sentimental, even childishly romantic about exploring the nuances of his shadowy past—despite his credentials of scholarship and authorship on a larger world. His Ford wheels over the bay, leaving Pensacola behind as a smear of green perching on red clay bluffs wading like cat paws in the placid bay; then, spreading before him—the rustic rural heartland of the region that Florida marketing professionals who write the tourist brochures have christened the *Forgotten Florida* or the *Other Florida.*

And now, as the miles roll with the slow tick of the dashboard numbers, somewhere up ahead, there's Ring Jaw, just a spot in the road, and the Chipola—majestic little river of boyhood, yonder beyond cattle-dotted pastures, blackjack scrub-oak fields, piney flatwoods, cypressed branch heads and rivers veining the old colonial province one governed by Spaniards and the Redcoats of Britain. There, like the Chipola, flow the rivers— Blackwater, Yellow, Shoal, Choctawhatchee. Green roadside signs signal West Florida towns born a century ago with the rails and fire-breathing steam engines of the Pensacola & Atlantic Railroad spanning the pine forests from Pensacola to River Junction on the Apalachicola River: Milton, settlement of sawmills and timber men early in the Nineteenth century; and then towns strung along the Old Spanish Trail that sprang from railheads— Holt, Crestview, DeFuniak Springs, Ponce de Leon, Caryville, Bonifay, Chipley, Cottondale, and finally Chipola Springs, the old nineteenth-century cotton town

on the limestone-caverned hills jutting up from the banks
of the tree-canopied river.

Now before him, exiting Interstate 10, the narrow
bending pine-bordered road that leads to the heart of
Chipola Springs and Andrew Jackson Avenue.

Chance drives slowly along Jackson Avenue, passing
the few remaining columned and filigreed houses standing
more than a century, manicured with verdant hedges,
flower gardens and live oak and magnolia trees; by the
Grecian-columned home of Civil War Governor John
Milton; by Saint Luke's Episcopal Church—scene of the
town's bitter defeat in ashes by a Union invasion column
from Pensacola in 1864. Grandpa said his pa, old
Jeremiah Cahoon, was here at the Battle of Chipola
Springs, culmination of the West Florida cavalry raid by
Union Brigadier General Alexander Asboth marching from
Union headquarters in Pensacola. The battle had been
burned in his boyhood memory by the bitterness of the
people of Redlands County lingering more than a century
after mounted black soldiers torched the town—and the
church—after a heroic but futile defense by a handful of
ragtag militia led by Major Malcolm Grant MacNab. The
young Confederate officer who had raided with Forrest
was home with an empty sleeve at his family's Magnolia
Plantation when Governor Milton sent word the Pensacola
raiders were riding toward Chipola Springs. He
commanded mostly boys shouldering ancient muskets and
old men with squirrel guns too infirm to march away in
gray to distant battlefields. That September day, in the
smoke of black arsonists in blue uniforms, Chipola Springs
turned to fire and ash and the lingering stench of defeat
and humiliation. Yet its few heroic defenders, Major
MacNab's Cradle and the Grave Company, including old
Jeremiah, gained a measure of defiant pride sealed in the
granite monument standing tall and sturdy and silent, like

a sentinel, for a century. In the shadow of the stone pillar they gathered, the generations, celebrating the courage of the old men and boys on that long autumn afternoon when the Civil War thundered in flames and fear and death on quiet, leafy Jackson Avenue.

The street widens at a traffic light; the granite obelisk on the grass-covered median sits in the shadow of the Chipola Springs Hotel. Little of this old river cotton town has changed—same storefronts—except the courthouse: now a contemporary building rising through the oaks of the square in sterile straight unadorned modernism weathered in stained concrete, sharply contrasting the old Southern gothic county building with a steeple clock threading vaguely through memory. Yonder, the oak—*the old oak still stands, a canopy spreading dark, sunshot shadows, outlasting the courthouse built in 1845 when Florida became a state. The shadetree once bloodied by the hanging corpse of young Buck Santee, dangling in blood-drenched tatters. The one Grandpa talked about. And the Square, ever in shadows, strewn with bloody fragments of clothing and muzzles of bayoneted rifles in the silent aftermath of the hellish lynching. And across the square the Old English lettering boldly swirls across the glass window:* The Chipola Springs Courier. Founded 1845. F. Moss Musing, Editor and Publisher.

The dark, taciturn man with a thick thatch of closely barbered white hair, sitting behind an antique oak partner desk layered with dust and yellowed newspapers, reaches for one of many briar pipes on a dusty bookshelf behind him. Striking a match to the tobacco, a small fume of smoke fogs his vision momentarily. The slender man turns his six-foot, still military-trim body in the squeaking leather chair and stares blankly at the yellow sheet of wordless paper rolled in an ancient Underwood typewriter. He catches a smear of sunlight filtering through the reversed lettering on the window. Afternoon sun shafts pierce the live oak squatting on the square, tossing shadows over the grassy courthouse grounds. A slow trickle of people and a few cars and pickup trucks move around the square.

Before him, on the desk, he looks at a shoe box with a thin line drawing of a bird and *Red Goose Shoes* in trademark red letters, held together with cotton string as if the pasteboard container he had taken from his office safe was a part of him. Then he turns back to the window, his eyes fastening on a man with carrot-red hair parking a Ford sedan beside his World War II Jeep in front of the *Courier.*

Finus Moss Musing stands, tugs at his blue polka-dot bowtie, and walks through the doorway onto the sunlit sidewalk. At age seventy five, he moves deliberately, confidently, wearing his years as if ten years younger. His eyes run the length of the fortyish man wearing a blue casual shirt, tan trousers and chukka boots as if a long memory now rushes, colliding with fresh reality. He sucks the pipe deep and blows the smoke into the hot afternoon air.

That must be Chance Cahoon.

"I just took a shot, calling you," Moss Musing says. He yanks the pipe from his lips, and grabs Chance's hand. "Knew you'd want to know."

"Kind of you," Chance says. "Give me reason to come back after all these years. Seems like a lifetime ago, Mister Musing."

"Call me Moss. Most folks do," the newspaper owner says, returning the pipe with a caked bowl to an ashtray. "Take a chair, young feller. Pleased you came. We don't get many big-city writers here. Not in this one-horse newspaper. Chance Cahoon, you were in your early teens when I last saw you down at your Grandpa's old house on River Road in Ring Jaw."

"Long time since *that* funeral," Chance says.

Moss Musing slides in his chair, grabs the pipe and looks at Chance as if some fragment of the past lighted in tired gray eyes. "Now, sadly, another." He pauses. "Can't get over it—spitting image of Roscoe Ransum. Sitting right here a quarter of a century after that brave man stood on a French parade ground being decorated for bravery. We got a lot to talk about. Let's begin with this old Red Goose shoebox that Roscoe left with me long ago. It's yours."

"Mister Musing, what can I say—"

"I'll say plenty, if you'll listen."

"I'm listening."

Two hours pass before Chance walks into the fading afternoon of lengthening shadows, the shoebox under his arm and the words of F. Moss Musing still fresh as when spoken in soft, measured professorial cadences. He turns, looking back toward the doorway, reluctant to depart. Already the editor, in shadows of pipe smoke, pokes the keyboard of the Underwood with the old self-taught, two-finger practice of his age of newspapering. On the sidewalk, Chance lingers, glancing at Moss Musing past the black lettering on the facade window—F. Moss Musing's mane of hair is like cotton in sunlight. He turns. The square before him is awash with sunlight, the gnarled oak limbs breaking the light into zigzag shadows.

Chance drives down a red-clay hill to the river, the old Red Goose shoebox, held together by twine, beside him, searching for the Riverside Lodge—*you'll find a good catfish supper there, Moss had said.* He slows at the bridge; the narrow, tree-shrouded stream is barely visible through heavy foliage bearding the banks. Leafy arms of oak and cypress and gum shawled with Spanish moss blot out the sunlight shadowing dark pools of the lazy current sliding along the limestone-crusted trough.

Moss Musing was insightful, sitting in that old leather chair, surrounded by his books, animating memories, puffing on a pipe, talking of the past not even past, quoting William Faulkner; as if he was still a young reporter probing dark mysteries of this narrow little valley, finding its sweep of humanity hidden yonder in nature's ever-changing raiments that robe the haunting beauty of waters dark and deep, running in whispers out of the silence of all the yesterdays.

The gold of late afternoon burns behind the horizon as Chance stands watching dying embers of sun flood the window of the limestone Riverside Lodge. He listens carefully, night softly coming, the breeze gentle in the trees. A rising hasp of crickets and frogs sing in the twilight, a chorus shrill, uneven.

He turns to the shoebox on the bed—an old torn and faded square pasteboard with its mysteries, now his, but for years secure in Moss Musing's office safe. *Red Goose—the owner of the Ring Jaw Mercantile Store once gave us boys a baseball bat with the red bird burned into the Ashwood that the shoe company drummer left to advertise his footwear.* He spreads the contents on the bed: two U.S. Army citations for bravery, signed by General Omar Bradley; a Distinguished Service Cross, Silver Star and a Purple Heart; honorable discharge documents dated 1945; two metallic identification tags with the name William R. Ransum; a small pile of campaign ribbons; a picture of young raven-haired Rachel Rebecca Cahoon cradling a baby in her arms, leaning against an oak tree with Look and Tremble shoal in the background; a yellowed snapshot of Private Ransum in combat gear, standing in a French town with another dogface infantryman, like GIs Willie and Joe in a Bill Mauldin cartoon; a letter scrawled in pencil, addressed to "My son" and signed "your father, William Roscoe Ransum."

Chance slowly unfolds the blue-lined sheet:

"Some day maybe you will be reading these words, and I want you to know I loved your momma and I did her wrong, running off, cutting the fool all of those years.

Your Grandpa tried best he could to bring you up to be a man. Then when he died, your momma took you away. Mr. Moss, he was a good officer over in France where they give me these medals. I was in a lot of hard fighting over there. Caught a Kraut bullet in my left shoulder that'll pain me to my dying day.

I come home from cross the water just to throw my life away. But I want you to know they was wrong, calling you all them names and trying to hurt Uncle Sol, for he was a good friend and he tried to do right by you. I may never see you again but if you someday read these words they are the only way I can express all the love I missed by not being with you."

Chance rereads the letter, then the two citations. He holds the pictures side by side—the young GI in war; a young mother with a son in diapers. His fingers move slowly over the medals, touching lightly, as if he were discovering a wisp of his soul.

The dream pokes holes in the night as Chance fights for sleep—*the medals and the ghosts of words clattering down the long echoing burst of machine gun fire and the soldier moving in the hedgerows with tank-tread teeth chewing the earth and bullets thudding and careening off tree limbs and there's the rattle of Death and then he's in Elleck Dunkane's store with a bloodied shirttail standing there at the red Coca-Cola cooler with a bullet hole in his back and asking about Momma and then his eyes are on me and he smiles and turns to hand me the medals and then, in a vapor, he's gone and Momma cries with a baby in her arms and everybody's eyes are on me in Elleck Dunkane's store and the grayed gathering of men whisper about the boy without a daddy and the one who they whisper was his daddy wearing olive drab was always high on shine and just plain no'count*—and the telephone rings: "You wanted a wakeup call, Mister Cahoon, it's five...."

"Yes, thank you." He sits up in bed in the curtained dark, the dream splintering in the jarring dawn ring. *Grandpa always said that early don't last long—savor the freshness before rushing the day.*

Chance locates a small green road sign with the names Ring Jaw and Estiffanulga, turning onto the narrow blacktopped highway. The sixteen miles are easy portraits of flat red fields rolling back against cypress heads and pineywoods on the horizon. Machines now crawl the dusty fields; split-level brick farmhouses dot the rich green tapestry of those who work the fertile Redland plateau between the Chipola and Apalachicola rivers.

Ring Jaw must be little more than a crossroads still, springing up on at the dawn of the Twentieth century with pine in abundance. Mill men chop through Chipola Country with their saws, and hardened men driving teams of slobbering oxen fill the flatcars pulled by the steam-breathing Red Level Line engines; then, the naval stores operators build turpentine distilleries to drain the long wood of its gummy essences—like the one on the Red Level Line at Mulehead Pond Plantation south of Ring Jaw. *With the new century, timber cutters and tupentiners— armies of axmen and chippers and cutters work with the stern horseback authority of woods riders and the melodious half-shout, half-cry of the lonely worker near debt-peonage. Grandpa always called them* turpentine niggers, *black and white, tolerating a simple uncomplicated life of can-to-can't work and the endless burden of credit at the company-owned commissary. The worker, white and black, has shelter in a simple tin-roofed Cracker house that called shotguns with clapboard shutters over glassless windows to shut out the weather and the night whistles through the cracks but provide for*

*him, his woman and a brood of children a home and safety in
a paternalistic system.*

*Some sing, but most sweaty, muscular laborers unleash
agonies of their imprisonment in lonely cries echoing through
pines: Boy, hear me—you are born into turpentine; you don't
go into it; it's something you get out of.*

Chance still clings to the words of the letter and the
vague smoky dream while driving by the peanut and
cotton fields and bubbling creeks and cypress heads into
Ring Jaw. The sun is wiping away the dewy mists as he
passes the boarded-up Dunkane store and then the
whitewashed schoolhouse where Moss Musing once
shared his love of books with eighth-graders in demin
overalls. His aloneness with old echoes vanish during
the conversation with the tattooed man with yellow teeth
at the Rebel Oil station. Then they return, buzzing in
the quiet of the Ford moving along River Road.

Now, beyond Ring Jaw, Chance hurries past
farmhouses and sloping green pastures and gullied red-
clay ridges, curving into the tight little Chipola River
valley.

He slips a cassette of classic country music into the
tape deck; suddenly a voice heard by millions long before
he was born fill the car with the blue yodel lonesomeness
from the ancient Mississippi voice of "The Singing
Brakeman" who rode the rails from Meridian, wailing the
hunger and yearning of a troubled land with primitive
but honest poetry,
Rather drink muddy watah
Rather drank muddy watah
Than to be in Atlanta, treated like a scolded dog
T for Texas,
T for Tennessee
T for Thelma, that gal done made a wreck outta me.
Grandpa's favorite, Jimmie Rodgers' words worming from

*the tired old lips in a gravelly, uneven imitating voice as he
fishes the Chipola depths for supper; sits on the front porch in
a broken rocker, whittling with his Barlow; chewing and
spitting and staring into nothingness in the cool of the evening
as whippoorwills whisper the long loneliness of an old bent-
over man trapped by fragments of cursed remembrance—*

Chance stands in the middle of Willis Bridge: below
him, the Chipola flows—time its steady rushing tannic
current, like eternity with no beginning, middle or end,
sculpting the mind, trapping cycles of yesterday fused with
now. Cypress stand broad-kneed on the banks, putting
down feet in wet eternity; beside them, above the dark
water, vines cling in an interwoven mass to bent old oaks
like old men who appear ageless against a cloudless blue
sky.

He pulls the small wartime photograph from his shirt
pocket; the sun strikes the bearded grin of the soldier
with the vacant, baggy-eyed look of the American GI.
He's typical of the "dogface" that Moss Musing had shown
from the book, *Up Front*, by cartoonist Bill Mauldin.
"We're now just an aging long gray line of old soldiers
walking gently into the shadows," Major Finus Moss
Musing says with sadness in his voice, speaking again,
his echo rising as if whispering from the river. He had
sat there just hours ago with his pipes and his books and
his one-horse newspaper speaking of Roscoe Ransum:
"Like old Uncle Sol told Roscoe when he left for Camp
Blanding, 'shoot em where they're the biggest and don't
go as far as hell for the love of a woman.'"

3

Bull of the Woods

*C*hance, let me tell you."

"I'm listening, Mister Musing."

The editor leans into the softness of his worn brown-leather chair; a slight soft smile lights his face as dregs of pipe smoke lift toward the ceiling. "Roscoe grew up poor'n owl dung," Moss Musing says. "His daddy William Hatchett Ransum peapatched around, cut fence posts, dug up stumps from new ground for a dollar a day. Mostly he cooked likker like others—in these days back in the Twenties and Thirties wasn't much shame in whiskeymaking in Chipola Country when a feller tried to put meat and bread on the table and keep family bellies off their backbone."

Moss chuckles. "Hell, old Will tried to bring up his boy without a mother—your grandmother died in childbirth less than a year after Roscoe was born. Will's wife Althea Gillwater—sister of Whiskey George Gillwater—was a damn good woman but awfully frail. But old Will couldn't make a go of it trying to grub out an honest living. He lived on a patch of sandbed ground across the river that was so poor two redheaded women couldn't raise a fuss on it."

"That's poor," Chance says, laughing.

"Like his father, Roscoe took up making whiskey like

everybody else when he was no more'n fifteen. Worked with Uncle Sol and those two colored men, Willy Santee and Uncle Charley Crowe, and old man Lige Reddoake and Whiskey George Gillwater. I hope you're not offended—"

"Mister Musing, I think I know; I seek the truth."

"Chance, you know gossipers spread a pack of lies around that your real father was Dr. Noddington Ambrose Easton—mostly folks called him Doc Nodd."

Chance laughs. "Oh, yes—I remember Doctor Easton. Grandpa said he was a helluva hunter on the scent of a fox."

"Now Doc Easton charmed the ladies, no doubt about that. And they were charmed by him. But, hell, they credited that old foxhunting buddy of mine with fathering every baby born out of wedlock in Fayette County—some others too, here in Redlands County."

"Legends spread in a country town," says Chance, laughing.

Moss Musing nods, grinning. "Doc used to laugh about it, sitting around a campfire on a hunt. Hell, he brought your mother into the world—and would have been there when you were born if he hadn't been off running them fox hounds in Bearthick Swamp.

"So it was Doc Dowling who came in the middle of the night. He thought you'd come stillborn, couldn't find any sign of life. But your grandmother Sarah Rachel grabbed you up and breathed life into your lungs. You were four or five when your grandmother died—she was the last of the Major MacNab's family. Your grandfather Jeremiah Cahoon, who fought alongside Major MacNab at Chipola Springs, died the year you were born."

"Your momma, Miss Becky, finally told me before she left here with you for Memphis that she'd been with only one man—Roscoe. They were no more than lovesick teenagers, slipping away at night, meeting down yonder at Look and Tremble."

Chance turns away. "Momma never talked about Ring Jaw. Kept it all to herself, even to the end—"

"She wanted Roscoe to marry her," Moss Musing says. "But back then Roscoe didn't want to be tied down to a woman—ran off, riding the rails, hoboing around. Pulled a hitch in the U.S. Cavalry in Wyoming. Said he got tired of shoveling hay and horse manure. Finally got a job as a welder's helper in a Mobile shipyard. After Pearl Harbor he hitchhiked home and enlisted in the Army. He lived to regret his running off, of course, but he never stopped loving Rebecca Cahoon. Sat right here, some years ago, crying like a baby—the day he give me the shoebox and money for the funeral.

"Roscoe came home from the war and tried to start a new life working at the Brewton Lumber Company at Tupelo Landing in Estiffanugla. But he couldn't stay out of the jooks, drinking and fighting. He had gotten into some bad trouble with Lige's son, Rufus—remember him?"

"Yes sir," Chance says. "He was a few years older than me. Ran around with a feller named Hunky—Hunky Hoggen. They were meaner than pure hell itself."

Moss Musing nods. "Yeah, Hoggen's back around here now, I'm told. That Reddoake boy come on Roscoe with a .45 Colt revolver in that old jook called Buttermilk Hill on the river south of Estiffanulga. He fired a couple of shots—a bullet clipped Roscoe's left ear. But Roscoe ran for a machete in his truck. Before the Reddoake boy could fire another shot, Roscoe swung the blade and mangled that young feller's left arm. I'm told that one-armed man's still around Ring Jaw—spent some prison time in Atlanta, I believe.

"No charges were brought against Roscoe. Hell, a deputy sheriff returned the machete to Roscoe. He told the deputy he was trying to cut that Reddoake boy's head off, and would have shot him if he could have gotten his hands on a gun.

"But Roscoe figured there'd be a killing if he stayed. Told me he'd been running from meanness all his life. Said he'd seen enough killing in the war. Packed up, moved away. Found an old shack over there along a creek near the Alabama-Mississsippi line. Folks said he was raising and selling goats, sort of peapatching around; trying to avoid trouble. Looks like he found it again.

"We didn't know his whereabouts for years. He'd call Elleck Dunkane, the storekeeper you might remember, asking how to get up with your mother—mostly when he was drinking. Elleck didn't know. Hell, I had to track you down after reading your book and calling the university."

Moss Musing pauses, looking bemused. "You know, Chance, Roscoe Ransum had some of the qualities of Bedford Forrest—"

Chance laughs. "You mean how he said to whip the enemy—'git em skeered and then keep the skeer on em.'"

"Yeah," Moss Musing says, nodding, "or 'war means fighting, and fighting means killing.' Like Sherman said, 'there will never be peace in Tennessee until that devil Forrest is dead.'"

"No doubt where Old Bedford stood."

Moss Musing lifts the pipe from his mouth. "Roscoe neither. Now, Roscoe never talked about it, and not many around Ring Jaw knew, but he was a *real* decorated American hero."

"I always thought he must have seen lots of action—"

"He was with my infantry unit at Normandy. Bravest man I ever saw. I still hear the surreal sound of the guns raking Omaha Beach. Men dying, screaming, bodies floating in the surf. Thought we'd never get onto that damn hell of a beach.

"We're lying there, pinned down in the sand and surf streaked with blood, and getting torn to pieces by German machinegun fire. And suddenly I see this private soldier scrambling hell for leather in the wet sand toward the guns—Germans raking the sand with constant machinegun fire, piling up bodies in the bloody surf. The soldier was Roscoe Ransum, yelling, 'Goddamn it, Major, let's meet em in hell!' And the men were following, many falling, some screaming pain and crying and vomiting their gunshot guts. But we were going, following Roscoe, getting the hell off that beach.

"When we finally reached the hedgerows, the Germans were getting ready to counterattack. Roscoe grabbed his M-1 rifle and stuffed his pockets with grenades. You'd have thought he was back in the Chipola woods, stalking a deer or wildcat. The Germans had set up positions about a hundred yards from his platoon's position. Roscoe was part of a reconnaissance.

"Crawling unseen through a gully, he came on a German machine gun. The citation says he then 'climbed boldly onto a little mound. He stood up behind a bit of brush and fired his rifle and threw his grenades so accurately that he killed two of the enemy and captured four others.'

"But going in he caught a slug in the shoulder, leaving a gaping hole. But he kept going. Medics found him in a pool of blood. I thought he'd die, lying there on that stretcher.

"The next time I saw Roscoe was in a London hospital, sitting there puffing on a cigarette and drinking Irish whiskey. He'd talked a little redheaded nurse into bringing him the bottle. He sat there grinning. Said it was almost as good as Chipola white lightning."

"Couldn't leave it alone," Chance says.

Moss Musing pauses, smiling. "We had a toddy or two. I told him I thought he was going to die, back there on that stretcher, but he said, 'Hell, Major, I been shot before and overed it.'

"I told him that his action that morning had started our breakthrough. We'd recommended Roscoe for the Congressional Medal, but the brass said no. He'd made the mistake of leaving his guard post before we left England, chasing a young Welsh woman he met in a pub. Then he got into a drunken fight with a British Royal Air Force sergeant over another woman. But we were alerted for the invasion; charges were suspended. Hell, Roscoe didn't care—he said medals were for the heroes who didn't come home.

"I told Roscoe, 'looks like you bought a ticket back home.' But he said, 'Major, I want to go back to my old outfit.' Roscoe requested combat again, and was awarded the Silver Star for clearing out another nest of Germans, just before we reached the Rhine River. Helluva fine piece of soldiering."

"I don't remember hearing any of that," Chance says.

"Never talked about it—said he just wanted to forget," Moss Musing says. "I can still see him, standing there near the Rhine River, his shoulder wound finally healed, being decorated by General Bradley."

"Mister Musing, will he have a military funeral?"

"Chance, I called Fort Rucker for a rifle squad and a flag for military honors. And I tried to hire old Charley Crowe to dig the grave—Charley's up in age now, but you may remember him as the one who dug your grandpa's grave. The government will provide a bronze headstone. Best I could do for a real hero that few people know about.

"They're bringing the body to the Chipola Gardens Funeral Home tomorrow. I know few details of his death, other than the sheriff said they found him dead of knife wounds in a trash pile beside the Blue Bay Bar west of Mobile—"

"Trash pile?"

"Yes. Suppose Roscoe died the way he lived. Real bull of the woods, but a heart of pure gold."

"Like they say around here, Roscoe Ransum would treat you so many ways you're bound to like one of them. Hell, he'd give you the shirt off his back."

Chance laughs. "You must have cared for him."

"Yes, one of my best soldiers. Hell of a shame, him dying in a pile of trash, all alone in the world."

Chance sees tears well in the editor's tired gray eyes the color of old pewter. "Mister Musing. I have vivid memories of him—my first when I was about seven; he was drunk and had been shot in the back during a jook fight—"

"Yes, he talked about being shot and a little redheaded boy standing there in Elleck Dunkane's store."

"Then, I remember when he came home from the war, drunk, sleeping in a pile of trash outside the pool hall. Such bitter irony. True glory serving his country, and now all they will remember will be that he died so ingloriously in a trash heap."

"Chance, I hope you now have a clearer understanding of the bravest man I ever knew," Moss Musing says, striking a match, the curling flame lighting his eyes. He sucks on the pipe; tiny puffs of tobacco smoke drift ceilingward. "I've been sitting here all morning, trying to write a story for the *Courier* about Roscoe Ransum. He should be remembered."

"He will be," Chance says.

"Chance, you go on now, back to Ring Jaw; go down to the river."

"I'll begin there in the morning—"

The *Courier* editor stands, walks around the desk and grips Chance's scarred hand. "I know how that scar must have tormented you—"

"Not really anymore. A small lesson in growing up."

"We all have been scarred in some way. Remember your grandpa and your real bloodkin father—"

"Their scars burned deep; no one will ever know the miseries they endured," Chance says. "Mine is only a small patch of ugly wrinkled flesh from a moment of childhood foolishness."

"Chance, all of us are scarred in our own way. Our past is ever a part of us, haunting us, guiding us into the uncertainty of tomorrow. You may not physically see and touch them, but your father and that pretty little Becky and old Uncle Sol Cahoon are with you. They may seem only wisps of the past, but they really are the sum of your soul. They will write your book for you."

4

Look and Tremble

The early morning sun climbs the cloudless sky, slanting golden blades of light, and awakening summer heat. Chance feels a soft feathery breeze brushing the dewy pine needles and tree leaves, cascading shrouds of shadow beneath sunshot green canopies.

He walks the winding sand road, walled by dark thicket edging the moist bank of the Chipola. Chance's nostrils fill with a winey fragrance of wild flowers enlivening the aroma of river freshness. With soft sand and decayed leaves underfoot, Chance sees spears of sun glinting off the gnarled architecture of the forest. He feels the unheard sighs from the boughs of juniper, cypress, magnolia.

Before this green cathedral of trees, he walks, feeling a whispery wind move the leaves of oak, bay, laurel and tupelo gum. On the river, visible through a latticework of ferns and reeds, a Coosa bass breaks the surface of the opaque water. Dragon flies hover over the river on their airborne missions of morning. Frogs abandon the bank as footsteps approach. On the leafy forest floor, scratchings of raccoon and possum tracks mark paths of thirty migrants.

Chance feels the rhythms of nature's eternal nurturing in timelessness as if the past and present were a solitary soul. He senses and hears and feels the throbbing, the

71

unseen organic pulsations, self-renewing, often brutal and deadly in the womb of survival, yet magnificently alive.

Moss Musing said it, reluctantly, honestly—a validation: *here, one night, long ago, as if now a voice of the river*—

By the light of a flinty moon poking through tatters of cloud, the tall, muscular boy counting eighteen years brushes away the foliage; old leaves and twigs crunch under his eager movement. And in a frame holding the river and the dark bearded mass of the live oak tree, he sees the thin, lithe girl sitting on the blanket, her browned firm breasts loose under a cotton blouse. Alone she watches shadows and the swift rush of the river before her.

"Becky!" comes a soft whisper.

She turns at his footstep. "I've been waiting. I'm chilled, scared. No place to be alone—"

"You're not alone."

"Yes—"

The girl moves catlike toward him, jerking away her blouse, long tresses of raven hair falling over her white shoulders, the silvery light striking her breasts, her eagerness to embrace the boy apparent in her awkwardness and clumsy girl-like rush of passion.

"I love you," whispers the boy and the girl repeats the whisper.

Now, before them, as groin pushes against thighs, and the belly of the girl takes a spurt of the boy's seed, the river flows—

Shimmering under the July moon, a sheet of water surges into a jagged, deep-creviced pocket of the river, crashing against the rocky shoals—twisting and swirling, tossing white-foam tongues and fingers, and sliding like liquid snakes over the webbed-rock formations, a wild frenzy of dancing, gurgling turbulence ... then, in the calm beyond, returning to the quiet discipline of its swampward journey.

A light breeze stirs.

Above them, the two as one, making new life, stars wink as if the galaxy is forever.

Chance stands now in the shadows, by a live oak he remembers, watching Look and Tremble, a watery symphony of the ages bathed by the radiance of the morning sun. At the shoal, rags of blown foam curl from the dancing whitecaps of the main current, eddying around the outcroppings and then bleeding into the rapid drift of the stream. Downriver, a blue heron stands in soft sand, motionless.

Even before Hernando de Soto trudged through Florida wilds, the Chatots claimed the river and the valley as sacred, their paradise for game, waterfowl and fish. In folk tales passed down, they challenged these shoals in awe and in fear, riding the white water in hewn-treetrunk canoes, giving origin to the name that evolved with the Creeks, Seminoles and early American settlers: *Big Look and Tremble.*

So it is still, centuries later, a wild tameless struggle of nature, cast in picturesque beauty and boyhood memory—a landmark characteristic of Chipola Country, hidden in a wilderness with its phantasmorgic past and living legends.

Chance walks the moist river bank, still shadowed by the lichen-braided oak, old and bent before he was born, jutting crooked, moss-bearded limbs over the white water. He picks up a small broken limb, and removes a pocket knife from his khaki pants pocket. *Grandpa's Barlow, a whittler's blade.* He rubs the scarred hand, feeling the hateful jagged ridge. *Never out of sight. That night, right here before a fire, so long ago.* He caresses the knife, then pulls the blade open, feeling its once razorlike sharpness.

Back then, Grandpa always whittling and chewing and staring into the moment: And deep sand paths hot to bare feet; spat-spat rain watering Chinaberry trees. And Grandpa

THE OLD MAN
OF RING JAW

on the front porch of the old dogtrot house pushed against a
clump of pine and magnolia. And hot unmoving nights
longing for the cool whisper of the river; moon silver bleeding
through beards of moss.

"Hear it?"

"What is it?"

"The wind, the river. They speak."

"I cannot hear, Grandpa—"

"You will, youngun. Someday you'll hear clear as if the
past sneakin up on you...."

There, before him, as if speaking throaty reality, the
Chipola River gushes a familiar voice—all the stories and
the scars, the summer the twentieth century turns fifty.
And the hot searing sun lights the way for a barefooted
boy on the footpaths and in these woods watered by his
river of remembrance, in a small place called Ring Jaw.

I come to know again.

I come, hearing a river.

Part Two
That Summer

Ochesee Oak,
Apalachicola
River

'94 CARLE
BOWDEN

5

Roscoe Ransum

The soldier wearing a rumpled olive drab Eisenhower jacket with Private First Class stripes and matching Army trousers sleeps in the Sunday morning light. The man with mussed red hair falling over his closed eyes sprawls, his thick legs spreadeagled in dirt-soiled, grass-matted pants amid the refuse tossed from the rear screen door of Hasty Ponds' Pool Hall.

He snores in short shrill whistling intervals, followed by long, harsh, quick-ending and choked gurgles, like a saw ripping into the smaller limbs and then gnawing the fat trunk of a pine log. He draws in the humid summery air and expels heavy, irregular grunts through his widening nostrils, lips bubbling and quivering with each breath and heave of his chest.

The soldier sleeps in the shadow of the sign splashing *Spearman Beer—The Pure Water Does It* across the pinewood wall fronting the sand-rutted River Road. A cluster of campaign ribbons and an infantryman's badge are a palette of gold and red-white-blue flag colors, brightening the chest of the unbuttoned jacket. A stained tan Army tie dangles from an unbuttoned shirt, snaking over crimson tufts growing profusely from his chest. Loose laces fall about scuffed brown combat boots. Rays of sun bathe the tossed-away empty beer, wine and

79

whiskey bottles, and rain-soaked newspapers and torn cardboard boxes about him. Only the snoring breaks the silence of sleep.

"That's Roscoe Ransum," Chance Cahoon says, standing near the porch, approaching the sleeping disheveled soldier exhaling sharply in dirt and brown burnt grass. He giggles. "Ol Rattler, happy as a dead pig in sunshine."

"Drunk agin, Lil Sol," Ben Henry Swinnard says, sliding off the edge of the porch. "Heck of a durn place to sleep it off—Hasty's trash pile."

"Come home day before yesterday," Lil Sol says. "Saw him step off the bus over yonder. Nobody met him— he just walked cross the road, went in Hasty's place. Guess a soldier home from the war had a right to celebrate."

"Rattler don't need a reason," Ben Henry says. "Pa says drunk when he left, gonna be three sheets in the wind if he comes back. Pa was right—"

"Bet he can tell some stories," Lil Sol says, looking at the striped ribbons dotted with tiny stars and gold clusters, rising and falling with snored breathing.

"Reckon he killed any Germans?" says Willy Buck Santee, standing behind Chance Cahoon, his dark eyes fixed on the sleeping soldier. "Ma says my Pa killed lot um before he died over yondah cross the water."

"Well, they didn't kill him, Willy Buck," Lil Sol says.

"Nobody could kill ol Rattler Ransum," Ben Henry says. "Pa says the Lord looks after fools and drunks."

Lil Sol moves nearer, looking at the dirt-caked soles of his unlaced Army boots and his closed eyes partially hidden by tufts of red hair falling over his brow. "Might be drunk but he's no fool, Ben Henry. Never forget the first time I remember seeing Roscoe Ransum—"

Willy Buck steps behind Lil Sol. "When?"

"In Mr. Elleck Dunkane's store one time—"

"Before my Pa and him went off to the Army?"

"Yep, your daddy was with him. Roscoe had a big bullet hole in his back, standing at the counter. I remember Mister Elleck and Moses Trottah and some men were listening to the radio and talking about war coming. I thought the German war planes might fly right over Ring Jaw—"

"Hey," says Ben Henry. "Remember watching them German prisoners from the Chipola Springs camp working Doc Nodd's peanut fields over by the Pine Thicket? Big soldier like ol Rattler stood near that ol cherry tree guarding em with a machinegun—"

"Betcha them Germans went back home," says Willy Buck. "That soldier shoulda shot them mean ol Germans. They killed my daddy—"

Lil Sol looks at Willy Buck. "Americans don't shoot prisoners of war."

"I know, Lil Sol," Willy Buck says, his eyes wet with tears. "Them Germans—all brown from the sun and with that long blonde hair—they looked just like white folks here. But my daddy aint coming back."

The boys then stand silent, hearing the snoring soldier.

"That Sunday morning," Lil Sol says, "Mister Elleck gave me a big candy bar. And Roscoe Ransum—they were calling him Rattler—bought me a Coca-Cola."

"Bullet hole? Ouch! Boy, bet that hurt!" Ben Henry says.

Lil Sol pauses, squinting into the soft morning sun. "Would have killed most men."

"Yeah, there he is, ol Rattler," Ben Henry says. "Home from the war. Pa says he was a real bull of the woods. Don't see any bullet holes—"

"Mistah Elleck gimme a cold drink once—NuGrape," Willy Buck says, backing away, side glancing wide-eyed at the sleeping and snoring soldier. "Lil Sol, c'mon, let's go on down yonder to the calaboose. R.C. said he'd meet us there. Ol Rattler might wake up madder a wet hen and—"

"Yeah," Ben Henry says. "We'll tell stories, play guns, go down yonder to the Pine Thicket and ride the Flying Jenny. But first, Lil Sol can finish telling bout seeing the bullet hole in Rattler's back."

Storekeeper Elleck Dunkane stands by the screen door, a broom in his hand, watching Sunday morning awaken. Edges of the sun's crescent, throwing light into two dusty windows, flame the pine-tree horizon. He moves a lighted match over the bowl of a briar pipe, and expels a cloudlet of tobacco smoke.

He's a rather tall man, sandy hair with flecks of gray mostly gone except for a bushy fringe about his ears. His crumpled cotton trousers are the same as yesterday and many yesterdays—soiled with motor oil and food stains of a working man bagging groceries and patching inner tubes and pumping gasoline and selling snuff, Charmer coffee and White Water Rose self-rising flour since opening the store in 1925.

Elleck hears the static of the Emerson radio and voices of a cluster of men gathered around the wood stove heater. Voices from England and Europe blare, then crackle amid static, colliding with muted store voices. The cluttered wood store on the slagged highway across the athletic field from Ring Jaw School has about it a fresh awakening—sweetened by aromas of ripened bananas, tobacco, hooped cheese and green coffee beans. The slender storekeeper watches the approach of a small redheaded boy toting a kerosene can, and steps into shadows of the canopied driveway leading to two Pan-Am gasoline pumps.

"Mighty big can for such a small boy," Elleck says, laughing. "Chance, how's your grandpa?"

"Fine, sir. Gone fishing."

"He hooks them shellcrackers, don't he? Bet your momma's getting ready to heat up a frying pan."

"Yes sir."

"Nothing better than a good mess of Chipola bream and shellcrackers for Sunday supper, young feller." Elleck then jams a small withered Irish potato into the spout of the kerosene can, having filled the half-gallon tin container for the redheaded, barefooted boy standing at his feet. Oily fluid sharpness spilling from the can lid hangs in the humid Sunday morning air as the seven-year-old boy in denim overalls follows the storekeeper through the screen door into the store.

Moses Trottah and a knot of men stand and sit in a shadowy corner around the wood stove heater, talking, sometimes laughing, knife shavings from their whittling at their feet. Elleck places the pipe on the counter, and pokes a wad of Beech-Nut tobacco in his jaw. He walks to the radio, and twists the volume knob; the men turn, listening.

The boy stands at the counter, the radio voices now louder; Elleck and the men huddle around the Emerson radio, as if they hear it coming, as if on swishing wings of vultures, zigzagging dark shadows on a troubled land far across the Atlantic.

Radio voices bleed through the pop and crackle of annoying static; the drumming martial music echoes the far distant calamities, clanging as firebells in midnight dark shadows spreading a holocaust across a raging sea. The men drawn near in the jumbled-up interior of Elleck Dunkane's store know the world rolls on the jagged edge of war.

There, from the Emerson, sitting on the wooden shelf next to the fan belts and inner tubes, comes the static-bitten description and commentary—words crafted for the palette of imagination: thud of the hobnailed German jackboot, humming drone of gasoline-fired winged gunships; snapping banners emblazoned with the Swastika that now has been a frequent image in *Life* magazine. And the voices—hurried and English-correct baritone—conjures the torment of war by the grinding machinery of an invading army plunging its brute force on the grinding tank tracks and infantry hordes and aerial bombs across the quiet boundaries of a place called Poland.

"Told you, Moses. War's on us agin," Elleck says, turning over the Beech-Nut cud as if about to spit. "This feller Adolf Hitler's gonna try to conquer the world."

"Hell, yes, Elleck, afore long we'll be in just like before," says Moses Trottah, the wool-hatted town blacksmith with heavy years on his lean, sunbaked face. He whittles slowly, methodically with a Barlow knife. The wood shavings drop as if leaves caught by wind. He takes careful aim, spewing brown tobacco saliva in a tin can beside the weathered rocker creaking under his two hundred pounds. "Hell, seems like yesterday we were in them damn lice-infested trenches, fearing mustard gas more'n ol Kaiser Bill."

"I gotta feeling this one's gonna be the big one," Elleck says.

"Yeah. That's what they said in 1917, Elleck. I went over there with Blackjack Pershing's Rainbow Division. Fought to make the world safe for democracy. Hell, we never got that bonus they promised. Now it's coming agin. Shorely as hell hit will."

A lean peanut farmer in starched overalls and white cotton shirt spits tobacco juice in the woodbox, clears his husky smoky voice and snickers. "Helluva way to end a depression."

"What depression?" says Moses, his eyebrows shooting up. "Hell, folks round heah so pore they didn't know when the panic started. Only way outta this pohouse or leaning on a WPA shovel is to join the Army for $21 a month and shovel horse dung. Like ol Rattler Ransum, who jined the cavalry out west few years ago. Said he got tired cleaning stalls and smellin hoss poot."

Elleck cups an ear, listening to the radio voice through the din of gathered voices. "I gotta feeling we'll be drawn in eventually, and when we are—look out. Every family in Ring Jaw will feel it."

"Mistah Elleck," Moses says, "that boy yonder's waiting for somethin—"

He sees the boy, standing at the counter. "Yes, Chance. Son, I'll be with you in a minute."

The boy hurries his words. "Grandpa said he needs chewing tobacco, too. Said put it in on his account."

"Bloodhound, Uncle Solomon's brand, Chance," Elleck says. "Sometimes, though, he chews Bull o' the Woods, or Day's Work." The storekeeper laughs, handing the boy a cellophane-wrapped wedge of dark brown tobacco tagged with a red metal image of an animated hound. Elleck smiles. "Wait a minute, boy, got somethin for you." He pulls a candy bar from the wooden case. "Here, have a big Baby Ruth."

"Don't have a nickel, sir."

"No nickel? Aw, you don't need one. My gift to Uncle Sol's fine boy."

"Thanks, Mr. Elleck."

"Keep that tater tight on the spout, Chance. Don't you spill none, now. Yore momma, she'd be upset."

"Yes sir."

The boy pushes the Baby Ruth deep into his overalls pocket, and smiles. His nostrils stinging with kerosene fumes now gather rich aromas of ripened bananas, hooped cheese, onions, green coffee beans, oranges, winesap apples, flour, corn meal. His eyes roam the shelves: canned food, patent medicine, Grove's Chill Tonic, small tins and brown gullets of Rooster, Railroad, Navy, Dental,

Peach and Buttercup snuff. But his eyes fall onto the circular glass encasing rows of Baby Ruth, Butterfingers, Milky Way, all-day suckers, jawbreakers, tinfoil twists of chocolate Kisses, packets of Juicy Fruit chewing gum, boxes of Crackerjack laden with mysterious prizes, Moon Pies.

"Damn, look yonder, Elleck," says Moses, walking into the window light. "There's a messa trouble for you."

"I see them."

Outside the sudden tearing crunch of tires on gravel causes the storekeeper and the boy and the men to look into the sun-spangled window toward the gasoline pumps. The click-click chug of a car engine falls silent. Car doors slam. Four men stepping from a mud-streaked Ford sedan follow the wobbly path of a tall redheaded man wearing a stained white unbuttoned dress shirt, exposing a patch of crimson tufts growing from his chest, the tail dangling over soiled khaki pants.

Moses Trottah laughs. "Look like them fellers been rode damn hard and put up wet. Ol Rattler Ransum, much of a man, helluva big stand up in the road, drunk agin."

Then other voices:

"Strong as an ox."

"Sting worser a yellowjacket."

"Ol Rattler, though, never fails to stand up as a man for his friends agin all who challenge his nerve and his strength."

"Yeah, them who take him on tote scars and miseries of their mistake—"

"Y'all member that time ol Rattler on hossback rode into the front door of Ruby's Cafe after that feller who cut him, crackin that ol black snake whip cross his backside—"

"Yeah, scared the hell outta Ruby's customers, shucked oysters spilling to the floor, them folks scattering. But, you know, ol Roscoe come back, apologized to Miz Ruby Barefoot and paid her for the mess he made."

"Law don't wanna mess with Roscoe Ransum...."

Chance Cahoon turns for the screen door, and a shadow streaks the pine floor before him. A brawny mass of manhood—youthful muscle and bone joined in toughened hardness—floods the frame of the door. Suddenly, the boy hears the creaking hinges of the insect-darkened screen, and the drunk man staggers inside. Quickly the boy dodges the man's shuffling booted feet, his carrottop head striking a stalk of overripe bananas hanging from the ceiling. Morning sun filtering through the dust-smeared windows falls on his broad shoulders covered with a rumpled white cotton shirt splotched and stained red as if dipped in blood. Dried crimson droplets widen at the loose tail of the shirt—large as a man's hand— falling over khaki-covered thighs. He stands there, Sphinxlike, as if a wind-whipped statue footed firmly on the floor, a hulking specimen six feet and more, biceps bulging tightly in torn rumpled sleeves, wheezing from a heavy torso and barrel-band waist, a heavy shadow blocking out spears of dust-flecked light flooding the pinewood floor.

The boy hears the redheaded man's heavy irregular breathing. Heat and whispery mumbling and rasps of the screen door fill the store as the four jittery companions move behind the redheaded man. Then, standing before the counter, Roscoe Ransum turns to the storekeeper. "Mawnin, Mistah Elleck," Roscoe says, a faint crooked smile parting his lips. "Been gunshot."

Elleck sees the blood stains and smells the stale sweat and sour sting of liquor trapped in the hot still morning air of the store. "Hell you say, Roscoe. Who shot you?"

"Some goddam yellerbelly down yonder at the Silver Dollar Bar. Bastard shot me in the back. Look heah."

Bracing his meaty right hand on the red Coca-Cola cooler, Roscoe uses his left to slowly lift the tail of his shirt. Dry-mouthed, Chance sees Elleck and the bunch of stoic-faced codgers move nearer, muttering and whispering. Then Chance moves slowly into the window light falling on a patch of adhesive tape near Roscoe Ransum's spine. Smears of dark fingerprints stain the white bandage; the bullet hole outlined by a circular indention. Roscoe staggers, grabs the icebox to steady his legs, and pain radiates over his unshaven face. He fishes a crumpled pack of Lucky Strike cigarettes from a shirt pocket. "Somebody gotta light?"

"Here, Roscoe," says Willy Frank Santee, holding a flaming match, trying to light the cigarette. But Roscoe grabs his hand, wobbly trying to connect the flame with the Lucky Strike. "Hell, Willy, you light it. Likker shorely numbs the belly pain, but, hell, can't see straight. Light me this heah readyroll."

Willy Frank puts a lighted cigarette to his thin pale lips; Roscoe pulls, then exhales sharply, smoke trailing from his nostrils. The slender black man says, "Mistah Elleck, sir, we gotta git Rattler to the hospital in Dothan. He's been bleeding bad all night down yonder in the river swamp—"

"Hell, Willy, I'll be awright," Roscoe says, weaving and staggering, laughing hoarsely, then gazing across the wood counter at first Elleck, then Willy Frank. "Gimme another snort of yore likker; pain back on me. Mistah Elleck, open me one of them cold Nehi orange sodewatahs and gimme some gas. Ford bout empty."

The boy keeps to the shadows, watching, listening as the men move about, their broga120ed feet scuffing the pinewood floor. They speak in nervous jerks, colliding words gravelly, high pitched, floating in air stirred by the slow rotation of wooden fan blades of a ceiling fan.

"I tell you, that sonofabitch came on Rattler with that tater blade," snaps Runt Rivers, a reed-thin man with stringy muscles. "Roscoe, heah, hell, he aint never backed up on nawbody. He aint feared of nothun or nawbody—"

"He kept comin"—a bowlegged man, Cowboy Sardee, lifts his hoarse tobacco voice to finish the sentence—"and Rattler put him on the floor with a fist to the jaw—you could hear it crack—and grabbed the Barlow and pushed the blade agin his throat. Everybody was screaming like hell at Roscoe. Then that man running the Silver Dollar Bar scooted behind the counter and came with a forty-five revolver firing. Slug caught Rattler in the back. But he kept standin—"

"Damn, we had a helluva time getting Rattler outta there." Runt says, shaking his head, long blond tufts falling over his forehead. "The owner threatened to call the law, but, hell, ol Rattler heah, he was still ready to fight."

"We finally pulled Rattler out of the door," says Gasoline Brunce, whose red-veined nose spread over a thin hatchet face like that of a damaged prizefighter. "Willy Frank hit the back roads out of Estiffanulga, and we headed for the river woods. We cleaned up Rattler best we could down yonder at Look'n Tremble and waited the rest of the night in the river swamp while he slept. One time thought he'd die on us. We went by Doc Nodd's house, but, hell, he's off foxhunting somewhere in Redlands County."

"You can't kill ol Rattler," says Big Bone Stakewood, towering over the others, his hard emerald eyes sweeping the men about him.

"Lotta men try; most um live to regret it," says Cowboy, snickering. "Real booger in a fight. Aint many men roun heah gonna mess with ol Rattler."

"Mistah Elleck," says Roscoe, pulling a bloodied shirt

sleeve across his mouth, "that feller told me if I brung Willy Frank in that ol jook that I was gonna carry him out a dead man. Said he didn't like colored folks—"

"He said the wrong damn thing, I'll tell you," says Big Bone, his round face drawn.

"Hell, Big Bone, " Roscoe whispers, coughing. "I just told that sonofabitch if he didn't like Willy Frank Santee he didn't like me or any of my friends. *Right?*"

"*Damn* right," says Cowboy; others hurriedly echo the words.

Roscoe straightens. "I said I like Willy Frank a helluva lot better than any low-down white bastard who's got nothun better to do than hate a man cause of the color of his skin. Then he pulled that knife and I...."

Suddenly Roscoe bends. "Damn gut killin me."

"Aw, c'mon heah, Roscoe," Runt says. "We gotta get you to the doctor somers. Hell, you bleedin inside. It's fifty miles to Dothan."

"Relax, Runt," Roscoe says, gulping a long swallow from the pint liquor bottle; quickly following with yellow sodawater. "Mistah Elleck, heah, he's gone take care of us. Mistah Elleck—"

"Yes, Roscoe."

"There're two gallons of good beaded drankin whiskey under the cooterhull of my Ford—"

Cowboy grabs Roscoe by the arm. "Aw, come on, Roscoe. We gotta go find you a doctor."

"Awright, awright. Put the tank of gas and them sodiewatahs on my account, Mistah Elleck. Pay you next Saturday."

"Your word's your bond, Roscoe." Elleck says. "Credit always good here. Let me go fill that tank. You boys better hurry."

Chance nervously leans on the Irish potato bin when Roscoe Ransum turns for the door. The drunk man's curly red hair hangs like straw over dark bushy eyebrows, hiding tight dark brown eyes darting cat-like, seeming to float in flecks of blood. His reddish nose, strong like a knife blade, sits above thin taut lips in a square bulldog-jaw face burned by sun and raw wind. He swivels, peering at the boy. Then, as their eyes meet, the drunk man's face warms in a gentle smile.

"Howdy there, young feller," Roscoe says, looking down at the boy's overalls cut off at the knees. "What's your name?

"Chance. Chance Cahoon."

"Yeah, Uncle Sol's boy, huh?"

"Yes sir. He's my grandpa."

"Don't make men any better than Sol Cahoon—he'd give you the shirt offen his back, go your bond. He'll raise you right, boy. How old are you now?"

"Seven last September."

Roscoe tries to laugh, steadying himself against the counter. "Seven? Why, you aint bigger'n a nanny goat. Your mother must be Miss Becky—"

"Yes sir. Rebecca Cahoon."

"Fine lookin woman best I remember. How's your momma?"

"Doing fine. She cooking for Ruby Barefoot at the cafe."

"Well, you're a fine looking gentleman, a real dirtroad sport. Where'd you get all that red hair?

"Don't know, sir."

Roscoe laughs. "Willy Frank, tell Mr. Elleck to give this boy a co'cola and a stick of candy. I'll pay for it."

"Mister Elleck already give me a Baby Ruth."

"Elleck Dunkane's a good man. Willy, open this young feller a cold dope."

Chance pulls the candy bar from his pocket. "Yes sir, he gave me this—"

"You take care of yourself, boy. Your momma must

be right proud of you. And ol Uncle Sol, that old cutter, you better mind him—he'll raise you right and put a switch to your beehin if you misbehave."

"Yes sir."

The screen door whines; Roscoe staggers onto the wood steps; the four men at his heels follow him to the gas pumps. Chance grips the green bottle momentarily, flecks of ice chilling his fingers. Then he lifts the Coca-Cola bottle to his lips, feeling the cold sweet amber fluid in his throat. He stands in the doorway as Roscoe and the other men crowd into the Ford sedan, three tightly in the front seat and Roscoe and Big Bone Stakewood in the back. And Elleck Dunkane screws on the gas tank cap and turns, hanging the nozzle on the pump.

"Put it on my account, Mistah Elleck," Roscoe says, glaring up at Elleck from the back seat. "I bought Uncle Sol's boy in yonder a cold dope. Pay up Saturday."

"Gotcha, Roscoe," the storekeeper says. "You boys better get on the road. Roscoe needs to see a doctor damn quick."

"Yeah," says Willy Frank, his black muscular arm on the open window of the driver's seat. "The law might be on us, anyway—"

"Don't worry," Elleck says. "They don't like to tangle with Roscoe. That jook feller who shot him aint gonna stir up a stink. Anybody who'd shoot a man in the back aint gonna call the law."

"Cowardly," says Willy Frank, turning the ignition key, and squinting dark hard eyes in the morning sun.

The wheels of the Ford stir a swirl of dust as Willy Frank Santee stomps the accelerator and the automobile rolls onto the slagged highway. The back trunk cooterhull sinks low to the ground as gears groan and the motor coughs, and loose slack spurts from the whirring tires.

Elleck Dunkane stands by the gasoline pump as the car crowded with Saturday night drinking buddies speeds along the narrow highway, the engine's roar and the trunk-heavy sedan shrinking in the distance. He turns for the screen door as Moses Trottah steps into the sunshine.

"Think he'll live, Elleck?" Moses says, with a chuckle in his gravelly voice. "Roscoe's bad shot."

Elleck shakes his head. "Roscoe's a tough young feller. He just can't seem to avoid trouble—mostly standing up for his friends. But he'll over it."

"Like they say, Elleck, you couldn't kill Roscoe Ransum with a two-by-four or a fat lighterd knot. Though don't know bout being backshot, so close to the spine—"

"Roscoe'll make it. Always has. The Lord may be on his side, him defending a colored feller. Aint many around here would do that—"

"Reckon so. That likker may save his life."

Elleck Dunkane walks back toward the screen door, watching the seven-year-old boy carrying the kerosene can walk along the weeded edge of the slagged road, the feather of dust from Roscoe Ransum's Ford sedan now settling gently in the bright warmth of the Sunday morning.

"Boy! Shot in the back like that, and him living to fight all through the war," says Ben Henry, the words of Chance Cahoon fueling his imagination. Ben Henry leans against the cold dark stone wall inside the calaboose, sunlight filtering through the rusted iron bars of two small slits and the broken rusting metal door drooping from the hinges. The light falls on him and the two other boys listening to the one they call Lil Sol.

"Mistah Elleck said that Dothan doctor cut out the bullet—didn't damage any vital organs," Lil Sol says. "Clean missed his backbone."

"My Pa killed lots of Germans," says Willy Buck, sitting on the stone floor near the door. "I remember when he got on the bus with Roscoe Ransum, going to Camp Blanding—him waving at me and Charley Crowe through the back window. Never saw him agin. Buried somewhere in France, Grandma Hattie Santee says. She still cries when I talk bout him. But she's got a right, what with Pa killed in the last days of the war, and his older brother, Shawky Santee, blowed up on that battleship *Arizona* at Pearl Harbor. Shorely wish Uncle Shawky and my Pa coulda come back like Mistah Roscoe—"

Lil Sol looks into the sad eyes of the black boy. "Ol Roscoe surely stood up for your daddy. Willy Frank was a brave soldier. Lots of those fighting men didn't come home."

"Wish my Pa had."

"Shoot, Willy Buck," Ben Henry says, "Lil Sol aint got no daddy."

"I know, but he's got Uncle Sol Cahoon."

"Well, Willy Buck, you've got ol Charley Crowe."

The black boy jumps to his feet. "Aint the same. Uncle Charley walks the highway ever Sunday, cuttin Grandma Hattie stovewood. He looks after Grandma and me best he can, but he has to work all the time, digging graves and cutting sugarcane for the cane mill. I shorely wish I could member more bout my Pa—"

"C'mon, y'all let's go to the Pine Thicket," Lil Sol says, watching another boy approaching. "We'll swing on the Flying Jenny. Here comes ol Hickernut Hickery."

"Yeah, boy," Ben Henry says, walking through the broken door into the shade of a live oak spreading a dark canopy over the small one-room jail. "Two riding, two pushing. Me and Lil Sol riding first."

R.C. Hickery saunters under the oak. "Pigpen Swinnard always wanting to be the first rider."

"Yeah," says Willy Buck, "I'm always last."

"Not this time, Willy Buck," Lil Sol says. "You and me riding first. Ben Henry likes to push—"

"Okay, but you better not skin up my head like you did last time," Ben Henry says. "Swole up like a turkey egg."

R.C. giggles. "Pigpen, you skint your own head."

Willy Buck turns to Ben Henry. "Gotta duck and jump outta the way—that ol pine pole swinging on top of that stump will knock the daylights out of you if you forget to duck—"

"I ducked," whines Ben Henry. "Still hit me up side the head. Hurt for two weeks—"

"C'mon," says R.C., "Let's go get our guns and we can play cowboys and Indians. Let's go!"

"Why must I always be the Indian?" says Willy Buck. "Cause I'm black?"

R.C. snickers. "Naw. Cause Lil Sol thinks he's the Lone Ranger, and you're his sidekick Tonto."

"Bob Steele fights better than the Durango Kid," Ben Henry says. "Remember that time the *real* Bob Steele stepped out on the stage in the Tupelo Theatre, two six shooters blazing away. Boy, now that was somethin. Bob Steele coming from Hollywood to Ring Jaw—"

"I still believe Charles Starrett could out-draw Bob Steele," R.C. says. "Remember Gene Autry in that serial, *The Phantom Empire*, fighting them strange creatures living under a mountain?"

"Yeah, but Bob Steele don't sing—he fights better," Ben Henry says. "I don't like cowboys singing to their horse all the time."

R.C. frowns. "I still like Charles Starrett as the Durango Kid. He's better'n Lash LaRue—"

"Shoot,' says Willy Buck, "I Like Wild Bill Elliott as Red Ryder and Little Beaver—"

"That's cause Little Beaver's an Indian" says Ben Henry, laughing. "You're Tonto, remember."

"And you're the outlaw," Willy Buck says. "Aint he, Lil Sol?"

"Look yonder coming," says Lil Sol.

Walking toward the River Road, the boys hear in the distance the growling gears of an approaching pulpwood truck. The groan of the engine increases as the cab with two teenaged boys passes.

Lil sol squints in the sunlight, smelling the sour acrid leak from the muffler. "That's Rooster Reddoake and crazy ol Hunky Hoggen. You can smell them."

"I'm glad they didn't see us," R.C. says. "Hope they don't come down yonder to the Pine Thicket."

"C'mon, they're goin the other way toward Hasty's Pool Room," Willy Buck says. "I shorely don't wanna be pestered any more by them mean boys. Always poking my feet with that old hot piece of haywire, making me dance, calling me ugly bad names. They don't like the color of my skin. Shoot, can't help being black—"

"Willy Buck," Lil Sol says, watching the truck swallowed in a cloud of road dust, "they don't like anyone. Even themselves. Forget it. Let's go play. We'll come back by the mercantile store. Maybe Grandpa will be there and tell us a story."

Willy Buck hesitates, dragging a toe in the sand road. "Uncle Sol Cahoon always sittin there, tellin stories just like you, Lil Sol. You just like him, except your hair grows red as that soldier Roscoe Ransum."

Lil Sol laughs. "Willy Buck, betcha Rooster and ol crazy Hunky don't go messing with Roscoe Ransum."

6

Rooster and Hunky

White spumes of exhaust leak from the ruptured truck muffler, and vapors hang soured in the still summer air. The stink doesn't bother Rooster Reddoake and Hunky Hoggen. They slump in the hot cab, dark slick sweat clinging to the corded muscles of their bare backs pressing against the broken seat, metal coils worming from the torn fabric like bones of a decayed carcass.

The teenagers had found a cool shade, hiding from the stinging sun in the middle of the afternoon. Rooster had braked the rattletrap of a paperwood truck, letting it cough to a stop beneath a live oak tree. A breeze stirs as they turn their eyes across the sand-rutted river road to the limestone store building.

Through the dust-caked windshield, Rooster sees the Old Man, sitting alone, faintly perspiring, slouching on the wooden bench. Nailhole straws of sunlight streaming from the curled tin roof bathe and halo the Old Man. Light strikes silver on the great mane of hair. From this distance, the webbed shadows frame Solomon Jackson Cahoon like a grayed, grainy portrait shimmering in the July heat.

Rooster jerks a shoulder and straightens; he stretches his sun-browned arms, smells the sour stale sweat of his armpits, and quickly shoves his left leg through the paneless cab door window. He gnaws at a Barlow knife, pulling the blade out with his teeth. Rooster aims an eager surgical eye on the nail growing jaggedly over long from his scaly and dingy big toe now bathed by sunlight and standing like a rifle barrel sight. "Hunky, gimme one of them readyrolls."

"Dammit, why don't *you* buy some?" Hunky asks, whining his minor hurt between gulps of beer from a brown Spearman bottle.

"Gimme a cigarette, *dammit!*" Rooster says. He squints his left eye and fixes the other on the Old Man. He wiggles his toe into the line of sight. Rooster aims the knife blade like a pistol—"Bang! You're dead, old man!"—and pokes the other empty palm toward Hunky, nervously fishing the last Domino cigarette from a crushed pack. "Gimme a swig of beer."

Hunky grunts, wiping foam from his cracked lips, his dark eyes darting. "Hell, Rooster, smoke my last cigarette and drank my last swallow of Spearman. *Damn!*"

Rooster giggles. "Cool off, Hunky. Maybe we oughta hit the watah down yonder at Cooter Landing."

"Gawddam sure hot enough," Hunky says. "Aint nothen to do in this God-forsaken town before sundown. Slap these gawddam ol gnats and wait for early frost."

"Hell, Hunky, we got four boars, two whores—"

"And whole lotta nothin cept Purple Martin gourds."

Rooster grins, pointing. "Yeah, look who's coming yondah."

Four barefooted boys bob aimlessly along the weeded pigtrail like tattered remnants of an army platoon returning from combat. They approach the porch of the Ring Jaw Mercantile Store.

Hunky cackles. "Lil Sol and them other tiny farts, with Dink Santee black as ink right behind."

"Yeah, Lil Sol's Army, armed and ready to fight,"

Rooster says, shifting his elevated leg, sighting his big toe toward the approaching boys in denim overalls.

"But scarit of their shadows," Hunky says. "And the ol peglegged headless ghost down on the rivah."

"Hey, *boy!*" Rooster yells. "Bang! Bang! You're dead!"

"Hey, *boy!*" Hunky mocks, pointing the empty bottle like a six shooter. "Draw! This heah town aint big enough for bof'us. Which one's Bob Steele? Ken Maynard? Look at Injun Willy Buck—Lil Dink playing with the palefaces!"

"Playing with his pecker mostly," Rooster snickers, the cigarette paper sticking to his bottom lip. "Hunky, somebody oughta cut that old man's head off."

The boys stop, turning toward the truck.

"There they are, always pestering Willy Buck," says Lil Sol. Red tufts of hair riot from holes in a straw hat; from his denimed hips a holster stitched from tire rubber dangles a western cap pistol with eggshell-white plastic handles. "Don't say anything."

Willy Buck glances at the old truck, darkly embraced by the oak canopy. "I aint going that way—I'm going on down to Uncle Charley's house."

"Wait!" says Lil Sol. "Grandpa might tell us the story bout your cousin Buck—"

"Uncle Charley said don't talk bout that. Booger might get me."

"Aw, c'mon, Willy Buck, it's just a story," says Ben Henry, cradling a cork-stopper double-barreled shotgun in his right arm.

R.C. brings up the rear of the pigtrail column with a whittled board and clothespin rubber gun and a sharpened-stick saber with a tin handle cut from a Prince Albert tobacco can in a wide black belt. Two steps back, Willy Buck, the black caboose everybody calls Dink, trails as the Indian with a chicken-yard feather protruding from a ragbag band circling his head.

"Dink, the Lil Nig—dance a jig!" Rooster laughs.

"What y'all got tween your legs?" Hunky asks, chuckling. "Something to play with? Say, boy, wanna play pocket pool down at the rivah?"

The boys quickly dart away from the truck without looking, their feet stirring dust, and run for the store porch.

Rooster bangs a fist against the trunk door. "Hey, boy, why you always run for your damned ol grandpa?"

Hunky stares blankly. "Betcha he's sitting there, telling them big lies like he does every day."

Rooster bellows again: "*Hey*, boy! —"

Lil Sol stops, turns toward the truck, his voice trembling. "You quit talking about Grandpa. He's an old man and he's almost blind."

Rooster mumbles: "If ever an old sonofabitch needed killin, it's that old man—Uncle Solomon."

Hunky keeps giggling.

Rooster sucks in the smoke of the last Domino and laughs. Slowly curls of smoke drain from his nostrils. He carves the half-moon nail from his big toe, looks at the growth closely and tosses it in the weeds. He sights again across the big toe, watching the boys reach the porch. Knotting his right fist, Rooster rams his knuckles against the dashboard. "That ol basturd's always showing that ol knife to somebody. Maybe I oughta show him the nut-cutting edge of this heah tater blade."

"Yeah, Rooster, yeah—" Hunky sucks the cigarette; ashes fall in his lap like dandruff—"You man nough to try?"

"Wanna try *me*?"

Hunky slaps Rooster on the shoulder, and laughs. "Ol buddy, it's a helluva lot more fun sitting heah in the shade,

pesterin buncha snotnosed little pissants playin cowboys and Injuns."

Rooster draws back like a coiled rattler. He thrusts the knife in Hunky's face. "Keep your gawddam dirty paws off me, heah? I'll cut you, Hunky!"

Hunky jumps back. "Cool off, Rooster. Hell, forget it, man. Let's go back to Hasty's Pool Room, get a beer and head for Cooter Landing."

"You buying?"

"Yeah, readyrolls, too."

"Hunky, that's better'n snuff and not half as dusty."

"Better'n jacking off?"

"Not quite."

"As Pa says, second best thing is loping your mule."

They laugh.

The engine sputters, coughs and gas-fires. Grinding gears and the roar of the motor snuff out the last echoes of laughter.

Exhaust fumes hang heavy in the still July air. The old truck muffler leaks a sour stink as Rooster and Hunky move along the River Road in front of a feathered shaft of dust and smoke.

The boys reach the porch of the store where the Old Man sits alone in lengthening shadows of lazy afternoon. He turns, as do the four boys, hearing the last faint echoes of the truck engine.

"Keep away from them good-fer-nothing fellers," the Old Man says, his voice like gravel.

"Aw, Grandpa," says Lil Sol, "it's just ol Rooster and Hunky—"

The Old Man's eyes darken; his lips curl and moisten. "More like rattlesnakes in palmettos. Keep yo distance— you know what I'm talking at?"

"Pa says Rooster Reddoake's meaner a coiled rattler," says Ben Henry, climbing onto the porch.

The Old Man looks at Ben Henry, then turns his eyes into the sun. "Crazier'n a skunk-squirted dog, foamin at the mouth. Ol Lige, off in the gang, shovelin and sweatin on the hard road, and his yearlin boy yonder huntin trouble. He's gonna try to hurt somebody yet."

"Just bullies," says Lil Sol.

The Old Man coughs. "Stay outta his shadow. You *heah*?"

"Tell us that story, Grandpa."

"That shirttail boy with a daddy wearing convict stripes up to no damn good like lotta heathen folks I knowed in my time—"

"Tell em, Grandpa."

Look and Tremble Shoal,
Chipola River, West Florida
© Jesse Earle Bowden
Limited Edition

7

The Heathen

"Tell us about the lynching, Uncle Solomon." The thin
shrill youthful voice breaks the stillness of the humid July
afternoon on the shadowed porch of the Ring Jaw
mercantile store. Other jabbering voices chorus the plea
as the knot of barefooted boys crowd nervously around
the Old Man sitting alone on an Oakwood bench. "Tell
us about the time you saw that colored man hanging from
the limb of an old oak tree."

"Grandpa, tell them," says Chance Cahoon, sweat
beads reddening his freckled face and arms. "Please sir,
tell them."

The Old Man called Uncle Solomon by almost
everyone in Ring Jaw seems to awaken to Lil Sol and the
others hunkering down around him.

All tanned legs and arms, they're no more than
thirteen. Only moments before they had been animated
boyhood, chasing their picture show cowboy-and-Indian
fantasies and idling away another hazed summery
afternoon in the Pine Thicket and along the nearby
weed-edged pigtrail; hurling rocks at tin cans, tussling,
swatting gnats and swapping smalltalk.

They gather around the Old Man in anticipation.
Shaded from the sun in the shadows of the porch, the
boys continue knocking away gnats pestering their matted

107

manes, sweaty faces and shirtless torsos. The gnats don't bother the Old Man. He stares into emptiness. Whopperjawed, a cud of tobacco buried in the pocket of his stained mouth, he rolls over his wad, purses his lips and skeets an amber rope of juice over the wooden porch, and draws the back of his hand across his mouth.

. "You younguns know better'n to talk bout such things," he says, tumbling his chew in rhythmic consistency. "The booger getcha shonuff. Oughta whup you with a gallberry switch. Got no bidness knowin bout nothun don't mean nothun to you."

He continues his blank stare. "Remember, younguns, what it said right there in the Good Book. Ol Jeremiah, who had the same name as my ol Pa. *Thus saith the Lord, learn not the way of the heathen, and be not dismayed at the signs of Heaven; for the heathen are dismayed at them.* My momma used to preach that to me back yondah when I was bout your age...."

Again, he's silent.

His old eyes are drawn beyond shadowy angles of the tin roof and the town's vistas before him: sagging storefronts squatting along rutted sand streets; two sleepy motionless hounds, shaded by a rusting cowshed roof; clusters of live oaks and pecan trees; miasmic shimmers of heat waves wilting another vanishing day.

Out of the stillness come low groans of a wagon's rickety wheels grinding through fine deep sand, stirring swirls of dust. A farmer's mule bobs along the crusted River Road crossing the slagged highway.

Behind the Old Man, inside the store's windowed showcase—lined with farm tools, animal harnesses, sewing thread, ax handles, pocket knives, brogans and Red Goose shoes—an ancient pineywoods trophy of menacing dimensions spreads like a mosaic over the back wall: a diamond-patterned skin of a rattlesnake, headless, scaly and faded, stretching vertically more than seven feet, with sixteen rattles and a button.

"You killed lots of things, didn't you, Grandpa?" Lil Sol draws close, less fearful than the others, crossing his tan legs, sitting in front of the Old Man, looking straight into the washed-out eyes of the boys' favorite storyteller whose daily perch is what townspeople called the loafers' bench. "Even that big snake hanging yonder in the window."

"Yeah, son—some folks mean as that snake long time ago," the Old Man whispers hoarsely. "Meaner, maybe. Serpents and varmints and such always lurking in the garden, don't you see."

Ben Henry finds courage: "Uncle Sol, sir, tell us bout the ghost of Look'n Tremble?"

The Old Man coughs. "*Ghost*? Who says so?"

"Come on, Pigpen, he don't want to talk about that," Lil Sol says.

"Shoot, everbody knows Uncle Solomon was the one dug up that murdered one-legged man from the graveyard and cut off his head," Hickernut says, his words worming through buck teeth.

"Says who?"

"Pa said the sheriff got your grandpa to dig up that man who got knocked in the head with a pump-point down on the river at Look'n Tremble. Cut off the head so they could tell how he was killed."

"Says who?"

"Pa says they boiled his head in a lard can in the jailhouse yard. Pa saw the skull, right there in the courtroom the day they sent the murderer to Raiford. Pa said the sheriff gave your grandpa a twenty dollar bill and a gallon of whiskey to cut off that head—"

"Shut up, Pigpen!" says Lil Sol. "None of your concern."

"Shoot, Lil Sol, you know folks around here say the headless man they called Pegleg Whiskey George still walks the woods at night, down yonder at Look'n Tremble shoals—"

"Hell no, boy," the Old Man says. "Whiskey George's long dead and buried. You too tender to hear such a scary thing like that. And I warn you: stay away from Look'n Tremble at night. Some ol booger down there grab you snotnosed younguns."

The Old Man laughs. "Ghost! What a lie!" He spits again, his eyes following the squirming boys.

"Come on, Willy Buck," Lil Sol yells at the speck of brown flashing white buck teeth, standing in the sunlight. "Grandpa's going to tell the story."

"No sir," Willy Buck says. "Uncle Charley'll tear up my bee-hin with a razor strop. Better just get on home. Bye!" The black boy darts down the River Road, following the dust of the wagon. In a flash, he's gone.

The Old man turns. "Chance, that Willy Santee's grandson?"

"Yessir. He's Willy Buck. The big boys call him Nig or Dink."

"You call him Willy Buck, heah? That's a good name, Willy. His grandpa was a good friend long time ago. Miss him still."

"Uncle Sol," Hickernut says, "you ought to see Nig dance a jig when them older boys threaten to brand him with red-hot haywire."

The Old Man straightens. "Leave that youngun alone, yuh *heah*?"

"Tell us the story, Grandpa."

"I might and I might not. Aint no tellin."

The Old Man perches here most days now, on the porch near the snake trophy he had brought from the turpentine woods in his own youth. Now little more than a shabby shadow of time past, tobacco juice oozing over pale lips, staining brown lines in the wrinkled corners of his mouth. His gnarled hands—hands that severed the snake's head and cut away the skin with a Barlow pocket knife—grip the curved handle of a hickory-wood walking cane now his crutch and constant companion. He holds the cane upright between long gangling legs covered with faded and frayed khaki, sockless feet cased in scuffed brogans.

The Old Man sits here and tells stories often now. His body is bent like an old mossy oak weighted down with branches and time. Shadows thicken around his cottony thatch of once-black wiry hair crowding his forehead and growing like a summer weed patch. His white mane almost touches craggy gray brows above tight dark rheumy eyes set deep in a square face sagging around a blue-veined bulbous nose. A knife scar protrudes from other facial erosions, running jaggedly from his left ear over a tight-set jaw into leathery layers of skin forming a massive neck.

Chipola country folks whisper: The Old Man had Creek Indian blood mixed with his Scots-Irish. Chained in a painfully arthritic body drained of youthful vitality, the Old Man sees through eyes washed into dimness in the latter years of a turbulent life now in its eighty-fifth summer. His clouded vision turns to mere fogged mists of eroded time.

He came out of the past like a creature of the woods, smelling rosiny, his reluctance and strangeness mystifying the youthful gawkers. He's *Old Age* to those who know him and watch him, the sunset of all his yesterdays. Yet, sitting here with baggy-lidded eyes, he's a facade of his former self: stubborn independence born of pride and an arrogance hiding inward fears.

He'd turned into mysterious myth—old West Florida

vinegar and piss, cracked as old pottery shards. He gazes into the sun, hunting some sharper recollection in its blinding heat.

"Grandpa, you told the grown-up folks all about the lynching the other day, sitting right here," Lil Sol pleads.

"Awright, awright, boy," the Old Man says, words tangled in a rasping cough. "But I might cut off your tallywhackers and feed em to the hawgs!"

The boys giggle. Lil Sol says, "No sir, you won't neither, Grandpa. Tell them the story!"

"Well, younguns, it was back'n thirty-four when it happen up the road yondah, don't you see," the Old Man says, tracing aimless patterns on the floor with his cane. "Long time ago. Men were meaner then. Meaner'n pure hell itself."

The Old Man pauses again, glancing into Lil Sol's alert brown eyes. He runs stiff fingers through the damp red hair of his grandson. "Son, you remind me of your great grandpa, ol Jeremiah Cahoon. Fought Yankees in the ol Confederate war. Purty damn mean hisself—specially that day back'n 1864 when them Yankee niggers rode into Chipola Springs burnin and killin—"

"How mean, Grandpa?"

"Mean enough to sack a treed wildcat with a crokersack. Mean enough to scare shoes right offen a nigger in a watermelon patch."

The boys giggle.

"Yessir, mean enough to stand and fight them Yankee basturds who come roaring into Redlands County. Yessir, and when I was a young man myself, folks roun heah was mean enough to run most of the niggers out of Redlands County, don't you see? Didn't come back for more'n a year...."

The Old Man's voice trails off in a hacking cough. Silent again, staring blankly, as if memory fails him.

Uncle Solomon knew mustang violence and primitive spirit of West Florida backwoods and crossroad settlements during the rawhide and lawless timber-turpentine days. He lived close to the earth, like his father before him, harvesting its fruit and its pine and hardwood and barreling its rosin and its liquor. He stood in the throat of adversity in the bleak, dirt-poor years of a new century merely a continuation of a frontier of woodcutters, turpentiners and sawmillers. In the woods, he saw back-talking *uppity* black men die in a spray of buckshot from the trigger fingers of white woodsriders. In poolrooms and whiskey dins he smelled and tasted hot blood of some *Big Stand Up in the Road* challenging him with animalistic aggressions, fortified with sharply whetted pocket knives or icepicks with "Drink Cola-Cola" emblazoned in red on the handle ... or with other expedient weapons: two-by-four board, fat lighterd knot, car tire iron, fat end of a pool cue or an iron rib from a Model-A Ford body axle spring.

Outwardly he wore his scars as badges of self-perceived honor, affecting a robust and *much-of-a-man* confidence and independence setting him apart from the hardscrabble, stoical country people walking the same three-trail roads, sweating in the same pineywoods, and fishing the same bream and shellcracker beds of the narrow pristine Chipola River.

To Ring Jaw youngsters, eager for legend and thrill in an otherwise country boy's mundane and monotonous regimen, the Old Man—snake killer and survivor of dozens of knife fights and a few man-killings—is a fascinating mossback, a dinosaur of an ancient age. He's a primitive so distant from their world that his reminiscences ring with heroic fantasy. His earthy experiences epitomize the essence of long-gone yet revered *meanness* of all their town's yesterdays.

Even Ring Jaw boys know the Old Man's time was now seeping into darkness, his memory flickering like a dying campfire flame caught by wind.

For them, only the most bizarre and violent episodes will survive webbed intricacies of memory, and that too will be warped with embellishments emphasizing the most bloody and horrendous kinds of *meanness*. These latter-day spectators, watching from some time-distant arena, shouting for victory and vengeance, cheering the brave in lockstep with *meanness*, make folkheroes of old busthead-drunk heathen defying fear with bullet and blade.

"I heared bout that lil girl gettin raped and killed one cold mawnin," the Old Man says, his rheumy eyes suddenly alive and darting. "Purty lil thang, Beulah Callie Baskum was. No more'n nineteen. She didn't come home for supper, and her Pa and some of them boys found her bloody body covered with logs and brush in the river woods. Her haid busted open with a clawhammer they'd been usin to fix the fence.

"Lots of folks powerful het up over the killin, don't you see. They knowed it was a nigger right out. Warnt long fore the sheriff found that black basturd hidin in the corn crib. Found a piece of cloth at the murder scene that fit his tore jumper jacket. Word spread through this heah country like fire in tuppentine woods.

"Course the sheriff knew a mob would gather. Hid out the nigger over'n the Washington County jail.

"I tell y'all. Folks from everywhere swarmed in there round that ol Baskum farmhouse up yondah near the Chipola, north of Chipola Springs. Cars come from Alabama and Georgia. Lotta us ol fellers from roun heah went up there too, drinkin busthead and makin damn fools of ourselves—"

Ben Henry, on his knees, feet clotted with dirt, asks, "You help kill Buck Santee, Uncle Solomon?"

The Old Man's deep-set eyes are unmoved, filling with water. His long twisted fingers tighten around the handle of the walking stick, and momentarily he shuffles his heavy brogans against the grit of the wood floor. Without expression, the tobacco wad locked in his jaw, the Old Man brings up his cane, and then brings it down, wood striking wood, with sharp thudding. He shifts his eyes to his hands:

—*hands* gripping the leather reins of a woods pony during the twenties when working as a turpentine woodsrider....

—*hands* holding the wood stock of a plaited rawhide bullwhip hanging from his saddlehorn coiled like a Diamondback—often unleashed as lightning tongues, severing the head of a rattlesnake; sometimes lacerating the backside of a turpentine nigger causing his torment....

"*You sonofabitch! Talk back to me, and I'll cut you in two and leave you for the hawgs and buzzards.*"

—*hands* holding the handle of a Barlow pocket knife with its razor's edge, whittling while watching the red flames of a woods campfire...

—*hands* guiding the Barlow blade when likker-induced violence opens a white man's belly and the gash runs red, spilling onto the barroom floor like a stuck hog...

"*Back off, you bastard. Call me a liar and you'll tote your guts back home in a washtub!*"

—*hands* pulling the trigger of a thirty-eight caliber revolver, stopping dead in his tracks a busthead-drunk attacker who surely would have knifed him to death....

"*Sheriff, I told that tub'uh guts not to come on me with that knife. Told him I'd kill him show's the world.*"

—hands filling a half-pint whiskey bottle with carbolic acid in the dark midnight and delivering the lethal brew to a black man through the calaboose window bars. And in the sunup of the wintry dawn the town marshal found his prisoner, charged with the murder of a turpentine woodsrider, dead on the cold stone floor with his frightening eyes glaring at the steel-cage ceiling and his rosiny hands clutching his burned-out throat in the black rotting silence . . .

"Hey, boy! Wanna drank of good busthead likker?"

"Yassuh! Yassuhree. Much oblige."

"Sho settle your nerves so you can sleep before the sheriff gets heah in the mawnin. Here's a half-pint. Keep the bottle."

"Yassuh, capm. Thank you, capm."

—hands working a shovel along the hot torturous miles of hard road, moving truckloads of dirt for a year-and-a-day as a state prisoner in black and white stripes, repaying the law for fermenting and hauling rotgut whiskey from Chipola River canebrakes...

"Bossman, can I have a drank of watah to cut the dust, pleasesuh?"

"Watah boy! Give him a dipper full. Move yo black ass!"

"Yassuh, capm!"

"Thank you, capm."

"Move that dirt, white boy! We got miles to go before sundown."

"Yassuh, bossman!"

"In the jailhouse now, in the jailhouse now!"

"Rather drank muddy watah ... rather drank muddy watah and sleep in a holler log ... than to be in Atlanta treated like a scalded dog!"

—hands in the chilly river mists of the October night the men bring Buck Santee back to the scene of the crime of raping and murdering pretty young Beulah Callie Baskum on the banks of the Chipola River; with men mutilating and slaying the black laborer in shameless

humiliation that was the wild surging and cold dark terror of a maddog lynch mob lusting for blood and venegeance....

"Aw, goddam, Sol, if a nigger ever needed killing, this one needs a slow, painful death. Somebody gimme a sharp knife."

"Well, blood's already on our hands...."

The Old Man looks up from his hands, staring into the sunlight, his squinting eyes fixed on something beyond his hands and beyond the store-porch gathering. His lips move. There was no sound, no words. The Old Man stares with nothing worse than a malevolent leer into the stillness embracing him.

"Uncle Solomon," Ben Henry says.

"Huh?"

"You help kill Buck Santee that night?"

"Naw, not really," the Old Man says, his raspy voice sinking into softness, his leathery face expressionless. "Mostly just there, in the crowd. Some of these ol fellers roun here had a hand in it, though. One of em bragged bout his knife castrated the nigger. Coulda been. But we were all there, running hawg-wild like frisky bucks, shoutin, cussin, drankin lots of busthead whiskey.

"Never seed as many hawglegs and scatterguns and tater blades as I did when that bunch gathered at the Baskum farm. They was mighty mad white folks. They kept talkin bout them Yankees burning Chipola Springs and how they'd run all the colored folks out of Redlands County. But suppose you could say we was all guilty as hell."

The Old Man is silent again. His eyes tighten in furrows of wrinkles, deep lines spelling the rigors of his years; gray hair like snow atop a mountainpeak; breath laden with midday toddy. He looks at the tin roof leaking sun light. He squeezes his eyes shut, lowers his head, then opens them, staring at the wood cane. "Been roun trouble all my life," the Old Man says in a low voice. "Never as bad as that night back'n thirty-four. Nevah! I'd stand up to any man, like my Pa Jeremiah. Hell, I kilt a nigger or two and a white man that needed killing. But I aint nevah seed nothun like that."

"Grandpa," Lil Sol says, "you ever meet your match?"

"Suppose so. But I'm still heah, younguns. I made it to old age. But that aint worth a goddam, don't you know. Caint do nothun no more. Outlived all my ol buddies roun heah. Nothun left but memories of this heah place I knowed all my life. Younguns, remember: you make your own memories."

Ring Jaw.
Shabby, leafy, sun-hazed, green in summer, gray and smoky in winter; sandbed streets splotched with horse tracks and droppings and mule dung and horse flies and thin rubber tire ruts and big-toed footprints of shirttail boys moving through their seasons of giggling, frolicking youth; weathered old store buildings and shotgun houses bunched on back roads of another West Florida backwash—far in mind and in miles from that unknown mysterious world yonder in haste of faceless outsiders; people hunkering down in everyday monotony of sunup-to-sundown sweating labor; people hardened with squinting eyes and hollow faces radiating rigors and despair of dollarless days that were their straitjacket long before the desperate seasons of the Great Depression; a greasy-spoon town cafe where the woman behind the cash register sells lightbread sandwiches and collard greens and fatback pork and salted mullet and charred round steak and sugared tea and Martha White cornbread; creaking wheels of old farm wagons rolling behind plodding mules with their heads bobbing misery in the stinging sun; a motionless parade of down-and-out codgers lining the doorway of the poolroom, watching curiously the slow

traffic of the one-stop-a-day bus station and the patent-medicine drug store, and sipping Co'Coler and Spearman beer; groan and roar of engines of pulpwood trucks with grinding gears in mists of stinking exhaust fumes; men in the woods living by muscle and courage more than by mind; ambitions dwarfed by the simple urge to survive and find contentment, heightened by the peace of hooking catfish from dark river pools and passing the likker bottle; street gossip spreading like wildfire among folks of narrow lives in an isolated backwater of societal tides and time; manwork limited to land and its nourishment and its hewn wood for a few dollars pay on Saturday morning; white men cynically calling themselves *turpentine niggers*, sharing miseries with colored folks living down the road in Shantytown; blacks coming to the back door and asking permission to enter—removing hats from the back of heads and calling every white man *Mistah* or *Capm*, and punctuating each muttered thought with *yassuh* and *nossuh*—crowding stores in the twilight of long hard days in the woods and in the farm fields, dirty and dusty, nervous in a white man's world of commerce; security of tradition—embracing home-bred folks as neighbors and confederates and casting suspicion on outsiders: *damyankees* talking too fast and not eating grits and taters and not understanding Southern customs where whites and blacks sit on riverbanks and fish for supper and talk and laugh and sometimes share a fruitjar of moonshine whiskey; husky-voiced men with red necks and brown, muscular arms guarding chain-gang convicts, standing in shadows with the authority of a shotgun loaded with buckshot, watching men build hard roads with leg-irons clanking, sharp metal cutting their ankles, and blood oozing in their brogans; nocturnal whiskeymakers and bootleggers cooking moonshine with store-bought sugar, chicken-feed mash, and steel nerves—and selling brew rotting the guts of strong men drowning fears and frustrations with likker deep in their bellies; hard men the churchwomen call *heathen* drinking and fighting and fornicating in a wild and lawless frenzy, proving they are much-of-a-man or a coward, living in fear they too will go into the earth in a pool of blood; and bloodshot eyes of young bucks in church on Sunday mornings with the little woman and the younguns, knowing they have to get right with the Lord or they will go to hell as heathen, their souls burning forevermore; a small place where change remains inevitably the same.

"Where'd y'all find Buck Santee, Uncle Solomon?" Ben Henry asks.

"Warnt easy. A damn long wait, it was. The sheruff, he kept hidin out that boy in jails—over at Chipley, then Panneemaw City; then over yonder roun Pensacola. The law got scarit. Everbody had a gun, looking for that black boy. Finally the law hid him over the line at Brewton, Alabamer.

"When some of them ol boys found out, they hit the back roads of Alabamer and grabbed Buck Santee from a scarit deputy guardin the Brewton jail in the middle of the night.

"I heared tell that high sheruff in Pensacola worked over Buck Santee with a blackjack and got him to confess it all. Didn't much matter; they tell me that long ride back to Redlands County warnt no damn joy trip for that scarit boy. Them fellers picked at him with pocket knives all the way.

"Ol man Hiram Hagar Baskum was a sad sight, all juiced out by the sun; eyes red from cryin and lack of sleep. Mad sonofabitch he was. Swore he'd kill that goddam nigger rat there in his own front yard. And he waited a long spell with a hawgleg in his hand before that crowd. Must have been two thousand of em with

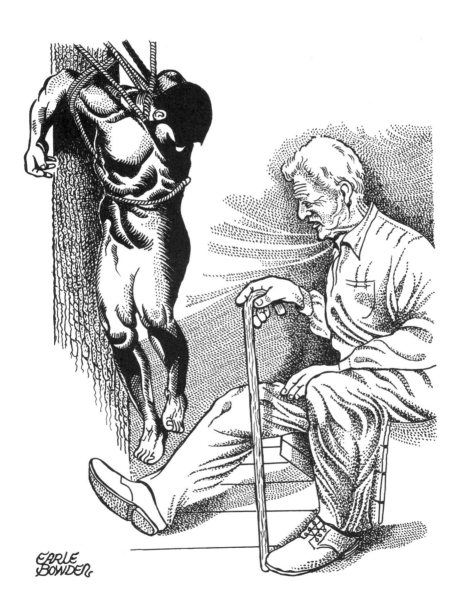

their guns and their headlights shinin all over the cornfields.

"But ol Mistah Hiram finally broke down, squallin, standin rat there on his own porch. Cried like a baby. Said he couldn't kill the basturd there. Never be able to live on the ol place agin. Couldn't blame him none, his baby daughter murdered on the place.

"It was just as well; that mob done took him to the river. They meant bidness. Cut off his privates and made him eat em. They'd pull the rope round his neck and cross the limb of an oak tree, and he'd kick like hell and almost strangle. Then he'd be back wallerin on the ground—and you could see the knife blades shinin by the light of the fire and the moon. Finally that nigger was a bloody sonofabitch. The torment went on it seems like hours. But a quiet come ovah that crowd when they finally realized Buck Santee was deader'n a butchered sow on a cold winter mawnin.

"Then they tied the body to the back of a car and drove back up the road to the Baskum house. The crowd rushed round the car; they dumped the dead nigger right'n front of ol Mistah Hiram. That old man was shaking, tears gushin from his eyes. But he stood right there, pumpin three pistol shots in Buck Santee's bloody head.

"Bunch of boys bout your age, I reckon, they stuck sharpened sticks in the corpse till somebody told them to quit.

"Sometime roun three o'clock that mawnin another bunch yellin and cussin hauled that dead man to Chipola Springs and hung it from that old oak tree beside of the courthouse. Goddam wild bunch, cussing, getting drunker and drunker. Warnt no stopping em, like wild bull yearlins. You was with em or you got stomped.

"Bout sunup, reckon it was, the sheruff cut down the body. But that wild bunch was still crazy for blood. They tried to knock down the courthouse door demandin the sheriff give up the nigger's body.

"By this time hundreds of folks was pourin into Chipola Springs. And fights broke out. Somebody said a nigger hit a white man with a beer bottle. Fore long they was whuppin the hell out of niggers all ovah them streets and roun the courthouse square. Runnin whole nigger families out of town. Warnt no stoppin that wild bunch.

"Nevah seed as many bloody faces and tore and bloody shirts as I did roun that courthouse that day.

"But that crowd of loudmouths cooled down purty goddam quick when them National Guard soldiers marched up the hill into Chipola Springs and set up machineguns on the square. They yelled and cussed at them soldiers as they marched into town—some folks even spit on them. But the sight of them rifles and machineguns done took the wind out of them ol boys' sails.

"Most of em just turned away and went on back home to their families. It was about over. I come on back home myself and sobered up. Just tried to forget it. Warnt nothun evah done bout it neither. I did hear tell there was lots bout it in the papers. Some folks up yondah in Washington and New York raised hell with the governor. Far's I know, nothun much evah come of it roun heah."

The Old Man is again silent, as if tired of telling his nightmare; as if suddenly drained of its terrifying shame. He leans forward, opens his mouth and spits the moist brown cud over the edge of the porch. He puts his right hand in his pants pocket and pulls out a Barlow knife. He opens the blade, gleaming with whetstone sharpness.

The boys move back, Hickernut asking, "That the knife?"

"That the knife you had that night?" Ben Henry yells shrilly.

The Old Man coughs. Pulling a plug of Bloodhound chewing tobacco from his shirt pocket, he slices a fresh chew and buries it in his right jaw.

Momentarily he holds the knife before him, his right hand covering the bone Barlow handle. With stiff fingers, he feels the blade's edge. His eyes are cold and empty and rigid in a faraway stare—

The gnawing has been there since the cold October night in 1934—the inner self adrift in guilt and remorse; enmeshed by a malignancy; tortured by a self-inflicted thornbed of crucifixion. Suddenly older and nearer the grave, the dark bloody October night filters through thickets of memory. *Thirst*; thirst for another toddy: a big drank of whiskey; a man-sized shot; maybe a half-pint. *Evil* of the thirst of the turpentine nigger trapped in calaboose darkness; gnawing thrist while tortured by the hard-road inferno when the chain-gang guard allows a dipperful of water—cool water cutting the dust of his parched throat; gnawing thirst for a snort of moonshine whiskey.

An *aching*; a strange unexplainable feeling: same as aching hours waiting in the woods by the river in 1934, stomping around cornfields, warming backsides with cornstalk and lighterd-knot fires and coating thirsty innards with the numbing courage of stumphead likker; the night men's meanness reached its zenith and infected the years with a cancer of cowardice corroding the spirit and searing the soul.

I seed Buck Santee only that one time—the last tortured hours of his young life: black eyes swimmin in wept fear, dartin in desperation, flashin terror of his last earthly moments slidin into silence and sobbed acceptance.

At first, mutterings, gushin through hushed sobs:
"Kind sirs, can I have one of them cigarettes?"
*"Hell no, black boy, where you're goin you gonna smoke
like hawg guts strung up in a smokehouse."*
*"Yassuh, capm. Pleasesuh, I knowed I done wrong.
Yassuh, bossman. Pleasesuh, have mercy on me."*

*I seed his butchered body awash in his own hot blood: the
final moments ragin an eternity amid swirlin smoke from the
pinewood fire, hangin on the gray mists curlin over the
riverbank cypress and oak. Some men doin the meanness had
plenty of doubt bout his guilt. Was it our own guilt and
vanity? Besides Buck's uncle, Willy Santee, was my friend.
Loved the ol riverrat whiskeymaker like a brother. Buck Santee
nevah done nothun to me.*

Old phantoms whisper Momma's words: "Solomon, you
make your own memories."

The Old man looks up from the knife. "Now, you
younguns, get away from heah—or I'll show you how
they cut Buck Santee that night. *Who's first?"*

Squealing, laughing nervously, the boys bolt away,
jumping off the porch in the sunshine.

"Nosirree, Uncle Solomon, you won't neither!" Ben
Henry shouts, his blue eyes focused on the steel blade.

"Grandpa's just teasing," Lil Sol says. "Just teasing."

Ben Henry yells: "That the knife that castrated Buck
Santee that night?"

The Old Man laughs. "Could be," he says, shoving
the knife blade through the air with a swift slicing motion.
"Could be. Just might be. Aint no tellin. Just aint no
tellin."

8

A Legacy

*T*he Old Man laughs, touching a stiffened thumb against the knife blade sharpness stained with fragments of chewing tobacco. In the distance, he hears the fading screams as the boys race along the River Road. Quickly they are gone, their voices whispery in the dust. *I've told my old and timeworn tale of horror again. Oughten not be talkin that way to my grandson and them other younguns, no more'n thirteen, still wet behind the ears. But they gotta learn you run with heathen you become one yourself. Now, my memory races way back yonder, and the faces come agin, flashin before me—faces of my time:*

There's my fragile and tender Sarah Rachel, youngest granddaughter of Major MacNab, grieving all those years for our only son Adam—dead at twenty-two on the wooden floor of the County Line Liquor Store from stab wounds in the stomach after a long and bloody knife fight.

"Sol, my life's bout ovah. I loved my chilrun, Adam and Rebecca, and I tried to love you despite all your drinking and fighting. But the Lord's forgiving; maybe Heaven will be more peaceable—"

And Adam, long gone, and the word came like a knife puncturing the heart:

"As sheriff, Sol, I have to tell you that your boy was crazy drunk. He said something about proving he was as good a

man as his Pa and Grandpa Jeremiah. He died with his entrails in his hands, crying for his Momma Rachel—"

Sarah Rachel, quarreling about men's meanness, tormented by Adam's death; firm in her softness, like my own Momma before her—arguing that black folks should be treated the same as white folks and the day will come when we pay for our sins.

And Momma Savannah, a Primitive Baptist Christian angered by the wild meanness:

"They're heathen, Sol, wild and violent and no-damn good and just sorry white trash drinking rotgut whiskey and whoring with painted women no more than sluts and trying to prove themselves much of a man. Why must folks take advantage of poor and frightened black folks? Why are they blamed for all sins and suffer unforgivable cruelties at the hands of cowardly bullies?

Her words come again:

"Declare His glory among the heathen; his marvelous works among nations ... thus saith the Lord, learn not the way of the heathen.... Me and your Pa, rest his soul, named you Solomon cause it was from the Bible, hoping you'd grow up wise and be a leader of men; named your brothers Paul and Silas, hopin they would follow ways of the Lord—"

And older brothers Paul and Silas, long dead, like ol Jeremiah before them. Paul, a drifter with the gift of music playing tent-revival meetings and finally a piano player in a Pensacola whorehouse, dying in the 1918 flu epidemic; Silas, like Momma, always quoting the Good Book—a Pentecostal Holiness preacher railing against hypocrites and heathen, and finally an evangelist who sent ol Wiley Wickerd to Ring Jaw to preach and show his faith handling a Diamondback rattlesnake.

And ol Jeremiah, barrel-chested, hard-drinking timber cutter and teamster logging and peapatching Chipola woods until he got a job hauling crossties for the railroad being built from the Apalachicola River to Pensacola. He inherited his father Shawn Cahoon's homesteaded land at Ochessee Landing. Ol Jeremiah never talked about his Creek blood outside the family, hiding the fact that his Momma's family fled Alabama tribal lands for sanctuary along the Chipola River—escaping the onslaught of Andy Jackson, whose volunteers had swept south out of Tennessee with the blood of the Creek War flowing at Horseshoe Bend on the Tallapoosa River.

Jeremiah talked about his redheaded Irishman father, born in the Georgia's Chattahoochee Valley, scouting for Jackson's army in 1818. After Jackson's march across West Florida, from Fort Gadsden to Pensacola, the Irishman returned to Ochessee—where the American army was ferried across the Apalachicola. He worked with Stephen Richards, Jackson's interpreter during the First Seminole War, and was granted the lands along the Apalachicola River by the Treaty of Fort Moultrie Creek in 1823. He lived with the Indians, including the tribes of John Blount and Tuski Hadjo, who were among the five chiefs granted reservation lands along the Apalachicola by the U.S. Congress.

He hunted the pine forests between the rivers, fished the dark cypress sloughs of Ochessee Pond, and often camped at the rocky shoal the Indians called Look and Tremble. He first saw Jeremiah's mother standing in the shadows of a Spanish-moss bearded live oak tree: a young Creek maiden with shining black hair spilling over her shoulders and wreathing the finely chiseled face of a princess. He called her Dancing Waters.

He built a log cabin upriver at Ring Jaw Island. Jeremiah was born in the cabin in 1845, the year the Florida territory became a state.

The boy grew up part Indian, part Irishman; close to the river and creatures of the woods. He worked alongside his father, axing timber, snaking logs to the river with teams of oxen, and discovering the white man's world from woodsmen rafting pine and cypress timbers south past Federal shoals, Look and Tremble, Bullet Bend, John Clark's Landing, Abe Springs Bluff, Scotts Ferry and the dark sloughs spreading into the Dead Lake—on to the Apalachicola.

In 1864, with war reaching Chipola Springs, Jeremiah's parents had been in their graves near the Ring Jaw Island cabin for ten years.

Jeremiah often relived the Battle of Chipola Springs, back'n September 1864, caressing the old frayed Confederate jacket he had worn and the Yankee officer's broken-blade saber that he pulled from the ashes of the church after the bluebellies torched the town.

"One day a Confederate cavalry patrol come cross Federal Shoals headin north. I was down on the river roundin up scrub cattle for a Chipola Springs contractor workin with the army. Them cows we caught were so pore you could count their ribs.

"The captain tol me the Yankees from Pensacola were raidin east, a column headin for Chipola Springs. I put on a gray jacket they gimme and lit out with em. All I had was an ol scattergun my Pa Shawn left me. Pa scouted for Andy Jackson when the general was fightin the Seminole War in these parts.

"Hell, we didn't have much of a force—a few sick and wounded; few home on leave. Most of em militia—just boys and old grayback coots too crippled up to fit with regulars.

The major come ridin up on a black mare wearin a Navy Six and a saber, rallyin our little troop. He said General Alexander Asboth's force—bout seven hundred, colored and white—was at Campbellton. He told how the Campbellton Home Guard had fallen back toward Chipola Springs all shot up, and reportin the Yankees were breakin camp. That mawnin the streets were crowded with soldiers. The major had bout two hundred regulars and militia. He warned the town folks to stay in them homes, and we fell into line behind barricades of Jackson Street.

"Them Yankee basturds come on us roun high noon—mounted skirmishers first, shootin and yellin, follered by a full battalion of horse soldiers from up north yonder in the state of Maine.

"Helluva fight, son. Them black-assed bluebellies came at us with ball and blade. Major MacNab didn't have but one arm but he rallied our little troop folks later called the Cradle and Grave Company. Us boys and a few old men made our stand near the church—me with Pa's buckshot-loaded scattergun—when that damyankee general cut loose his nigger troops; soon smoke whirled over town and the Lord's house was afire.

The major feared his men couldn't hold off the charge. He yelled, "Fall back to the Chipola bridge," but them boys and old men refused—we just stood fast. But the regulars scampered back toward the bridge and ran smackdab into a hornet's nest of Yankees in the middle of town. Our Captain Jesse Norwood—he was a private in the Fifth Florida Cavalry—knowed we were trapped; he ordered us to fall back into the houses and behind the fences north of Jackson Street.

"And here come ol Asboth—he was Hungarian, from Chicago—a graying man with a thick droopin mustache, yellin like a foreigner, cussin them goddam nigger troops. He led em chargin down the Campbellton Road. I ran inside St. Luke's Episcopal Church, still firin at them mounted bluecoats. A bunch of them dismounted, waitin for Asboth's orders.

"I seed it plain as day. My buckshot wad hit that goddam Yankee general in the left cheek and arm, knockin him out of the saddle. He was bleedin like a stuck hog, and screamin with pain. He yelled at them nigger troops: 'Burn em out! Burn em out!'

"I got outta the church while it was burnin like hell, and ran smackdab into a mounted Yankee captain. He come at

me with his saber, but I swung my gunbutt agin his head, knockin the basturd off his hoss. I caught his wrist, grabbed that frogsticker and jammed the blade in his gut.

"Somebody said one of them Yankee officers saved the Bible off the pulpit, but them timbers was red with flames and them black basturds came like hell itself.

"Everybody was suddenly running, and I'd had enough. The major on horseback tried to rally us for a counterattack but he was unhorsed and captured. We fit all the way down that clay hill to the river, and scampered cross that planked bridge—bout thirty or forty of us. The regulars started tearin up the plankin. There were a few more shots, but we was safe.

"The Yankees come roarin through town, roundin up bout eighty prisoners—put em under guard on the second floor of the courthouse. Then them nigger soldiers and freed slaves sacked the town, stealin everything they could tote and all the hosses, mules and guns. We hid out cross the river til bout midnight when we heared reinforcements was on the way.

"Them Yankees musta had enough, too; they headed back to Pensacola, takin lot of my friends prisoner. Ol crazy Asboth was hauled off in a wagon, still cussin and hurtin from that buckshot. They left their dead and wounded, includin a Yankee major named Nathan Cutler, who got shot after goin into that burnin church and grabbin the Bible off the pulpit just before the timbers fell in. He was gallopin to the preacher's house with the Bible when two young boys yelled for him to halt. He drew his pistol but was unable to fire on the boys. He dropped his gun, and when he did this fourteen-year old boy Frank Baltzell blasted him outta the saddle.

"The Yankees captured the boy, but he fell asleep under a courthouse bench, and the bluebellies missed him when they pulled out to march back to Pensacola.

"That Major Cutler was nursed back to health by the folks of Chipola Springs, and after the surrender he come back over

heah as military commander. Folks thought highly of Major Cutler, he savin the Holy Bible.

"Next mornin after the fight we come back cross the Chapully and found dead all the over the streets, burned buildins, the church in ashes.

"Me and this ol nigger slave, Uncle Eph Santee, poked through the ashes of the church lookin for bodies. That ol darkie stole a pair of boots offen a Yankee corpse and put em on right there. Uncle Eph had a yardful of younguns—one was Willy Santee.

"I found the Yankee captain I kilt, the blade still in his belly, but the saber was broken in two by fallin timbers. I stuck the broken hilt in my belt as a souvenir.

I hid out awhile down on the Chipola near Bullet Bend, scoutin the swamps for beef cows.

"Heared tell ol crazy shot-up Asboth made it back to Fort Barrancas with a sore jaw and bout eighty prisoners, two hundred hosses and mules and four hundred head of cattle and six hundred freed slaves. I bet he never forget that September day in Chipola Springs. And them Redlands County folks sure as hell will never ever forget them black troops burnin their town.

"Then heared tell Governor John Milton rode his hoss back to his plantation in Redlands County, went in the back door and shot himself in the head roun the time General Lee was surrenderin to that drunken ol Sam Grant.

"Nevah seed a Yankee soldier agin til after the war. Them bluebellies come back over heah runnin things and tellin white folks they gotta give their land to the niggers. Lotta nightriders killin folks in Redlands County during Carpetbag days. Even now, Solomon, niggers better stay in their place. That lynch party for Buck Santee was a direct result of the bitterness from the Battle of Chipola Springs.

Them bluebellies kept Major MacNab a prisoner at Fort Pickens. The other prisoners burned in the sun of Ship Island

*off Mississippi. After the surrender, Major MacNab came
back, buildin the railroad and barrelin rosin for his own
tuppentine still."*

And Major MacNab—
a tall, wool-hatted shadowy figure firmly saddled atop
a black mare, the right sleeve of a cotton shirt tucked
under a broad black leather belt. Riding these turpentine
woods til he was in his seventies. He still carried a
holstered single-action Navy Colt—the one he used riding
with Bedford Forrest in North Alabama til a Yankee saber
blade tore away his arm at Sand Mountain in the long
chase of that Yankee Colonel Abel Streight.
I see him still: gripping the reins and a plaited cowhide
whip with that one arm. Turpentine chippers and
dippers watch him at a shadowy distance, silhouetted
against the sun and a cloud-smeared sky, motionless
in the hot still pines and snake-infested palmettos. Folks
who knew him say he ran his coloreds as if he were still
on military campaign—ever demanding, quick to
unleash his whip if any dare talk back to him; he
controlled the lives of turpentine laborers and their
families through his company commissary at Mulehead
Pond Plantation.
He won the major's gold braid raiding with Forrest's
critter company. In a running fight with a Yankee patrol,
a bluecoat horseman turned and slashed away his arm.
He kept riding until he fell unconscious, and then woke
up in a Rome, Georgia, hospital, looking at that bloody
stump. He came back to Chipola Country to recuperate
at his father's Magnolia Plantation and found himself
leading a home guard troop at the Battle of Chipola
Springs. Like General Forrest, after Appomattox, Major
MacNab turned to railroad building—first as a track
foreman for Colonel William Dudley Chipley, building
the Pensacola & Atlantic stretching across West Florida

from Pensacola to River Junction; then engineering the Red Level line tracking in front of his pinewood house sitting in the middle of a pecan orchard at Mulehead Pond Plantation.

And always the gossip: "Folks say that ol one-armed nigger whorechaser didn't want much—just all the land that bounds him ... folks say the sun sets daily on the Major's holdings, but it has to work at it."

The major's funeral was the largest most folks had seen in Fayette County. His tall granite tombstone with an American eagle is still the largest in Ring Jaw Cemetery, casting a long shadow just like the major put down the largest footprint.

And Uncle Eph's son, Willy Santee—
the little skinny booger with a sixth finger on his left hand, sharing the likker bottle and cans of sardines and pork'n beans and sodiecrackers and stoking the lighterd-knot fires and cooking moonshine whiskey deep in the river swamps; Willy, hightailing with brogan tracks in the river mud and plowed fields escaping from state and federal revenue officers; Willy, canepole fishing from the Chipola banks and talking and laughing and passing the fruitjar.

"Willy, gimme another shot of that whiskey."

"Mistah Sol, you can drank more likker than any white man I knows."

"Sho can, Willy. Specially if you run it off yoself. Always got a nice fine bead. Best batch you evah run; best I evah swallered."

"Mistah Sol, you say that evah time we cooks ups a barrelful."

"Willy, you just got a way with the sugar and that chicken mash. Damn fine drankin whiskey. Must be that extra lil fingah there on your left hand."

"Yassuh, capm. You powerful kind, Mistah Sol. Lemme pour you nother fruitjarful...."

Willy Santee, dying with buckshot in his back, deep in the dark river swamps, his bloody body heavy in my arms, his shallow grave by the river I dug for him with the pinewood plank I carved with my Barlow knife: *Willy, a friend.*

And now Becky, so like my momma Savannah and my Sarah Rachel, trying to raise Chance without a daddy; a daughter never speaking the name of the boy's father, running as he did when he learned she was pregnant; a daughter letting a grandfather teach Lil Sol to be a man like he was his own father; Becky always brightening the home at Christmastime.

"Pa, Chance will live in a different world. Your generation knew hard times, not much different from Grandpa Jeremiah and that bunch along the river sloughs and swamps. But Chance, call him Lil Sol if they will, his world's not for the likes of you old heathen. Don't teach him none of that meanness...."

"Becky, that boy's gotta learn to be a man."

Yes, a man. A man with the strength and the good heartedness of the father he's not known, Roscoe Ransum.

And Doc Nodd, helluva feller on the scent of a fox— more than a doctor, with that curly auburn hair and that polka dot bowtie. Many a time we ran fox. Loved to run them hounds. Music to his ears. Never knowed a man who knowed the mouth of a hound better. On a hunt one time he shinnied up a tree and brought down a wildcat in a crokersack slick as a whistle. There he was, hugging himself up the trunk of an old poplar with a crokersack clenched in his teeth, crawling out on a limb like a shirttail boy. And them four hounds leaping and yapping below. Yessuh. A feller without fear.

Smarter than a fox. No man loved women and runnin fox more. The stories I member—

Not many folks around Ring Jaw can handle a mouthful like Noddington Ambrose Easton. Even for the man doctoring aches and pains and sewing up knife and gunshot wounds and spanking babies to screaming life. Not even when he removes an arm chewed up in a sugarcane mill or a saw blade or removes a leg mangled by buckshot. Not even when he goes south of Ring Jaw into the Shantytown shotgun houses at Mulejaw Pond Plantation on Saturday night to repair damage done by straight razor.

Even if he's Ring Jaw's only medical doctor, driving the big Buick, always in a spotless business suit and tie and felt John B. Stetson hat even during the heavy sweat of summer.

In Ring Jaw homes and on the red-dirt streets he's just Doc Nodd. And town loafers in Ruby's Cafe and the storytellers in Elleck Dunkane's store talk about him as if he were special, driving the biggest car in town, ever if it's often mud-splotched from traveling the winding, wet-clay roads.

Especially not when he sits before lighterd-knot fires deep in Bearthick Swamp with ol dog-breeding codgers who spend long nights drinking, chewing tobacco and arguing which hound has the best mouth and nose. He's there sitting in his Buick, dressed up in what most folks called Sunday-go-to-meeting clothes, chewing a wad of King Pin plug tobacco and drinking Co'cola and listening to his fox hounds yelping and baying on the long chase across the fields and into the dark mystery that's Bearthick Swamp.

The faded, paint-chipped sign outside his River Road office says N. Ambrose Easton, M.D., but everyone knows him so well the shortened name fits the man who shows up with his black leather bag in their sickrooms. They know he came from South Georgia into West Florida, following timber cutters, saw millers and turpentine operators. He had been that breed of men in the South who as a youth on a Cairo cotton farm worked the hot fields wearing patch-bottomed blue denim overalls and daydreamed of practicing medicine. He worked his way through medical school in Nashville emptying bedpans and scrubbing floors and returned to rural cotton-patch Georgia, then followed woodsmen and their cutting blades and whining saws into West Florida pine forests. Following the sawmills, moving to another railroad crossroads town as the pine and cypress were sliced into lumber, he honed his surgical skills in a working man's world of aches, pains, saw-blade injuries and ill-nourished families wholly dependent on the timber companies.

By the 1930s Doc Nodd settled down to what most folks called gentleman farming with a large family in a big two-story pinewood house surrounded by pecan trees on Pea Ridge, north of Ring Jaw. His small office between the post office and the mercantile store where he dispensed his own medicine is always filled with hard-faced farmers in overalls, women wearing bonnets and barefooted younguns.

Everyone knows Doc Nodd, traveling muddy dirt roads, even in the long dark hours before dawn, delivering babies, tending the bedridden, and the gossip grapevine that runs from the post office to Ruby's Cafe to Hasty Pond's Pool Hall to Elleck Dunkane's store promoted the belief that Raw Jaw's only doctor was obviously a source of satisfaction for several women frequenting his small office complaining of female trouble.

No doubt, Doc Nodd carved out his own reputation with the love of many a good woman. After all, he's a handsome, broad-shouldered man of modest height with dark eyes and a warm, crooked smile, always impeccably dressed—dark wool pinstripes in winter, suntan seersucker in summer. And many a young matron or widderwoman will admit privately they find him charming; some are more eager, their flirting eyes flushed with hope he'd come calling. *"He can park his Buick at my front door anytime he wants to...."*

The men gathered in Elleck Dunkane's store snicker and grin and spit tobacco juice into the ashbin of the wood stove while telling their stories as if in manly admiration. The women in the Methodist and hard-shell Baptist churches whisper with long, shock-struck faces and suppress their snickering for fear they would be accused of spreading gossip. None know the truth, and could not swear on a stack of Bibles, but it don't much matter: stories grow like summer weeds with each retelling.

No one in Ring Jaw ever really counted, for they could not, but Dr. Nodd is believed to have impregnated many of his female patients with their blessing, of course. And at least twice he brought home a new wife. The willing spouses leaving their husbands' empty beds.

Now there's that Other Woman—the one he had knew in Chumuckla Springs in Santa Rosa County where he began as a sawmill physician for the Bagdad Timber and Turpentine Company. Suddenly Mattie Figg's at his side in the Buick, her dark mane of hair flowing over her shoulders. There's talk she's a grass widderwoman from Laurel Hill who had worked in Pensacola at Hotel San Carlos as a hairdresser. Folks say she's a friend of Jacqueline (Jackie) Cochran, who had been a San Carlos hairdresser before becoming a famous airplane pilot. Just as suddenly the first Mrs. Easton, the quiet, Sunday school-teaching mother of his five children, moved out to live with her oldest daughter, and there's a new Mrs. Easton keeping house on Pea Ridge.

For most folks in Ring Jaw it would have a nasty scandal, and the divorce was fodder for gossipmongers who spread quiet whispers like fire spreading through turpentine woods. But—as folks say—this heah's Doc Nodd.

"I'll tell you, ol Doc, now he's a ladies' man," Moses Trottah says, sitting yonder in Elleck Dunkane's store. "You know what they say—"

"What's that? "

"When Doc Nodd dies, they'll have to beat his tallywhacker down with a baseball bat to close to coffin lid."

And, always, they laugh.

Yet Doc's a cultured man, playing the church piano on Sunday morning, often accompanying a family gospel music quartet when Ring Jaw folks gather for all-day singing with dinner-on-the-ground at Sweet Bethel Methodist Church.

Doc Nodd has a reputation for exploding into violence with a blink of the eye, but few question his own independent ways of attracting women, specially frustrated husbands who rather than protest or face Doc Nodd's hot temper go back to empty beds.

Ring Jaw menfolk may fear Doc Nodd, but they marvel at his hunting smartness. The double-barreled shotgun he carries in the Buick backseat was but one of a large collection of weapons lining his large mahogany cabinet standing in the hallway. There on top of the cabinet stands the open-mouthed bobcat, preserved by a Macon, Georgia, taxidermist. Out front, on the broad green lawn, three alligators swim in a fenced concrete pool. He'd dove in the Chipola, snaring them moss-back gators.

Folks still talk about Doc going up that poplar tree with a flashlight, an ax handle in his belt, twine in his teeth and a crokersack over his shoulder while we stood there shaking in our brogans.

Once Elleck Dunkane looked out of the store window and saw Doc Nodd poking the shotgun barrel under the chin of a truck driver who was unloading groceries. Elleck knew Doc Nodd had been looking for the man, but sight of the gun under his chin sent him out the door, yelling. "Hey, Doc! Wait! Wait! Don't pull that trigger!"

"Dammit, this man owes me a dollar," Doc says. "Pay me now or—"

"Doc, Doc! Don't shoot! Don't shoot!" The frightened man collided his words in desperation. "I'm gonna pay, but I aint got no dollar right now—"

"Dammit, pay now or die," Doc Nodd yells, his rigid face darkened by hard, piercing eyes locked on the frightened, squirming man backed against the cab of his truck.

"Doc, don't shoot this man!" Elleck yells. "He's got a family!"

Doc Nodd clenched his teeth. "Dammit, I want my money now!"

"Here, here, Doc!" Elleck says, pulling a crumpled greenback from his pocket. "I'm lending him a dollar."

Doc Nodd grabbed the dollar bill, and quickly jammed it in his shirt pocket, and slowly lowered the barrel of the gun. Without speaking, without relaxing the taunt muscles of his face, he turned and walked slowly back to his Buick and quickly sped from the gas pump in a fume of dust.

"Crazy man, Mistah Elleck," the frightened man said, shaking. Jumping behind the wheel, he nervously fished to insert the key, repeatingly thanking Elleck for saving his life. "He would have blown off my head sho as hell."

Elleck laughed. "Naw, you have to understand Doc Nodd."

"I do now."

"Doc's a man of his word. Expects the same of others, even if it's only for a stray dollar."

Now, Doc knew the object was the chase, not to kill the fox—although at times the hounds will chew the animal to pieces. To him, it was the music of the night; Doc hated a closed-mouth dog. He'd sit there in the firelight, laughing, drinking a dope, listening—as we passed the likker—to our smart-assed arguments over who ran the best dog. He knew his Walker was usually the strike dog and the one out front. Ol Doc, he kept the night alive.

Silently, Doc Nodd rolls over his cud of King Pin as he steers his black Buick through the silvery moonlight of the July summer. His four hounds in the wire cage poking out of the cooterhull bounce along the narrow sand-pebbled road, knowing they were about to be worked. Already he anticipates the music of the hounds and the spirit of nocturnal chase. In the dark distance, he sees the tiny orange glow of a fire. He turns off the road, grinding across a sugarcane field and stops in a clearing on the edge of Bearthick Swamp. Flames of the lighterd-knot fire cast in the night dark as a black iron washpot the other hunters with their hounds in silhouettes, steam rising from their sawmill coffee spiked with white lightning.

"Doc, we've run that ol fox many a black night," Moses says, opening the wire cage. "Smartun, for shore. But we might scare up a coon."

"Or a bobcat," Doc Nodd says, laughing, as the hounds leap and turn in circles. "Don't pay to get too smart, Moses. These dogs are ready."

"Ever treed a wildcat, Doc?"

"Time or two. Hard to corner. They're gone about as fast as they appear. I'd surely like to bag one."

Jake Barefoot laughs. "I knowed a feller they called Scratch back up'n Alabama who went up a tree after one and come back down quick, bloody and bleeding. He had scars on his face and arms. Folks called him Scratch after he tracked and killed that cat and spread his hide on his wall."

"Doc, come heah and look at these tracks," Moses says.

"Could be a coon," Jake says.

"Naw, a bobcat," Doc says.

"Hell, you say," Moses says, holding the collar of the dog circling the lean, loose-hided neck of the hound. "Ol Trouble heah, he's rarin to go."

Away like bullets, the pack of hounds cut south across the field through palmetto flats. The hunters fell silent to hear the hounds way off in the darkness. In the firelight, the hunters follow the music of the dogs, imagining the hounds on swift feet onward into the unknown of night.

Down in the swamp they lurch, the sounds of their baying echoing all directions at once. Along the vined creekbeds, the young bitches lead the chorus in a shrill tenor; out in the open fields and hillsides the male dogs bolt in front, booming a powerful baritone.

Along the pine ridges, and whisking through the broom sedge, under the cool summer stars, rings out the mournful symphony. Sloshing through creeks, the hounds become animated trumpets, a cacophony riding the hot night air.

Then silence.

"They got him, Doc!" Moses says. "Cat, you think?"

"Sounded different this time."

"Could be."

Reaching the tree, they see the hounds, leaping and floundering and gasping and bleeding and slobbering. The dogs vault upward toward the mystery hidden in the leaves.

Then the dogs, sensing the presence of their masters, freeze in silence.

The men all hunker down, panting. The ground is damp and smells of moss and humus and swampwater. The sky, a velvet star-studded canopy, stretches close over the dank swamp. The men look up into the shadowy black tent of leaves bearded with Spanish moss.

Moses turns, feeling eyes on him. "Hell, I can't do it, Doc."

"Moses, who you think's man enough to go up there and sack that cat?" Doc says.

The hunters smile and giggle, their eyes searching the foliage. Then Moses turns, his eyes meeting those of Doc Nodd. "Hell, Doc, reckon you know better'n any of us."

The medical doctor laughs. "Moses, go back yonder and bring me that big flashlight and that ax handle in the back seat and crokersack in the back seat."

"You'll need a gun, Doc."

"Bring some twine. I'm going up there."

In moments the doctor's up the tree, moving as if he were a cat himself, a part of the thick foliage, the long flashlight in one hand and the crokersack in the other. He climbs quietly until he is level in the tree and his prey is precariously balanced on two limbs only three feet away, thirty feet up. The dark creature does not move. In a flash, the cat screams, breaking the silence of night, and blinded by the light, leaps unknowing toward the light—

That was a wildcat in that tree, and Doc knew its muscles were drawn tight from the chase. He went up there to spit him in the eye, sack him and bring up him down. He scampered down that ol tree trunk with that sacked cat, tied tightly with that twine he'd held in his teeth. We threw that cat in his dog cage, put the hounds in the back seat and got home bout three in the morning. Ol Doc, he had Moses Trottah build him an iron cage that sat out in front of his office for all to see. Hell, he even had that cat stuffed when it finally died.

"How'd you do it, Doc? " Moses asks. He smiles and says, "Charmed him, Moses, charmed him—just like loving a woman."

Never knowed a man who loved good warm women, Co'Cola and runnin fox more. Doc Nodd's something else, him and Moses Trottah talking the storekeeper into hangin that rattlesnake skin on his wall yonder.

And Moses Trottah:

once stepping into the sand streets wearing a black felt western hat, black coat and vest, woodland boots and a long-barreled hogleg dangling in a handmade cowhide holster, his strong baritone voice one of lawman authority. He won Ring Jaw fame, walking into the sunshine afternoon, firing a forty-five at point-blank range, and a whiskey-sotted hellraiser's chest ran red with blood.

Moses the town marshal carried the calaboose key on his gunbelt until Major MacNab's colored turpentine worker was found cold dead that morning. Moses up'n quit, joined the U.S. Army and was gassed while in the trenches in France; the town of Ring Jaw surrendered its charter over a bitter land dispute; now and then a county deputy drives up here from Estiffanulga when trouble's in the wind.

But Moses, bitter he didn't get the promised bonus for his combat service in the World War trenches, just became a jakeleg blacksmith and mechanic who could build and fix anything from hammering horseshoes to welding iron cages for bobcats and rattlesnakes. Moses became fascinated with rattlesnakes. He'd sit in a rickety old chair, drinking moonshine and caressing the scaly head of a Diamonback he kept in a wire cage. Then one day, his pet snake—like lightning—sank his venomous fangs in his arm.

"Damn snake bit me," he said, applying the only medication he knew—a gallon of Charley Crowe's white whiskey.

Then that old snake-handlin Georgia preacher Wiley Wickerd came to town and Moses found him a snake over in Liberty County.

And the serpents:

yonder on the wall—the broad Diamondback hide folks said was the biggest snake ever seen in Ring Jaw, and Doc Nodd and Moses had the storekeeper spread the skin on the wall for all to see. And then that night over yonder in Moses Trottah's ol blacksmith shed with them shoutin and screamin hypocrites and that ol foolish Georgia preacher standing there pulling that snake from the lard can in the summer-night dust. I tried to tell Belle and her old-maid sister Rhoady that snake smelled of death, slithering like Satan from that lard can.

Voices, threading through nightmares, the fog of fear on faces of many when the knife is pulled; screaming cold terror reverberating in the dark river swamps—heathenism leading to the grave.

Doc Nodd says Old Age aint nothun but a long memory. Hell, Old Age, it's nothun but a series of losses; with death waitin yonder in the dark shadows—waitin in Ring Jaw Cemetery with Jeremiah and Momma and the rest of my bunch in the dust.

And Momma speaks: "*Solomon, you've made your own unholy memories. Must you crawl of your belly like the serpent in the Garden?*"

TEAMWORK

9

Whisper Out of the Dust

"*R*hoady Rivers, snatch on your glad-rags!" Hurrying her sisterly command, Belle Rivers Sinbadde dabs her moon-round face with a damp bathcloth. She stretches her puffed pallid jaws, pinches her cheeks and blinks repeatedly. Staring blankly into the cracked mirror, she hates the deepening crevices near her tight brown eyes. "It's the last Sunday meeting. Brother Wiley says he's gonna do what he's been promising for three whole weeks."

"Hold yo hosses, Belle," Rhoady says. Her shrill voice cuts through the dull whine of the whirring fan blades gusting air through the open-windowed bedroom. "Corset's bout to cut me in two. I think I'll just leave it off. Nobody cares no how. Gettin bigger an ol heifer."

"Be lots more cooler, sister, sitting on them hard benches in this hot July weather. Vanity bedamned. I'm goin comfortable." Belle purses her lips. She threads a comb through her sweptback gray hair wreathing her face, and steps back from the mirror, filled with more poundage than desired. "I'm ready as I'm gonna get. Let's go, sister."

"You always ready to go, Belle. Like Grandma Rivers long time ago. Hitch up the mules—she was first in the wagon. Hope you'll hear some gossip. See something aint seen before."

149

"Well, you aint seen a preacher handling no rattlesnake, either," Belle says. "They say he's been bitten four hundred times. Imagine, sister. And still afeared of nothing; preaching the Good Lord's word. Now that's faith."

"Yeah. Might be just talk. Just talk," Rhoady says. "Aint seen him handle a snake yet. That's all he talks bout." Scratching to untangle the straps of the corset, Rhoady suddenly chokes back a weak giggle, her face wet with globs of sweat as big as honey bees. "You know what they say. He's putting a smile on some these widderwomen's lips."

Belle frowns. "Widderwomen! *Foot!* Aint that lucky. They say that bout ever traveling preacher who comes to Ring Jaw. Brother Wiley don't strike me as that kind."

"That's what they say!" Rhoady says, lifting her voice. Quickly she contorts her face into a roadmap of age lines. She turns, facing the fan, sweeps sweat beads from her brow, and jerks the metal hooks loose and the elastic snaps free. Wiggling out of the stiff corset, Rhoady angrily flops it onto the quilted bed. "They say he's still a lady's man, even at his age."

"Gossip! Just gossip," Belle says. "That's all they do in Ring Jaw—tend to everbody's business but their own. 'They say'—who's they? That preacher's seventy-five if he's a day."

Rhoady chuckles. "Still fire in the fireplace. Some these traveling preachers do more'n preach and flop down at your Sunday dinner table eating fried chicken. You know what they say bout buckeye baptists—preaching and praying til midnight; fighting and frigging til daylight."

"Mercy, Rhoady Rivers! An unmarried woman! Be shamed of yoself, talking bout good church folks. You been listening to Brother Wiley ever night for three weeks—"

"Now, Belle! What bout yo last husband, that ol

hypocrite, Brother Simon Sinbaade? Prowling at night with them foxhounds. Whorehopping. Running off with that grass widow from Wewahitchka—"

"Rhoady! None yo bidness."

"—Lordy me, how you wished Brother Sinbaade would crawl on his belly and eat dust!"

Rhoady shakes with a hack of laughter, remembering: *suddenly, coming out of July's heat, muting the hollow chug of the engine and the sand crunch of the tires, a gravelly voice from the loudspeaker atop the mud-splattered cab of the Ford pickup: "This is Brother Wiley Went Wickerd, from Cairo, Georgia. Blessed be the Lord. Brothers and sisters, join me for a revival at the old blacksmith shed on River Road. Love the Lord and save your soul from Satan...."* "—Well, Belle, maybe you right. Not many look a rattlesnake in the eye, praise the Lord, cuss the devil. But you know his old truck's been seen parked in front of Lucy Ducker's house. They say he's getting groceries on credit at Elleck Dunkane's store—"

"Lucy Ducker! *Lies!*" Belle pushes the screen door open and steps into the cool shadows flooding the fern-bedecked porch. "Let's go, Rhoady." She feels a light breeze against her face, and glances toward the sun spearing yellow ribbons through the pecan trees against the rust of vanishing day along the Chipola River road. "Sister, you know what ol Sol Cahoon told me?"

"*What?* What did that old fool of a snakekiller say bout all this?"

"Sol said a feller in Liberty County has had this six-and-a half-foot rattlesnake penned in a cage nine months. Sol said ol Moses Trottah found Brother Wiley a meanun."

The dusty screen door whines as Rhoady pushes onto the porch, straightening her rosebud-print cotton dress. "No meaner'n old Uncle Sol. He lies without trying." She slips a Chipola Gardens Funeral Home fan with a painting of Jesus Christ delivering the Sermon on the Mount into her oversized purse. "Well, Sister Belle. You and your preacherman. May the Lord watch over us this Sunday. Let's crawl on our bellies and eat dust!"

"Rhoady Rivers! Don't you make fun of the Good Lord's work."

From the porch, Rhoady and Belle see the rusted tin shed down the rutted sand road—a stained shadow against the pine-tree horizon. Already a crowd gathers.

After the short hot walk, with lengthening shadows fencing the day, the sisters are soon faces in the crowd milling around cars, pickup trucks and farm wagons. Insects whine like tiny saws; smell of sawdust mixes with the nostril-sting of horse manure in the still-blazing sun, pushing stray shafts of light flecked with dust particles thorough cracks of the tin roof. Women in plain cotton dresses, barefooted children, and rednecked men in boiled and starched white shirts crowd near benches and straightback stairs bunched around the pulpit.

A forest of hand-held fans chases gnats; the murmur builds amid squeals of playful children. The dust rises and sifts and settles into the still torturing light.

Rhoady and Belle approach Sol Cahoon, standing with Moses Trottah and a knot of men talking beside the preacher's pickup truck. "Well, Uncle Sol, this is the day," Rhoady says.

"Yassum, Miss Rhoady," Sol says. "Reckon so. See that lard can there in the truck. Big ol Diamondback. Meanun."

"That lid on tight, Sol?" Belle says in nervous laughter, her eyes fixed on the thirty-pound container riddled with icepick holes and ribboned with baling wire.

Moses and the men laugh. "That serpent's wicked," Moses says. "Lotta poison in them jaws, Miss Belle."

Sol spits. Wiping brown tobacco stains from the

corners of his mouth, he chuckles, turns quickly, and drums his fist against the side of the can. From within rises a piercing dry rattle: a muffled whirring as if it were the shaking of a baby's celluloid beads. "Feller from Telogia pulled that one outta the palmettos in Tate's Hell, over'n Liberty County—"

"Tate's Hell?" Rhoady says. "Nobody goes in that old hellhole of a swamp comes out the same."

"Yassum. Sho aint no Garden of Eden," Sol says.

Moses turns to Belle. "Feller from Telogia told me there's a hundred million snakes in Tate's Hell, all mean as that moccasin that bit ol Cebe Tate back yonder in 1875—"

"But Tate lived," Sol says, laughing.

"Sho did," Moses says. "Feller no more'n forty-five, Tate was farmin at Sumatra, went into the swamp one morning with three dogs huntin a panther killin his stock. He got lost trying to keep up with the distant baying of the hounds. One by one, the hounds' voices diminished in silence. He fell in a bog, lost his gun trying to free himself, and that huge coiled rattlesnake struck him just bove the knee—"

"Some say it was a moccasin, Moses," Sol says.

—"Hell, one's deadly as the other. Instead of dying, Tate stumbled and crawled round the swamp delirious with fever for ten or twelve days. When them folks found the stranger crawlin outta the swamp on the coast near Carrabelle, his hair had turned white as cotton. He told em, 'my name's Tate, and I've just come through hell.'"

"Lord with Cebe Tate all the way, Moses," says Belle.

"Hope the Good Lord with Wiley Wickerd," Sol says. "I warned that Georgia preacher in Ruby's Cafe just yesterday. He won't listen—said I doubted his faith. Hell, aint doubting nothing, other that whether he's got sense God give a billy goat."

"Now, Sol, he says he's been bitten four hundred times," Belle says.

"Not by this'un, he aint," Sol wheezes.

"Been handlin snakes more'n fifty years—ever since he was a farmboy up round Cairo," Belle says. "Your brother Silas told me that as a youngun he'd catch a black snake, stand on a treestump, preach the gospel—"

"Belle!" Rhoady says. "You aint seen him handle a snake yet—not even a black snake."

"Silas died a damn fool," Sol Says. "Y'all ever see a man snakebit? When I rode the woods, years back, I saw a nigger struck in the calf of his leg. Never saw the Diamondback. Struck like lightning. That leg swole up tighter a drum. The skin busted, and blood poured out the cracks before he died screaming in the back of a turpentine wagon. One time walking a logging road I come on a whirling dervish of snakes joined together in a ball big as a washtub. The moccasins with their heads sticking out an darting, were rolling like a ball of yarn—"

"Mating season, Sol," Moses says.

—"Helluva way to make love. Only a damn fool would risk being poisoned, even if he believes the Almighty will save him."

Moses laughs. "Snake bit me once, and I put my faith in a gallon of Charley Crowe's white lightning."

"You lucky, Moses, damned lucky," Sol says.

"Sol Cahoon, all us gotta have faith, even you," Belle says, giggling.

"Amen," Rhoady says. "Come on, sister. Let's put our faith in getting a seat up front."

Brother Wiley, tall and thin, his leathery face like cracked varnish, steps before the gathering, his every movement one of authority. Armpits of his white cotton shirt are circles of sweat. His liver-spotted hands clutch a Holy Bible. Standing behind the makeshift pulpit of stacked wooden crates, his tired gray eyes dart over the hushed congregation. Sunlight piercing cracks of the curled tin roof strike his long iron-gray mane and play on floating dust. "Bless you, my dear brothers and sisters, who come this last Sunday in love and repentance," Brother Wiley says, his mouth twisting wryly, his words thick and deep. "Yes, beloved, the Lord's house is everywhere if we know Him in our hearts—even here where once an old blacksmith heated and hammered iron and shaped tools for working hands in flames rising like fires of hell. Glory to God!

"Lord, help us revive the hearts of the humble before Your sight. Glory to God! Let us this day be true messengers of God as intended in the beginning. Let us pray. Every head bowed and every eye closed. *Glory to God!*"

Belle gulps a moan, holds it inside her throat, rolls it along her tongue and spits it out. She nudges Rhoady; their eyes fall on the lard can, now on the limestone floor by the pulpit. Rhoady ignores the preacher's string of words. *The evil therein—evil that seduced woman; the poison-fanged descendant of the serpent doomed to crawl on its belly and eat dust, as the voice from above commanded in that now far distant garden.*

Suddenly Belle and Rhoady rise with a rumble of feet, the once-hushed crowd quickly throating, "Amen! Glory to God!" Arms and hands—many holding cardboard fans—stretch upward. Out of muffled shrieks and basso rumbles, and rising above it soars a baritone challenge: "Who will come and go with me?"

The roar hurtles again, joyous in unison, weather-creased faces flushed with emotion. Suddenly surge-singing echoes off the tin shelter. *Some glad morning, when this life is o'er, I'll fly away*—Louder, faster,

hands clapping, tears welling many eyes—*O Glory, I'll fly away ... I'll fly away!*

Brother Wiley lifts his arms in blessing, roaring "Hallelujah! Hallelujah!" He strides into the crowd, flitting across the stone floor, darting glances from under his red eyelids. On and on he preaches, voicing shrill, staccato warnings of torments of Hell.

Shouts of "Amen!" and "Glo-ree!" punctuate the fiery phrases. Lucy Ducker jumps up from her bench, drops limply to her knees, screams and moans, "Lost! Lost! Now I'm found!"

Brother Wiley shivers to the floor with Lucy and other worshipers, wailing "Jeee-zus! Precious Jeee-zus!"

Belle drinks the preacher's words: distant echoes, flowing over mountains, into valleys, pitching shrilly against the hot still afternoon air. Her eyes like most others are on the lard can.

Suddenly Brother Wiley turns, lifts his right arm with bulging blue veins and speckled dried skin, squinting his eyes in sly triumph. He bends, jerks away the strings of baling wire and removes the lid. At his feet a dry nervous rattle breaks the hushed moment. The crowd moans; from rising heat muted screams flood the air as the snake stirs, its flat gray fanged head darting over the edge of the opening, its dusty eyes seeming to look at nothing.

Sweat streaming from his cheek, Brother Wiley reaches into the can, and then, with a jerk of his right shoulder, pulls back cautiously. The snake swings its head upward, its neck in a deep S curve, its forked tongue working constantly; and the tinny rattle intensifies. The preacher moves slightly, his long and bony fingers shakily poised, seeking the back of the snake's head; then quickly he grabs the rattler, and lifts it dangling, constricting, into the hot air: the hard eyes like glass, like frozen gems, unblinking— full of the unknown; a fragile, forked tongue quivers, searches. The Diamondback unwinds slowly, knotting its lengths in circles and a big figure eight, seeking to cling to the preacher's arm. Brother Wiley pulls the length of the snake across the pulpit, sliding his fingers across the glistening mosiac of elongated gray and black diamonds. "Brothers and sisters, this is God's messenger. We must not be misled as was that first woman in the garden. Satan chose the form of a serpent as his means of approaching Eve, and he beguiled her into eating the forbidden fruit. Praise God, his holy name!"

Fearful, Belle draws back, nervously clutching the pasteboard fan against her face. She watches Brother Wiley lift the snake with both hands. His right fingers firmly squeeze the thick scaly skin within inches of the fanged mouth and dark nostrils like pinpricks. He slowly walks into the crowd in steady silence.

Rhoady chokes off a whisper: *Fool! A man chancing his life so near deadly venom coursing fangs of evil.*

Brother Wiley pushes the rattler over his head—a living, slithering, twisting quiltwork of patterned scales, constricting, its skeletal rattle whispering in hoarse and urgent hisses. The snake slides its thick body slowly across his shoulders.

Many leave the benches, drop to their knees, weeping prayer muted by the preacher's shouted mysterious journey through Genesis.

Belle suddenly reaches out, cautiously touching the Diamondback's body with shaking fingers, and quickly pulls away.

"Belle!" Rhoady yells, tugging at her sister's skirt.

"Sister Belle, fear not, ye of strong faith," Brother Wiley says, holding the snake near, the forked tongue black as night on the ends and pink behind. "Touch, feel the serpent, ye who choose not to know the Tree of

Knowledge, as Eve did; as Adam did with his deliberate defiance and disobeyance of the Father, plunging all mankind into sin. Fear not the poison—defy the serpent, as we take back our birthright, the pure life, the fruit the serpent stole from all God's chilrun. Yes, praise God! We must test our faith for the flesh is weak. Only faith counts. Only faith conquers the wily ways of the serpent, whispering out of the dust the words of Satan...."

On and on he strides, the snake sliding around the many outstretched arms, and slithering across shoulders; the worshipers punctuating his rhythmic wheezing gospel. "Amen! Glo-ree to God!" Suddenly Brother Wiley turns, and backs toward the pulpit, pulling away from the outstretched arms. Slowly he lowers the snake's head into the lard can and, in fluid coils, the serpent slithers into the can out of sight of the worshipers writhing in moans and coughs and slurred words. "Glory! Sing Hallelujah!"

Fear grips Belle's throat, and her loosened cry joins other voices shrieking dry screams as her eyes, partially hidden by the hand fan, catches the repeated lightning plunges of the snake's fangs puncturing Brother Wiley's right arm. "Oh, Lord God!" she yells. Droplets of blood spurt from the punctures. The preacher writhes, claws at the snake's head, and falls weakly to his knees. The snake's hooked fangs cling to the flesh as a hawk's talons would seize prey. Belle searches frightfully, and in the moment's terror feels the pain of the needle punctures. "Somebody—somebody help Brother Wiley!"

With a lurch, eyes glazed and blank, his right hand clutching the bone handle of a Barlow knife, Sol Cahoon bolts through the screaming crowd, pushing aside stunned onlookers. "Get outta the way!" he shouts. Clawing at the snake's head, Sol finally jerks the fangs loose, and with repeated thrusts plunges the blade into the snake's head. He slices and twists the blade, tearing away the head, and flings the slithering body to the floor. Stepping back from the bloody, headless Diamondback still constricting in flopping loops and curls, Sol shouts: "I told you, dammit! I warned you!"

Those who had backed away in open-mouthed fear now rush around Brother Wiley, pained by the fevered skin of his arm already tightening and swelling.

"Leave me be," the preacher says, waving them back. "Don't fret. Been bitten many times. Faith in the Lord will cleanse poison from my veins."

Belle yells, "Somebody go get Doctor Easton!—"

"No! No! No doctor," Brother Wiley says, his voice weakening. "Have faith in the Lord! Let your prayers be heard." He staggers to his feet, his face drawn, his blood-spotted arm stiffening at his side; then he dizzily drops back to his knees. "Just let me have some air—"

"Take Brother Wiley to my house over yonder," Belle says.

"We'd better get him to Chipola Springs Hospital," Rhoady says.

Brother Wiley grimaces. "No! No hospital!"

"Let us help you! We love you, Brother Wiley!" cries Lucy Ducker.

"Preacher, you gonna die if somebody don't suck out that poison," Sol Cahoon says dryly.

"No! No need for the medicine of man," Brother Wiley whispers. "It's the work of the devil. Pray—pray hard. I'm gonna be awright."

Words of prayer rise from the knot of worshipers circling Brother Wiley, now stretched out of the wooden bench, his eyes closed, lips trembling, arm swelling and blood trails staining his long and bony fingers. Fragments of sun from the cracked tin roof fall on the fevered preacher. And only coolness of dusk-dark will diminish the dusty heat.

Into the long darkness they pray. The oscillating fan whirs as Brother Wiley, stretched out on Belle's feather-mattress bed, fights the snake's venom coursing his blood. Belle, Lucy and the other women bathe his face with cool water, whispering prayers. Rhoady wipes away goblets of watery crimson substance oozing from the pale broken flesh of his bloated hand.

"Yes, yes, Glory to God! Pray with me," gasps Brother Wiley, his once gravelly voice now whispery in his delirium. Suddenly he lifts his head from the wet pillow, crying out, "What's wrong with you people? Have you no faith in the Lord Jesus Christ?"

And still they pray, some silently. Some are wide-eyed, frightfully babbling prayers; others mute and stoic. Outside, hearing the weeping and moaning, pallid men stand or squat in the yard, shadows in the night. All night they come up, talk, move away; the house fills with people, awaiting dawn.

Sol Cahoon stands by the front porch, staring into the night, hearing the sobbed prayers. "Damn fool, just like my older brother Silas, dyin out yonder in Texas, messin with rattlesnakes—"

"The Lord's gonna call us all home some day," says Moses softly, breathing the moist night air. "But sho aint very smart to tempt him."

"A stubborn Christian man," says Sheriff Cicero Turnbull, turning from the bed. "It's his life, I know, Mrs. Sinbaade. But he's been bitten so many times he believes faith will pull him through. He still refuses help."

"Prayer's the best medicine now, sheriff," Belle says.

"Florida law forbids snake-handling, Mrs. Sinbaade—"

"Cicero," Belle sobs, searching for words. "Brother Wiley spoke to a higher authority."

The sheriff shrugs, then walk onto the front porch, the screen door rasping behind him. "You people seem to believe ever pennecost peckerwood who comes to Fayette County."

"Cicero, I warned that feller," Sol Cahoon says. "Most us round heah been living by Divine guidance and baling wire most our lives. Believe the Good Book, but don't believe it says go messing with snakes. I seed enough of em in the pineywoods and palmettos—them serpents will put poison in your blood quicker you can blink an eye. I aint much of a Christian man but I know The Word's love and salvation—better'n all the goddam snakes you pull outta a gopher hole."

"Reckon so, Sol," the sheriff says. "I'll have to report this to Judge Hannah Hawke. Reckon I'll have to call this one a suicide."

"He aint gonna die," Lucy Ducker cries. "Brother Wiley can't die!"

"Oh, yes he can," Sol Cahoon says. "He's just a man—foolish man tempting the devil, just like the rest of the ol heathen roun heah."

"Brother Wiley's gone home," Belle says. She steps softly from the bedroom, and closes the door. "He's with the Lord. Such a pitiful, painful passing. A man strong in faith until the end. I'll hear him screaming his last words all my days." *How cruel, death slipping up, a shadow spreading grayly into darkness. Whispers the dead voice in the still room: "Faith conquers all, even death...."*

Chilled, Belle steps onto the front porch. Dew glistens on the grass and the long fingers of green ferns. Her head turns giddy, her lips tremble; the words brush against her teeth, and fall back in her throat. Glancing upward, her watery eyes widening, she catches a smear of morning sun on the distant rusted tin roof.

"Sister, old Brother Wiley Went Wickerd taught us

something," Rhoady says. "Beware the wily, shrewd ways of the serpent for its evil stalks the garden—even here in a small place called Ring Jaw. We should be on the map now—the place where the king of the snake handlers handled his last. Folks gone have plenty to talk about now."

Belle's lips quiver. Words claw at her throat. But she doesn't speak. Out of the dewy mists, her ears gather the constant cooing of mourning doves mingling with fading whispers of wept prayer flowing from the dark death bedroom. Now night's gone, and the rising sun reddens the rags of cloud scudding the horizon, widening the light of another day.

Long shadows snake across the Mercantile Store porch, and a cool twilight breeze brushes the Old Man's brow. He moves his thumb along the Barlow blade edge, and in the silence he's still way back yonder, remembering the people of his now fleeting years. In the fading orange glow, his memory snaps back to his grandson, no longer a whisper on the sand road. About him in the aloneness night approaches. He closes the knife and shoves it in his pants pocket.

A shaggy dog with yellow eyes bolts by the store porch, barking, its wobby-toned yelps jarring the hushed silence.

The Old Man lifts and brings down the cane, the dull thud causing the whimpering yellow dog to run. "Git! You mongrel, git!"

He turns over the wad cheeking his ancient face. *Becky's youngun got lotta growin up ahead of him. Hope Chance and them other boys got the good sense to stay away from Lige Reddoake's boy Rooster and the Hoggen boy they call Hunky.*

Up to no damn good, them rowdies, like an ol mongrel dog foamin at the mouth. Like snakes crawlin out of dead night, poison in their fangs....

10

Ghost of Look and Tremble

The wind whispers softly, bathing the face of the barefooted boy standing by the live oak trunk in the gathering blackness. Near him, orange tongues of flame leap into darkness, curling over the moist, leaf-strewn Chipola riverbank. Fanned by the soft wind, the pinewood fire gnaws at the decayed limbs and brush, zigzagging ghosts of light and throwing shadows against the webbed green forest. Light strikes the boy's matted red hair and illuminates the white dancing shoal waters. Chance Cahoon watches the diamond sparkle reflecting the July moon's silver on the swift turbulence of the place Ring Jaw boys know as Look and Tremble.

"Willy Buck, they boiled yet?" says Lil Sol, turning toward the lighterd knot fire.

"Bout ready, I think," says Willy Buck. With a thin board paddle, Willy Buck stirs the green peanuts dancing to the surface in the steaming, roiling water. Fingers of flame lick the smutted five-gallon lard can. "Dern sho hot nough."

"Oughta be done," whines Ben Henry, hunkering down in the sand, watching the moon streak through skeletal tree limbs. "Been waiting long enough. Shoot, let's try em. I'm hungry."

"Yeah, put in nough salt," says R.C., fishing peanuts from the steaming water with a rusted tin can.

Biting into the hot wet peanuts, Lil Sol says, "Naw, let them cook awhile longer."

"Shoot, how much longer?" Ben Henry pleads. "It's gettin mighty dark roun heah—"

"Look at ol Pigpen, scarit of the dark!" says R.C.

Ben Henry turns, shoving R.C. toward the fire. "Aint scared, you ol Hickernut! But Pa, he's gonna be out looking for me. I don't want no razor strop on my back."

"Reckon that ol one-legged ghost will stir?" asks Willy Buck, his dark brown eyes darting, lighted by the flames.

Lil Sol shrugs, then snickers. "Why, Willy Buck, aint dark enough for the headless, peglegged man to walk these woods."

"Dark nough for me," says Willy Buck, mumbling his words, and sucking the salty juice from peanut shells.

"Me too," says R.C.

The boys laugh. Then, silence.

Steam curls off the rim of the can, clouding the spiderwebbed light ceiling into darkness choked with the shrill woodland voices of the brooding night. The boys—chiaroscuro silhouettes bathed in grayed smoky light of leaping orange flames—draw close, bracketed by menacing shadows coalescing on webbed edges of night. They hear the deep steady rush of the river.

The shoal shimmers and sings a steady cadence in the moonlight: a sheet of spidery white water gushing over the rock outcroppings, the bombardments slapping ghostly foam fingers upward. Silver particles of moonlight dance on the swirling waters. The sparkling water whips down into the rock river trough, racing beyond the sudden gurgling turbulence and hurrying past the boys up the riverbank as if swallowed by the wilderness night curtaining the blackwater cypress swamps yonder beyond the unseen horizon.

The boys had known of Look and Tremble most of their adventuring years—but mysteries of summer night now embrace them. They had heard the stories—many stories, told by older Ring Jaw boys; told in ever-embellishing fullness with frightening intensity. None intrigued Lil Sol and the other boys more than the macabre episode they heard repeatedly. They listened to varying versions of the story while swimming buck naked in the Mulejaw Creek washhole, and during the late-afternoon gatherings as shadows fell across the calaboose. Yarnspinning marble shooters playing winners-keepers in the Ring Jaw schoolyard told the story. And the brave aerialists of the Pine Thicket—whirling in a circle from the cornsack-saddle of the pine-pole Flying Jenny bolted atop a stump—told the story. The gray old men sitting in the corner of Elleck Dunkane's store talked and whispered in quiet reflection. And farmers and timbercutters stood by the long wooden counters of the Ring Jaw Mercantile Store talking and whispering. And the older teenaged boys told and repeated the growing legend of Whiskey George Gillwater, murdered on the banks of Look and Tremble. The older boys said Whiskey George, after all these years, still came out at night, stomping through the river woods on a wooden pegleg, searching for his severed head. The removal of the head had been from the blade of a Barlow pocketknife—three months after Whiskey George's pinebox coffin had been lowered into the deep clay of Chipola Cemetery.

In the morning the boys had followed Lil Sol down the long, hot sand road to the river woods. They roamed the vine-laced Chipola banks all afternoon, fantasizing as pirates, cowboys and Indians, and skimming rocks and pine cones across the surface of the river. "Let's boil some peanuts," Lil Sol had suggested.

By dusk they had filled two syrup buckets found beside the river with peanuts, after jerking the nut-warted vines from a farmer's field.

And as sun pushed west, lengthening shadows, Lil Sol kept repeating, "There's no ghost; Grandpa says it's a big lie." Willy Buck and R.C. said, almost in unison, "I'll stay if you will, Lil Sol." And Ben Henry, reluctant, finally agreed, saying, "Ghosts can't hurt you, can they?"

Now with darkness coming, bullbats nesting in the moist grass, and Big Dark shrouding the oaks, cypress, sweet gums and pines of the forest, they had buoyed their courage. They fought their boyish fright and were determined to stay at the shoal to know the river night like the older brave boys of Ring Jaw.

Standing by the boiling cauldron, the boys watch shadows, listening to the pulsating night.

Willy Buck coughs. "Y'all hear something?"

"Heck, just an ol hoot owl, crazy," says R.C.

"Naw," grunts Ben Henry. "Sounds like a low moaning noise—like something dragging through the bushes. *Listen.*"

Lil Sol laughs. "Probably an old scrub cow or pineywoods rooter."

"Or ghost," says Willy Buck, giggling.

R.C. backs away. *"Where?"*

"Dern you, ol Hickernut, out yonder in the dark," says Ben Henry.

"Shoot, aint no ghost—"

"Is too!" says Ben Henry. "You know what Uncle Solomon said—stay away from the shoal at night. Some ol booger gone getcha."

R.C. frowns. "Shoot, Lil Sol's grandpa's always fibbing us, telling them ol stories bout meanness."

"Yeah, Grandpa knows it's a great big lie," says Lil Sol.

"Gonna prove it, aint you, Lil Sol?" says Ben Henry, a frown etching his face. "You talked us into staying. You dared us to stay for a peanut boiling, like the bigger boys. Shoot, we could have boilt em before dark and been home for supper by now."

Lil Sol turns, facing Ben Henry. "Look who's afraid."

"I aint scared. Not me."

"You are too scarit," says R.C. "Look at old Pigpen Swinnard. Fraidy cat. *Fraidy cat!*"

"I aint neither, you ol half-cracked Hickernut!"

Willy Buck tightens his brown fingers around the paddle, his eyes wide, darting. "Wonder where they found that dead man with his skull busted—somers roun heah?"

"Right here," says Lil Sol. "At the shoal. Grandpa's got a detective magazine with the story. Mister Musing at Ring Jaw School wrote it. It's called the Look and Tremble Murder Case. Shows a big picture of the shoal—"

"Pa says ol Doc Dowling examined the body and swore ol Whiskey George was struck by lightning," Ben Henry says. "His shoe was knocked off and his pegleg was broken in two, as if electricity hit him smackdab on the temple of his head."

"Ben Henry," says R.C., "Why do you always say what Pa says? They found a pump-point in the river."

"Yeah, and Pa said they brought the old skull into the courtroom, and this heah smart lawyer showed how it fit exactly in the crack of the skull."

Willy Buck, still stirring the peanuts, wipes the smoke from his eyes. "Reckon Rooster Reddoake's ol convict daddy done it?"

"Some folks say Lige Reddoake didn't kill that feller," says Ben Henry.

"If not, he sure spending twenty years in Raiford for nothing," says R.C.

"Yeah, and Rooster done turned mean, like his Pa," Ben Henry says. "He's still upset about his daddy still on the hard road. He and ol Hunky Hoggen running roun, dranking whiskey, cutting the fool. Sho don't wanna run into them when they're out on a toot. Shoot, boy, Pa said the law run em outta Estiffanulga last Saturday night. Dranking and driving his pa's ol junkheap of a paperwood truck through the sawmill quarters near the Big River—"

"Shoot, Ben Henry, Rooster's a big bluff—a bully," Lil Sol says. "Now, old crazy Hunky, why he can't find the outhouse unless he's led by Rufus Reddoake. Let's try them peanuts."

Sitting by the fire, they remove the hot, moist hulls and eat the nuts hungrily.

The moon's silver cascades across the shoal; constant chirping and the hooting of owls and footsteps across the broken debris of the forest blend with the steady gurgling of water striking rocky depressions of the river.

"What's that?" says Willy Buck, turning toward the tree-canopied sand road. "Sounds like grinding gears."

They hear groans of an engine pushing through the night; suddenly two blobs of light poke through the pines.

"Must be a truck," says Lil Sol, smelling the exhaust fumes souring the night air. The ghostly light winks in the foliage, slowly approaching; Lil Sol hears rubber tires crunching the soft sand road. And then the lights vanish, the engine coughs and turns to silence.

"Where'd it go?" Ben Henry yells.

"*Quiet!*" says Lil Sol. The oily fumes hang in the air. "It's out there."

"*Whoooooo! Whoooooo!*—"

"Who's there?" Lil Sol yells.

"Whooooo!...Whooooo! I—I'm l—lookin f—fer m—mmmy hhhaid!"

"Who are you?" Lil Sol shouts.

Ben Henry steps back into the shadows. "Let's get outta heah!"

"Yassuh!" Willy Buck says. "I'm sho gittin!"

"Wait!" Lil Sol says. "It's somebody trying to scare us." He lifts his voice. *"Who's there?"*

"Whooooo! Whooooo! The ghooooost! The ggghoost of ol Whiskey George! Ol Pegleg gonna getcha! The ggghoost of Look'n Tremble!"

Then another voice, shrill, a hollow echo, slurring: "Look out, boys! The peglegged *g-ghooooost* walks these woods—*thump duh thump! Thump duh thump!* I'm looking for my bloody haid!"

Then, in the distance, voices trail into hearty laughter.

"Naw, aint no ghost," Lil Sol yells. "You're Rufus Reddoake, I betcha."

Lil Sol hears crunching footsteps. A shadow, quickly animated, hurries through the dark foliage; then another, slower, a blur, a fragment in the thicket. Then out of the darkness, with footsteps heavy on the sand, two figures appear; firelight turns the approaching shadows of two scowling teen-aged boys into grinning faces and nervous laughter.

Rooster Reddoake staggers near the fire, light striking his dark brown eyes. He cracks a crooked smile and lifts a Mason jar half-filled with white whiskey as if giving a toast. "We gotcha, boys!" He slowly turns toward Willy Buck, standing with the paddle near the boiling peanuts. "Well, I'll be goddamn if there aint lil Nig, blacker'n smut—lil ol Dink, down heah at night with the white folks. You oughta know better, boy!"

Willy Buck releases the paddle, backs away.

Hunky Hoggen, a half-step behind, staggers, his voice rising drunkenly: "Maybe Nig'll dance us a jig, Rooster."

He wipes his mouth with the sleeve of his shirt. "Maybe we can heat up a piece of haywire—"

"You leave Willy Buck alone," Lil Sol says. "He's got a right to be here."

Rooster laughs, brushing by Lil Sol and pointing his Mason jar at Willy Buck. "Nig, you got an extra fingah on your hand like your crazy ol grandpa?"

Willy Buck backs slowly into the darkness.

Hunky grins, mumbling, "Naw, Rooster—it's tween his legs."

Rooster turns toward Hunky, winks his right eye and drinks heartily from his Mason jar. The fire illuminates his bloodshot eyes. "Well, then, Hunky, whadda you say we just cut his pecker off and put it in this heah fruitjar!"

"Rooster, you're crazy drunk," says Lil Sol, pulling Willy Buck behind him. "Don't you pester Willy Buck."

"Get out of the way, you little basturd," Rooster shouts, staring long and rigid into Lil Sol's face, then shoving the boy lightly with his lifted elbow. Then, giggling, he turns, draping his drinking arm around Hunky's shoulders. "Black boy, you know folks roun heah keep nigger fingahs in fruitjars. Feller down in Estiffanulga got a jarful of em."

Willy Buck is silent.

Hunky giggles. "Want me to go get the rope, Rooster?"

"Yeah," says Rooster, "maybe Nig can dance a jig from the end of a rope. We'll just string him up on that old oak hanging over the river like they did his cousin Buck Santee."

Lil Sol stands stiff, his arm on Willy Buck's shoulders. He watches the two teenagers staggering and giggling. "They're bluffing, Willy Buck."

"Naw, Rooster," whines Hunky, hurrying his words, cigarette smoke trailing for his nostrils. "Let's just throw him in the rivah. *Gatorbait!*"

"Stand still, Willy Buck," Lil Sol says. "He won't hurt you. Just teasing."

Willy Buck slowly steps backward, seeking darker shadows.

"Hell we won't!" Rooster snarls. "Hold him, Hunky! Time to cut another nigger!"

Hunky suddenly strides toward Willy Buck, arms flapping and grasping drunkenly for empty twisting shadows as the black boy plummets into darkness behind the trunk of the live oak. "Dammit! You lil black basturd! I gone getcha!"

Rooster snickers, yelling, "Go after him, Hunky!"

"Hell, Rooster," says Hunky, panting, grabbing at shadows in the drunken merry-go-round with Willy Buck, easily eluding the older boy's gangling, outstretched arms. He stops, breathing heavy. "I'm too drunk, dammit! Thought you come down heah to give Lil Sol heah a little baptism."

Rooster giggles. "Baptism, right. Gonna chunk him in the river. Hell, Hunky, you right, ol buddy. We'll save Willy for another night when the moon's right."

Rooster, sweat beading down his face and a white froth of saliva in one corner of his mouth, turns toward Lil Sol. "Come heah, boy. Come *heah!*"

Lil Sol backs away. "What you want?"

"You that lil basturd who lives with that old coot Uncle Solomon Cahoon?"

"Uncle Solomon's my grandpa."

"And you're Rattler Ransum's basturd son?"

"I ain't no bastard—"

"Goddam sho are," Rooster says. "And your old grandpa's a basturd, too. Folks roun heah tired of his goddam meanness. Gonna give you a little message for that old sonofabitch—"

"Stay away from me, Rooster!" Lil Sol stands rigid, his fists tightening. "You're drunk as a skunk."

Rooster laughs, turning to the three boys backed in dark shadows away from the fire. "Come heah! Come *heah*—me and Hunky just wanna show you how to join our Browny Rouny Club. Just pull down your overhauls and get down on your all fours like an old sow."

"You aint gone cornhole me!" Ben Henry squeals, backing away.

"Me neither," says R. C., his voice shaky.

Willy Buck ducks behind a tree stump, the distant fire light striking pinpoints on his eyes.

"There's no such a thing as a Browny Rouny Club," Lil Sol says. "Just trying to scare boys smaller than you."

Rooster walks into the firelight, grinning. "Dammit, pull down your drawers, I said."

"Shoot no," Ben Henry says. "You ain't gonna get me! I'll tell Pa."

Rooster and Hunky laugh. They drink heartily from the Mason jar.

"Hunky, old buddy?" Rooster stares at Lil Sol.

"Yeah, whadda you say?"

"Changed my mind," says Rooster, wiping the moistness from his lips. "Besides, that old heifer down yondah in the pasture would be better—or maybe oneun ol man Swinnard's Poland China sows. Let's just get on with this heah baptism. Come heah, boy. Come *heah!*"

Lil Sol backs away. "What you want?"

"Come *heah*, boy!" says Hunky, plunging toward the fire, grabbing Lil Sol's arm and pulling the boy tightly against his chest.

"Let me go, you drunken fool!" yells Lil Sol, squirming to free himself of Hunky's muscular arms, his legs scissoring the night air, his feet churning the sand. "Lemme go!"

But Lil Sol stiffens as he sees the firelight strike the blade of the pocketknife, and Hunky giggles as he presses the sharp edge across the boy's throat. "Move, boy, and I'll cut your goddam throat!"

Lil Sol screams and so do the other boys.

"Go get the rope, Rooster." Hunky giggles.

"Please, please! Leave him alone!" Ben Henry bawls angrily. He backs up, Willy Buck and R.C. at his heels in the dark shadows.

"Let me go! Let me go! You bastards!" Lil Sol says, his voice choked and whispery.

"Naw, you holdin the knife, ol buddy," Rooster says. "Just cut off his haid like his damned ol grandpa done for ol Whiskey George."

"You better not cut me," Lil Sol says. "Dammit! Pick on someone you own size. Let me go *now!*"

"Fiesty lil pissant, aint you?" Rooster growls. He sits the Mason jar in the grass and steps in front of the boy struggling under the sweaty pressure of Hunky's arm. "Brought long a lil somethin just fer you." Rooster laughs heartily, and pulls a twisted wad of baling wire from his back pocket, and slowly, methodically straightens the thin metal. "Boy, you ever see folks brand a cow?"

"Please, now, don't you burn him," Ben Henry yells. The other boys are yelling, crying, their hurried sobbing pleas colliding with those voiced by Ben Henry.

Rooster turns to the other boys. "Shet yore damn mouth!" Then he turns back in front of Lil Sol. He slowly loops the long strand of wire and jerkily twists the metal together. "Boy, you know it feels, burning flesh?" He bends one end of the twisted strand, forming crooked crude curves. Holding the bended wire between him and the fire, he smiles: the letter S. "Boy, know what my brand will be?"

"Let me go!" Lil Sol says. "You better not burn me!"

"Hold him still, Hunky." Rooster says.

"Hell, I got him."

Laughing, Rooster pokes the S-shaped wire in the coals of the fire. "Boy, you'll know how it feels soon—" ·

"Please, please, don't burn me!" Lil Sol says as if an echo of his constant plea. He pants, tears trailing across his face, his eyes wide and darting, his ears filled with Hunky's throaty breathing, the knife blade rigid against his throat.

"Shuddup, boy!" Hunky yelps, spitting out his sour whiskey breath that stings Lil Sol's nostrils. "You wanna lose your head?"

Rooster laughs, watching the squirming boy locked in Hunky's sweating arms and smelling the searing heat of the coals and leaping flames turning the smoking wire glowing red. Rooster's still laughing as he lifts the red-hot wire and turns toward Lil Sol. Pursing his lips, he draws the twisted wire near his mouth and blows his hot breath on the heated S-form, its crimson heat glowing and smoking. A crooked grin spits his face as he moves nearer the boy's nose. "Damn you, boy, I'll put a brand on you that you'll tote to yore grave. Make you always remember the goddamn name Solomon."

Weak with fear, Lil Sol cannot speak. Rooster steps back, laughing. "You boys, come heah. Watch yore little buddy, scarit outta a year's growth."

Lil Sol sees the hot S-shaped wire slice the night air like a streak of red smoking vapor, circling, swirling before his eyes; he feels the sickening knife blade sting and Hunky's sausage-thick fingers and the smothering forearm crushing his bare chest like an iron vice. The screams in his throat are sucked dry in fear, chilling his mind as he smells the likker and hears the guttural laughter of two figures hovering like demons in the endless night as if Satan had fled the fires of hell.

Slowly Rooster lowers the branding wire past Lil Sol's chest and waist in a smoking, zigzagging downward thrust. And Lil Sol squirms, his lips dry as powder, his

eyes following the red glow of the wire down his body.
Suddenly the wire escapes his vision, and he feels the heat
building on his thighs as Rooster moves the crimson wire
between his legs. Rooster giggles. "Boy, that warm nough
down there in peckerland?"

"Dammit! Be still, boy!" Hunky says, turning the
blade deeper in the loose flesh. "I'll cut you!"

Lil Sol feels a sharp sting.

The other boys still mute, their screams now lodged
in throats of cold fear. They see a thin trickle of blood.

"You're cutting him," Ben Henry bellows. "Please,
please—"

"Hell, Rooster, you ever gonna get on with it?" Hunky
yells. "Lost your nerve?"

"Hell, no," Rooster says. "Hold him steady." Rooster
grabs Lil Sol's left hand.

Ben Henry screams. "Please, please, don't, don't—"

Rooster pivots like a threatened cat, searching shadows
in the smoke of the fire, facing the three boys, now gray
silhouettes joined with blackness of night. His mouth
twists. *Watch me!*

Draining the last whiskey from the fruitjar, and with a
nervous jerk of the shoulder, Rooster slurs, *Dammmn
you!"* and plunges the red-hot wire into the boy's flesh
between the thumb and forefinger.

Lil Sol screams; the other boys yell, fear choking their
whimpering cries.

The scent of burnt flesh hangs on the night air. The
drunken Hunky Hoggen, cackling, muttering to himself,
releases Lil Sol, who drops limply into the sand,
trembling, his legs numb beneath him. The burned boy
sobs, his body jerking in writhing distortion, pain
bleeding into rage. He rubs his burned hand in the
powdery sand, like an injured animal, and he tries to stand.
His legs—weak, rubbery—fail him. He crumbles back
into the sand. Searching his pained throat, Lil Sol tears

out a bitter cry: "Bastards! Bastards! Damn cowardly bastards!"

In the firelight, tear stains lining his face, Lil Sol finds visual focus from the blindness of rage and swirling smoke; he sees the silhouettes of Rooster and Hunky like smoky shadows, their nervous laughter fogging the cold emptiness. A cloud crosses the moon, further inking the cold blackness about him. Fingers of firelight crisscross the faces of Rooster and Hunky, illuminating their wild excited eyes like proud, prancing matadors as the saber-stabbed bull sinks into death of its own blood.

Rooster turns, staggers, looking down at Lil Sol. "Now a lil old haywire brand aint nothing to squall about, boy. I could've rearranged your goddam face."

"Cowards—goddam cowards, both of you," Lil Sol shouts, trying to stand, dropping back helplessly into the sand. "You're too scared to pick on somebody your own age."

"Lemme tell you somethin, *boy!*" Rooster says, his shrill whiskey voice rising. "Your old grandpa was the sonofabitch who dug up that man's corpse and cut off his head with his pocketknife. Everybody knows my Pa didn't kill Whiskey George Gillwater with no pumppoint—even if he had to tear off that ol sonofabitch's leg with buckshot. But your ol grandpa went in that graveyard with his pocket knife, and he put my daddy on the hard road for twenty years. Show that old sonofabitch that lil brand on your hand and tell him I wish I could have cut off his goddam head instead."

Sobbing uncontrollably, Lil Sol sits rubbing his burned hand, his chin on his sweaty chest, blood drops wetting his stinging neck, particles of sand and leaves matting his shoulders and legs. The other boys move nearer but keep their distance, eyes on Rooster and Hunky.

"What Grandpa did was to help the sheriff because the judge asked him to," Lil Sol says, his voice cracking.

"Help the sheriff, hell!" Rooster says. "All that old basturd's ever done was meanness. Cuttin off a man's head was just another of his heathen acts. Cuttin, killin—disturbin the dead. Damn right! Ghosts roam these woods at night. You found him alright! Remember, you still got yore head, boy. So don't go squallin bout some lil ol burnt hand—"

"Let's go, Rooster," Hunky says. "That's nough."

—"You lil pissant, basturd boy of that good-fernothing Roscoe Ransum—good a mind to take my knife and slice off your head right now, you *heah*?"

Hunky touches Rooster's shoulder. "Rooster, let's get the hell way from heah—"

"Oh, hell, wait a minute—what frightened you?"

"Time to go, dammit. That's nough."

"Hell, wait a minute," Rooster says. "And you other boys—you keep your mouths shut bout this or I'll come after you. You *heah*? And it won't be no goddam ghost neither."

"Dammit, Rooster, let's go *now!*" Hunky rasps, his shrill voice rising. "Somebody might come up."

Rooster and Hunky turn into the night. With a few footsteps on the sand road, they vanish. In the dark distance, the boys again hear the engine and the grinding gears and smell the exhaust fumes, and night swallows the sounds that are soon silence.

"They gone?" says Ben Henry.

"Merciful God, I hope so," says R.C.

"Praise the Lord, sweet Jesus, hep us," says Willy Buck. "Been prayin hard as I could."

The boys hunker around Lil Sol.

"Lil Sol, burnt bad?" Ben Henry says.

"Pain killing me," Lil Sol sobs.

"They crazy, crazy as a bed bug, doin somethin bad like this," R.C. says. "Hunky cut him. See the blood?"

"Aw, just a nick," Lil Sol says, sobbing.

"Lemme get a bucket of cold water for your hand and neck," Willy Buck says. "Back'n a minute."

Lil Sol jerks, sucking back tears; rubs his hand and pours sand over the reddened wound. "Y'all don't tell Grandpa. He'll kill them."

"Lil Sol, wrap your hand in a bandage and say you burnt it while building the fire," R.C. says. "I aint tellin."

"Yeah," Ben Henry says. "Let this be our secret."

"Yeah, our secret," R.C. says.

"Don't matter," Lil Sol says. "I just wish now that we hadn't come here—"

"Remember," Ben Henry says. "Uncle Solomon warned bout boogers down here at night. Maybe that was the kinda ghost folks talk bout. Lotta meanness in these woods. Lotta meanness at Look'n Tremble."

"Lotta ol crazy heathen, you mean," says Willy Buck, sitting a bucket of water in front of Lil Sol. "That's what Lil Sol's grandpa meant and what Uncle Charley Crowe warned me bout lotta times."

Lil Sol bathes his hand in the cool water, and through the tears watches the boys douse river water on the fire and fill their pockets with boiled peanuts.

"I'm bringing you a pocketful of peanuts, Lil Sol," Ben Henry says. "Let's go home."

Willy Buck sits in the sand with Lil Sol. "Yeah, we gotta get on home and bandage that bad burn."

Lil Sol stands, placing his burned hand on his chest, his eyes fogged with tears. "Let's go."

The moon breaks loose from layers of dark clouds, filtering grayed light on the foliage of the river. Amid shrill woodland sounds of night, the steady gurgling sweet roar of the shoal is soon behind them as they begin the long walk home in moonlight.

Reaching the back porch of his Grandpa's house, Lil Sol quietly walks to the water bucket and pours a dipperful over his burned hand, then sluices his face and the dried-blood cut. He watches the other boys on the River Road disappear in the night, walking back to Ring Jaw. He quietly pulls open the screen door and tiptoes past his Grandpa's bedroom, hearing the irregular rasping sounds of the Old Man snoring, wondering if the thumping beat of his heart might awaken him. With moonlight spearing light on the window, he feels his way by the bed to a corner closet. He wraps his pained hand in a remnant of a torn bedsheet.

Falling across the bed, his face matted with trails of tears, Lil Sol feels fevered; coldness stabs his body, and his fingers fall across the pencil-line cut. He jerks the bed sheet over him, shivering.

"Chance! I was worried sick," whispers Becky, now a shadow in the doorway. "Your grandfather thought you were in your room studying."

"We were just down on the river," says Lil Sol, turning his back to his mother, hiding the wrapped hand in the folds of the bedding.

"River? At *night*? You know better—"

"Yes m'am. We just boiling some peanuts. It got dark before we knew it. But we could see good in the moonlight."

Becky sits on the edge of bed. Her fingers move over his forehead. "You're not sick, are you?"

"Just a little hot and tired, Momma. It's a long walk."

"You know you disobeyed, Chance. You know what your grandfather says. He will want to tan your hide."

"Yes ma'am. I'll tell him in the morning."

"You sleep now. We will talk in the morning."

"Goodnight, Momma."

From the front bedroom, his Grandpa's snoring shatters the silence as it always does in the dead of night, and Lil Sol cries, muffling his misery in the folds of the bedding. Moon rays flood the window, falling on the pillow moist with his tears. He sobs in the long darkness, chasing a sleep-tormented nightmare and searching the cold vacancy of night for the warm embrace of morning.

Grandpa warned us: *"Stay away from Look and Tremble at night. Some ol booger down there mess with you snotnosed younguns."*

The Old Man of Ring Jaw knows all about the real ghosts of Look and Tremble—

Sleeps finally comes, but there—floating from darkness into ghostly firelight and smoke, the limp, swinging body of Willy Buck dangling from the rope above the sluicing river; two dark animated shadowy figures, a sharp cutting edge of a knife blade blazing bloody in firelight; screams and yelps in fretful, frightened echoes tear the night as if endless Satanic scars of terror; burning flesh framing a searing quivering inferno. A muscular arm crushing his chest—the sour buzzard-wing stink of sweat colliding with the sting of whiskey breath; the swirl of blood-red metallic heat before his watered eyes; the pain throbbing, searing his soul; the helplessness, the humiliation; the hateful, cruel laughter of brutal conquest; then, bubbling from boiling waters of the flame-licked lard can, a chalky cracked skull of a man rises, speaking Sol Cahoon's warning: *Stay away from Look and Tremble at night—*

Chance Cahoon suddenly jerks awake, tangled in the bedding, wet from rivulets of sweat coursing the gully of his spine. He bolts upright, sweat sticking to the sheet, a dry near-scream tightening his throat—and the lingering residue of Hunky Hoggen's knife blade gleaming in the moonlight; the red S-loop of the heated haywire swirling before his eyes—

Then the dark silence: the half-awake reality that another hateful river night is but a cruel dream whisk away on nightmare wings. Chance opens his sleep-tortured eyes. Only ghostly moonlight spills through the open bedroom window, falling over clumps of bedding. A lingering fragrance of summer sweetens the stillness. He drops back on the pillow, pulling the bedding over his shoulders, the dark night embracing him in the feather mattress softness.

Just beyond the pinewall, the rhythmic reality of the Old Man's gravelly snoring chases the fear and steadies him in comforting peace. *Grandpa'll kill them.*

Then he finally sleeps again, the sounds of night dissolving into uninterrupted slumber.

Down along the Chipola's trembling waters, chirps of birdsong and footsteps of wandering forest critters fade into the bosom of the river wildness. And summer wind rises, cleansing, gentling the booger night.

11

The Pool Room

Storekeeper Elleck Dunkane quickly snatches the thumb-flipped silver dollar from the stale morning air, and slaps the coin on the wooden counter by the cash register with a metallic pop. Covering the coin with his palm, the storekeeper looks up with a crooked grin. "Call it, Roscoe."

"Heads."

Elleck lifts his hand, staring at the coin. "Heads it be."

"Got you agin, Mistah Elleck," Roscoe Ransum says, grinning.

"Let's have a dope, Roscoe."

They stand by the red Coca-Cola cooler, drinking the amber liquid, their fingers gripping the ice-specked bottles subtly woman-shaped, as some store gossipers observe, like movie seductress Mae West, maybe like GI barracks pinup Betty Grable. Roscoe shakes his bottle, sloshing the liquid; with long swallows he empties the six-ounce bottle and purses his lips. "Mighty ice-cold, Mistah Elleck. Much oblige."

"Glad you're home, Roscoe."

"Hell, weren't much. Lost some friends aint comin back."

"But it's over, thank God."

"You know, Mr. Elleck, many a time fore the war I'd

185

pull a cold yeller Nehi outta your icebox. Sodiewater's better'n Co'coler as a chaser—"

Elleck chuckles, emptying his bottle. "You ought to know, Roscoe."

Roscoe laughs, lifts the bottle and nods. "Thought bout your icehouse when I was yonder cross the pond— many a time you tied a string round a nickel's worth in your ol limestone icehouse, and I toted the small block home, meltin faster I could walk. Get home with piece no bigger my fist, about enough for two tea glasses. Many a time ovah there in France and England I dreamed about cooling off in your icehouse."

Elleck laughs. "I still got that penny postcard you sent from somewhere over there, asking me to send a nickel's worth of ice and tie a string around it."

"I was in a hospital in England, Mistah Elleck—"

"Rough in them hedgerows, huh?"

"About as rough as it gets round here."

"Roscoe, remember—musta been the summer of 1939—before Pearl Harbor, you stood right here with a forty-five slug in your back, drinking an orange sodiewater?"

"To be young and drunk and twenty—too damn crazy drunk to know a bullet might kill. I overed it. Them Army doctors didn't find no damage. Lucky, I reckon."

"Thought you gonna die that Sunday morning."

Roscoe turns toward the screen door. Shafts of sun pour through the store window. "I remember Becky's little carrottop youngun that Sunday morning, looking up at a crazy drunk with a bullet deep in his gut. About them boys. Seen em?"

Turning to the red cooler, Elleck lifts a thin steel pick off the counter and pecks slivers from a glistening block of ice melting on capped drink bottles rowed like tiny helmeted soldiers. "Yeah, Roscoe, them boys come by here this morning. Got five dollars worth of gas in Lige's old truck. Folks say they hang out at Hasty Pond's place most times. Hasty's probably got em hauling likker up roun Donaldsonville. They known to prowl at night. They're known for pestering colored folks."

Roscoe bends, places the bottle in the wooden Coca-Cola case beside the cooler. "Up to no damn good."

Elleck spews slivers of ice, falling like a blanket of snow on the bottled drinks. "Becky's boy, Lil Sol, up here earlier. Playing round the icehouse. Don't think he went home. Wandered over yonder under that ol oak in the school yard. Looked like he'd burnt his hand—wrapped in a piece of cloth soaked with salve. Looked a mess. I put a chunk of ice on his hand. Wouldn't talk about it, though. That Hickery boy with him they call Hickernut yapped on bout Rooster and Hunky down on the river—"

"Hell, Mistah Elleck, should've knowed," Roscoe says. "What's that?"

"That Reddoake boy grew up hating everybody for Lige going off to the gang. Now that he's eighteen, he's fool enough to think he can hurt somebody. Been talking roun about Sol Cahoon."

"Yeah," Elleck says, "Sol in here the other day talking with ol Uncle Charley Crowe. Sol said something about that Reddoake boy pestering his grandson."

"Don't think he'll mess with Uncle Sol, him uppen age. If he did, he's never know what hit him. Somebody's gotta stop that wild youngun—"

"Be careful, Roscoe. Still just a boy. Watch your temper. Sheriff deputies run him and Hunky out of Estiffanulga other night. Let the law handle it."

"Never thought I'd see the day I'd have to bring in the law. But, hell, he's just a youngun. Could be trouble. Hell, I'm callin the sheriff."

"Telephone's in Silas Haymoor's garage. I'm sure Cicero Turnbull will send a deputy."

"I need to talk to that boy first."

Elleck walks to the door and pushes open the screen. He points to two figures sitting under the spreading canopy of the live oak, silhouetted in shadows. "Roscoe, he's over yonder, under the oak tree."

Rooster studies the eight ball, dabbing chalk on his pool cue. The slender boy with Tarzan-length dark hair wipes his hands on a dingy white Navy t-shirt tucked in war-surplus dungarees. He bends under the bare-bulb spreading light over the green felt of the pool table. Dust hangs in the still air. He sights the cuestick toward the dark striped sphere in midtable.

"Betcha a beer can't drop it," Hunky says, grinning, his lean face hid in shadows and cigarette smoke across the table.

"Hunky, ol buddy, aint no bet—you just bought me another Spearman," Rooster says. He stares at the ivory cue ball, figuring a path to the eight ball. Hunky's wild shot had left the balls scattered, the desired money ball nudging the three-ball. He grins, glances up at Hunky, and his eyes drop to chance a clear path for the black-ringed eight ball from the midtable cluster. Rooster snickers, pulls the Domino cigarette from his teeth and places it on the edge of the table.

"Can't do it, ol buddy," Hunky says, giggling.

"Watch me." With a jerk of his shoulder, Rooster rams the cuestick. With a sharp thud, the cue ball strikes the three ball, propelling the black ball against the cushion; then, whirling to the opposite side of the felt cover, strikes the two ball and wobbles into the side pocket.

"Rack em, Hunky."

"*Damn!* Rooster, you luckiest pool shot in Fayette County."

Rooster lifts the cigarette to his lips and draws deeply.

"Hunky Hoggen, whip yo rusty ass any ol time." He turns toward Hasty Ponds, his wool hat and oversized overalls bathed in shadow, standing with a straw broom at the counter cash register. "Hey, Hasty! Nother cool un. Spearman Straight Eight. Haywood Hunky Hoggen's buying."

Hunky turns away, banging his cuestick on the floor. *"Damn!"* He flips the wet, half-smoked cigarette across the table toward Rooster, hearing the winner cackle like a rooster crowing morning, and plops down onto a wooden crate jammed against the back wall. "Damn you, Rufus Reddoake."

Hasty Ponds mouthing the unlit stub of a Red Dot cigar moves nearer the screened doorway flooding light onto his felt hat and thin bare shoulders. He slides a hand inside the bib in the denim overalls, scratching his hairy chest. He turns toward Rooster and Hunky, and leans the straw floor broom against the wall near a hand-scrawled sign, *No Credit—Let's Be Friends!* "Want another brew?"

The pool room operator walks behind the counter to the red Coca-Cola cooler and pops the cap off a brown Spearman beer bottle. "Come get it," he says, sliding the iced bottle in a smear of water over the scarred wood. Then, lifting an ice pick, Hasty hacks slivers from a small chunk of ice over the rows of beer and soft drink bottles. He watches Hunky collect the balls and bunch them in the triangular rack. "Owe for another game, boys."

Hasty Ponds can rack balls on his two green-covered tables and scrape up the coins almost as quickly as he could pry open two brown bottles of Spearman Beer.

His business is mostly beer and 10-cent pool games. Loafers spend the day in the smoky hangout, and nights are for nine-ball gambling, rarely more than twenty-five cents a game—although the stakes escalate with the laughter and the bragging and the intoxicated emotions as the dark hours lengthen.

The pool room is Hasty's own hangout, but everyone knows he quietly directs a moonshine whiskey operation threading north into the sawmill shantytowns across the Chattahoochee River along the Georgia line.

A tall, stoop-shouldered, gaunt man in his early thirties, Hasty Ponds has never worked a day in his life, other than running whiskey and polishing his deft skills as a pool shark of fearsome Ring Jaw reputation. Folks say Hasty made a small fortune during the war years.

He doesn't know the whereabouts of Poland or Germany or even Pearl Harbor, for he cannot read, having dropped out of Ring Jaw school in the fourth grade after drawing a knife and threatening the teacher. He grew up hauling whiskey out of West Florida into Georgia; his scarred tubercular lungs kept him from military service.

Hearing him talk in Ruby's Cafe while he devours fried eggs, grits, hogback ham and cathead biscuits his listeners know he figured out how to make a buck because he peddles what folks wanted.

He sits there, talking about white lightning as if it were a nectar of the gods. He says it whitens the teeth, perfumes the breath, and makes childbirth a pleasure. "Ah, some folks say busthead tastes like a lighted kerosene lantern, or two cats fightin in your mouth. Does it improve with age? Well, I kept a quart jar of it a week one time, and I couldn't tell that it was one bit better than when it was new and fresh."

"Hunky's paying," Rooster says. "Hand me my beer, Hunky. You know what they say—the Pure Water Does It."

"Pure water, hell. Somebody's hoss over in Pensacola got bad kidneys."

"No worse than Hasty's old rotgut. Pay the man."

"Hell, I will, smartass."

"Hunky, throw nother quarter in the jookbox. Wanna listen to Lefty Frizzell—"

"Aint got no quarter. Hell, you pay for somethin."

Hasty jabs the metal point into the wood counter, jerks the brown tobacco stub from his jaw, and pushes through the screen door onto the wood-planked porch. Two men sitting on the edge of the porch turn from whittling. Long twilight shadows fall on the post office where the two boys sit and on Silas Haymoor's tin-shed garage across the slagged road. "Nother goddamn scorcher," Hasty says, striking a flaming match to the cigar stub. "No rain again to settle the damn dust."

"Sho hot'un, Hasty," says Cleve Cutter, pushing a Barlow blade across a cedar board, dropping thin curls of wood at his feet. "You see Roscoe hurryin in the garage?"

"Yeah," said the other whittler, Jake Barefoot, spurting tobacco spittle off the porch, "just a few minutes ago he was over yonder talkin with Uncle Sol's boy on the post office steps. Sho looked in a hurry."

"Wonder what the hell happen," Hasty says, looking up to see the redhaired man in a khaki Army shirt striding across the road toward the pool hall. Reaching the porch, Roscoe Ransum hesitates, drops a cigarette and crushes the butt under his Army boot heel. He grabs a wooden post and swings onto the floor of the porch, his eyes searching the dusty window.

"Rattler, what's your hurry?" Hasty says.

"Where'n the hell them boys?" he says, pushing by Hasty, grabbing the screen door.

"Rooster and Hunky?"

"Yeah, them two cowards in heah!" he says, jerking open the door. "Deputy sheriff on his way."

"*Sheriff?*" Hasty says, his right hand moving to the forty- five automatic sagging from his rear overalls pocket.

"Dammit, Rattler, don't want no trouble in heah now. I run my place right. Try my best to keep law away. What the hell you doin?"

"No need gettin your dander up, Hasty. You'll know soon enough."

Rattler walks to the table where the two boys stand in shadow, gripping pool cues. "Rooster, you down on the river last night?"

"What's it to you, Rattler," Rooster says, bending over the table, squinting an eye on a new rack. Hunky turns away, coughing, sucking cigarette smoke.

"Plenty. I'd break your goddamn head if the sheriff's deputy wasn't on his way."

Rooster straightens, breathing heavily. "Sheriff? Why'd that ol pussel-gutted whorehopper send a deputy up heah?"

"*You!* And Hunky. Gonna put both of you in jail."

Rooster turns from the table, and through the smoky light sees the muscular man bending over the table, sweat stains ringing his khaki shirt; small flames from the downward pool of bare-bulb light striking his dark brown eyes. Hunky swallows, drops a cigarette to the floor and mashes the stub with his heel, and backs against the pine wall. "Don't mess with me, Rattler. You get hurt—"

"You're nothing but a lyin sonofabitch, Rooster Reddoake!" Rattler yells, his words spewing over the green felt. "Goddamn it, you and Hunky, burning that boy's hand out of pure goddamn meanness. Oughta kick yo cowardly ass, throw you to the hogs with the other stinkin slop."

"Whoa, heah!" Rooster says, straightening, pointing the cuestick wobbly toward Roscoe Ransum. "Not us. Hell, I was home helpin Ma fix supper. Hunky, heah, he off cross the river chasin some gal."

"*Liars!* You and Hunky down on the river, scaring them boys—you're damn cowards!"

"Well, Rattler, why so concerned? One of em wouldn't be that boy livin with ol Uncle Sol, would it?"

Roscoe straightens, his face reddened in the dim light. "You know, goddam it! You branded his hand—you lowlife good-fer-nothing sonofabitch!"

Rooster bumps a shoulder against the wall, and tightens his fingers gripping the wooden cue. "Now, Rattler, I know you much of a man—real hell-fer-leather bull of the woods, so they say. Big soldier home from fightin a war. Come at me, I'll lay this cue stick up side your damn thick skull."

Sitting on the post office porch steps, Lil Sol hands R.C. Hickery a safety pin, and rewinds the salve-soaked cloth covering his burned hand. "Don't pin it too tight now, Hickernut."

"I'm not," R.C. says, punching the pin into the cloth. "Oughta go back to Mistah Elleck's for some more ice."

"Felt good then. Feels fevered now."

"Mistah Elleck might give us a bellywasher—RC Coler or a Nehi. Gimme a Baby Ruth and some raisins one time. Nehi grape would taste mighty good—"

"*Ouch!* Pin the cloth, not me," Lil Sol says, jerking his hand away. "Roscoe Ransum said sit here til the sheriff comes."

R.C. sticks the pin in the cloth. "Hold still."

Both boys glare across the road. The two whittlers stand bending, peering around the red and black letters, *Hasty's Pool Hall*, painted on the storefront window. The pulpwood trunk that they had heard the night before at the river sits in the shadow of the building, obscuring the wall-sized painted sign: *Spearman: the Pure Water Does It.* Lil Sol says, "Roscoe went in there—"

"Boy, better git," says R.C. "Pa says stay away from

Hasty Ponds' mean ol place. Pa says that man's got a forty-five automatic in the back pocket of his overhalls."

"Go if you want, R.C."

"Naw, I wanna see the sheriff's car. Wonder what Roscoe's doin in there?"

"Roscoe never backs up, Grandpa says."

R.C. squirms. "Where's that durn sheriff's car? Don't hear no sireen."

Lil sol frowns. "Crazy, not going to tell he's coming. Where's Willy Buck and Ben Henry?—"

"Right heah," says Willy Buck Santee, flashing buck teeth, suddenly sliding onto the edge of the porch quietly, timidly, as if fearful of being seen. "Me'n Ben Henry playin yonder roun the calaboose and down at the washhole. Ben Henry's whittlin a flutter mill. We saw an ol hoot owl fly out of the jail. Bout scarit me to death."

Ben Henry Swinnard walks from the dark side of the building, a slingshot dangling from his rear pocket. "Hand feeling better?"

"Some better," Lil Sol says. "Roscoe Ransum just went in the pool room after Rooster and Hunky."

"Hotdam!" barks Ben Henry. "He'll kill em!"

"Sheriff coming," says R.C.

Ben Henry drops onto the porch steps. "Sheriff?"

"Yeah," says R.C. "Rattler called him—"

"Hope he locks em up and throws the key in the river."

Willy Buck looks across the street. "That redheaded feller don't need no law. Charley Crowe says he'll bite you quicker a rattlesnake. Chewed a feller's nose and ear off one time and spit em out. Ol Uncle Charley said Rattler got in a fight cross the river one time and bit off the nose of a feller. They laid it on a stump with that feller's ear and kept fightin til sundown—"

Lil Sol frowns. "Willy Buck, now you don't know bout that."

"Shot'n in the back one time, I know," Wille Buck says. "You said you seed the hole, Lil Sol, him standing there one Sunday morning in Mistah Elleck's store with blood on his shirt tail, dranking a yeller sodiewater. Ol Rattler, he don't need no gun."

"Nose? Ear? Bet that hurt," says R.C. "Imagine goin roun with no nose, ear chewed off."

"Shut up, Hickernut," Lil Sol says.

Willy Buck still looks across the road, watching the doorway. "Uncle Charley's got a forty-five automatic. Kick him like a hoss. Saw him shoot a maddog in his collard patch. Foamin at the mouth. Said been bit by a crazy fox."

Ben Henry turns, slapping Willy Buck on the shoulder. "Shoot, that ol blacksmith Moses Trottah yonder, he sometimes carries a forty-five revolver in a cowhide holster—just like in the picture show. Pa said he was marshal back when Ring Jaw was a town. He locked up many a meanun in the calaboose. He got thumbs thick as a cucumber. Nobody messes with ol Mose—"

"Betcha Doc Nodd's got more guns than anybody," R.C. says. "Houseful. Carries a loaded shotgun in that old Buick. Pa said he clumb a tree once and brought down a wildcat in a croker sack—"

"Ol Rattler don't need no gun," says Willy Buck.

"Yeah, got sharp teeth," Ben Henry says, chuckling.

Willie Buck keeps his eyes on the pool room across the highway. "Uncle Charley says he's a big stand up in the road. Said he kilt lotta Germans cross the water in the war. Betcha Rooster don't try to brand him like he done last night—"

"*Shut up!*" Lil Sol yells, his eyes like the others fixed on the pool room. Frowning, he caresses the bandaged hand as R.C. fastens the safety pin. "Heard enough about biting and branding. Roscoe said the sheriff'll tend to them bullies in the right way."

"Rattler, we goin out that door," Rooster says, sliding along the wall, the cuestick held with both hands on his shoulder like a club. "Get out the way!"

The redhaired man steps in the shadow of Rooster. "Going to hell if you try, boy—"

Rooster turns away from Rattler, his eyes on the ice pick that Hasty left on the wooden counter. Nervously he darts around the pool table, and grabs the edge of the counter. Turning, he moves catlike, his back sliding against the counter, his eyes on the light-filled doorway.

Rattler pivots, eyes fastened on the boy. "Run but can't hide, boy!"

Hunky stands frozen, his dry lips surrounding another cigarette. Then, eyes on Rooster moving nervously along the counter, Hunky parts his voiceless lips, the unlit cigarette dropping to the floor.

Rooster abruptly turns and pulls the ice pick from the wood. "C'mon, Hunky, we goin—"

Hunky does not move.

"Goin nowhere," Rattler says, bolting toward the boy, his eyes on the cuestick and the thin steel pick.

"Dammit, Hunky!" Rooster yells, lunging toward the redheaded man, the ice pick in his left hand. He suddenly swings the cuestick wildly in empty air until Rattler's in front of him, breathing heavily. The larger portion strikes Rattler's shoulder and the cue breaks, the upper half skidding across on the pool table felt and thudding against the pine wall. Rattler keeps coming. "Boy, you gone get hurt," Rattler yells.

Plunging the ice pick, stabbing empty air, Rooster turns toward the door. "C'mon, I'll put it in your gut—"

"Hell you will!" Rattler rushes swiftly, eyes fixed

on the ice pick. The redheaded man feints, dodging Rooster's downward plunges of the steel point. And Rooster still stabs wildly, tumbling off balance, wobbly scampering toward the door. Suddenly Rattler grabs the boy's forearm in midair, his fingers suspending the arm as if snared by a steel trap. "Give it up, boy," Rattler yells. Slowly Rooster's fingers release the ice pick; the pointed metal tumbles to the floor and pierces the pinewood near Rattler's Army boot.

"Damn you!" Rattler snarls, his hot breath heavy on the boy's sweating face; with the back of his right hand, he slaps the boy's jaws repeatedly. Rooster slides limply to the floor, his long black hair falling into his half-closed watering eyes. "Git up, you sonofabitch!" Rattler says, his wild shrill eager voice hanging in the stale air. "You aint hurt."

Hunky sleeks stealthily into a shadowy corner, avoiding the gray dust-pocked light spilling through the back window. He stands mute in a far corner as if shadows hid him, his eyes fastened on the muscular redheaded man hovering over Rooster Reddoake. The heavy sounds of Rattler's booted feet pounding the floor still hung on his ears; the cursed emotional moment, not fleeting, lingers in the shameful moaning of embarrassed defeat. The ice pick with Cola-Cola blazoned on the wooden handle had quivered like a half-driven nail as it punctured the wood board near Rattler's booted foot. A shattered stob of cuestick had rolled against the wall near the dusty front window where the two whittlers still stand, their eyes searching the dim-lit interior.

Then Hunky shifts his eyes to Hasty Ponds, standing behind the counter, his dark eyes ablaze and darting, his right hand quickly dropping to his frayed and sagging rear pocket. His fingers surround the brown handle of the forty-five automatic. From beneath the counter Hasty lifts a baseball bat. Hunky's eyes fall on the Red Goose Shoes trademark etched in the ash wood.

"Now, goddamn it!" Hasty says, his gravelly quivering voice rising. "Hold on heah! Just hold tight!" The pool hall operator, his face flushed, his hurried words caught in a nervous tobacco cough, jerks off his felt hat and slams the Red Goose bat on the counter, wood striking wood in a sharp deadening groan. "Damn troublemakers! Bring the law up heah!" he mutters. "Aint gone have no trouble in heah, goddamn it!" Hasty then slowly lifts the Army forty-five from his pocket, and slams the weapon on the wooden counter, a metallic thud shattering the sudden silence. "Now, reckon we'll wait for the deputy shore nough or I'm gonna crack some heads."

"Sheriff comin," Ben Henry says, darting from the edge of the road back to the post office porch. "Yeah, see that big star on the door and that big red light on top."

"Don't hear no siren," R.C. says.

"Crazy, no need for a siren," Lil Sol says.

The boys watch the Fayette County sheriff's cruiser slowly approach Hasty's Pool Hall, the tires crunching the slagged road and rolling onto the soft sand fronting the porch. The lean green-uniformed deputy steps from the car, his face hidden by dark sunglasses and a wide-brimmed hat. He slowly climbs the porch steps, chatting with the two whittlers. Then the boys hear the screen door creak as the deputy walks inside.

"Shoot, man, let's go over there!" Ben Henry says.

R.C. jumps up from the post office porch. "Yeah, let's go—"

"Nosirree, aint going," Willy Buck says, moving

away from the boys. "Uncle Charley beat my bee-hin. Said stay way from Hasty's place and the law—"

"Law's come to help, Willy Buck," Lil Sol says. "Look yonder—Roscoe's coming out now. Deputy's got Rooster and Hunky in handcuffs. They going to jail!"

"Thank you, Roscoe, for calling about this," the deputy says, slamming the rear door of the cruiser car. He turns from Rattler, glaring at the two boys in the back seat. "Helluva heathenish thing to do, branding a boy, scaring younguns to death."

"See them boys cross the road?" Rattler says. "They can tell what happen—specially Lil Sol Cahoon, that carrottop with the bandaged hand."

"Uncle Sol's grandson?"

"Yeah, he won't talk much bout it," Rattler says.

"Well, likely the judge will send these rowdies to the reform school in Chipola Springs—"

"Ought send em to the county road camp or down to the state pen at Raiford—"

"Goddam you, Rattler," Rooster yells from the back seat, ramming his cuffed hands against the window glass. "Oughta knowed you'd stand up for that young basturd!"

"Shut up, Rooster," Hunky whispers. "We in nough trouble."

Rattler steps to the car window. "Boy, you cross my path agin, and I'll put a brand on your sorry ass you'll tote to the grave."

Rooster turns away, lowering his head, his long dark hair shadowing his eyes.

"Come over heah, boys!" Rattler yells. "Deputy wants to know what happen." The three boys race across the pavement, leaving Willie Buck sitting on the post office porch.

"Don't be scared," the deputy says. "Just tell me what happened—"

Ben Henry stands drymouthed, R.C. snug behind him, in the shadow of the deputy; Lil Sol lowers his head in silence.

"Come on, boys, let me hear," the deputy says. "No one's gonna bother y'all now—"

"Tell the man," Rattler says.

"We just boiling peanuts when they came out of the dark, yellin like crazy that it was that ol ghost, trying to scare us," says Ben Henry. "They said they were gonna hang Willy Buck to the oak tree like they did his cousin Buck—"

"Yeah!" says R.C., "they said they'd cornhole us—"

"—but Lil Sol, he tried to protect Willy Buck; then they turned on him. I thought Hunky was gonna cut Lil Sol's head off when Hunky grabbed him and jammed that ol knife blade agin his throat. Then Rooster twisted that piece of haywire and put it in the fire—"

"Yeah!" says R.C., "branded his hand like a cow."

"—and Lil Sol yelled for him to stop—"

"Yeah!" says R.C., "Lil Sol tried to fight em off, but Hunky held him, said he'd cut his head off if he moved."

"—and then Rooster grabbed Lil Sol's left hand, cussing him and his grandpa, and you could smell the burning flesh."

"Boy, Lil Sol!" says R.C., "he sho didn't act as scarit as we were. They scarit the daylights out of me. Just comin up out of the dark, like ghosts, holding and brandin a boy just cause Rooster hated Uncle Sol. I aint never goin back to Look 'n Tremble again at night."

"Me neither," says Ben Henry.

The deputy turns to Lil Sol. "Got anything to say, boy?"

"They should not have burned me."

"No, they should not, son," the deputy says. "You take care of that hand."

"Yessir."

"You boys may have to talk to the judge and testify in court," the deputy says. "Understand?"

"I'll ask Grandpa," Lil Sol says.

Ben Henry and R.C. are silent.

"They'll testify," Rattler says. "I'll see to it."

The deputy slides behind the steering wheel. "Never heard such a thing, branding a human being, specially a boy no more'n a sprout. That boy'll be scarred all his natural life."

"Oughta keep them two in stripes sweating on the hard road," Rattler says.

"Judge might do it," the deputy says. "Such a cruel assault on underaged boys—threatening sodomy, disfiguring the boy's hand. Likely the judge will want to talk privately with the Cahoon boy. Give that youngun credit—he tried to stand against overpowering odds. Got spunk, Roscoe."

"He's scared but didn't back up," Rattler says.

"See you round," the deputy says, covering his eyes with the dark sunglasses; he turns the ignition key. Turning the sheriff's cruiser around on the slagged road, tires crushing gravel, the deputy drives speedily toward Estiffanulga.

"Goddam redheaded basturd," Rooster mutters from the backseat, lifting his handcuffed wrists to wipe sweat-wet hair from his eyes. "Hunky, dammit, you shoulda hit him from behin—"

"Me? Some tried, regretted it. Not none of me. All I know, Rooster, we got real trouble now—"

Rooster raises his voice. "All I know is someday, somewhere I'm gone meet up with ol Rattler and—"

"Shut up, Rufus! We staring a bad trouble now.

Aint wanting no reform school or striped suit shoveling roads—"

"Goddam you, Hunky, yeller all over."

Hunky coughs. "Damn it, you done it, knowin you could. We shoulda gone lookin fer them girls cross the river."

"Dumb-ass pissant, just standin there. You coulda knocked hell out of him with that pool rack."

"And wound up with a skint head, or worse."

"Pissant."

"Shut up, Rooster!"

The deputy sees the teenagers squirming and jabbering in the rearview mirror. "Hey, back there—simmer down *now!*"

Rattler and the boys stand near the pool room porch, watching the car move away, the shadowed heads of Rooster Reddoake and Hunky Hoggen visible in the rear car window.

"Chance," Rattler says, looking into the eyes of the redhaired boy, "let this be a lesson. Some folks crawl outta the night as cowards, doing meanness, ganging up on folks. In daylight they crawl lower'n a damn snake. I heard them boys saying how you tried to stand up against Rooster and Hunky and didn't squall to nobody about what happen."

"Yes sir," Lil Sol says. "Grandpa was right. Should not have gone to the river—"

"Your Grandpa's lived long time. He knows what's right for you."

"Yessir."

"Chance, ever time you look at that scar you remember ol Rattler. Folks roun heah used to call me a sorry no'count, but, boy, you gotta learn to be a man and stand up for yourself just like your Grandpa. Aint nobody ever put a brand on ol Rattler Ransum. Never will.

"You mind your Grandpa and your momma. She's good woman—take care of her. Stay with your schoolin. Make somethin of yourself. Behave, *heah?*"

Lil Sol lifts his bandaged hand, gently placing his fingers in Rattler's thick outstretched fingers. "Yessir. I'll always remember."

Roscoe runs his fingers through the mussed coppery tufts falling over the boy's brow. He sees tears welling in the boy's eyes. "I'll never disobey Grandpa again," Lil Sol sobs. "He warned us. He's right about meanness at Look and Tremble."

Ben Henry, R.C. and Willy Buck stand on the edge of the road in the twilight, their bare feet in the gravel, long shadows before them. The orange sun, dropping beyond Mulejaw Branch, spins coppery spangles across the dusty sky. Hasty Ponds turns sourly with his hand on the screen door, the Army automatic no longer sagging from his rear pocket. The two whittlers squat on the porch, breathing the silence, squinting toward the road where Roscoe and Lil Sol are now two shadows facing one another in the coppering light of dying afternoon. The man smelling of sour sharp sweat gently wraps his arms around Lil Sol's shoulders and pulls the sobbing boy close to his chest. "Good boy, *good* boy."

"Grandpa's going to be mad with me," Lil Sol says.

"Naw, boy, Sol Cahoon knows bout all this. He loves you."

"Reckon so."

Pecan Winter '87

Earle Bowden

Pecan Winter
in Rural West Florida
© 1987 Jesse Earle Bowden
Limited Edition

12

The Headless Man

"Chance, warned you bout prowlin the river," the Old Man says, his rasping whiskey voice booming a knife-edge of fear, floating up to the porch's tin roof, hanging in the morning heat. He straightens, arching his neck from the creaking ladder-back rocking chair, and turns slowly and feebly toward the boy, a shadow framed in the doorway. "Lemme see that hand, youngun."

"It'll be awright, Grandpa," Chance says, walking into the morning sun slanting across the Old Man's chair. Stammering, slowly approaching The Old Man, the boy's words squirm on his dry tongue. "G-ggone be awright, aint it, Grandpa? Don't hurt a bit. Put some more salve on it, kept it wrapped. Momma took me to Doc Easton. He said it'll heal up good as new. Gone be fine."

The Old Man touches the bandage with gnarled fingers on a hand with mottled aged flesh. He squints. "Can't see much. Bad burnt?"

"Feeling better now, Grandpa."

The Old Man turns over his tobacco cud, and strikes the planked floor with the hickory walking cane. "Gonna leave scar."

"Be well soon, won't it, Grandpa?"

"No, Chance. Afeared be long time. Long time."

Tears pool in Chance's eyes. "Never going back to

that durn old crazy river again. We should have come home before dark like Ben Henry said. Just wanted to show them—"

"You didn't listen, boy. Not a-tall. Them two buzzards, sneakin up on a bunch of younguns, scarin up damn foolish torment. Warned you. You learnt a lesson, boy?"

"Yessir."

"Better mind me, boy. You aint even half growed. These woods full of boogers and ol sorry folks who'll cut yore belly open or knock you in the head for no good reason. Like a rattlesnake, waiting to strike and poison innocent flesh. Pays to stay outta them snake-crawlin palmettos less you wearing man's high boots. You get my drift?"

"Yes, Grandpa," Chance whispers as sobs throttle his voice. "Promise. I promise."

"You better, boy, if you wanna grow man high. Oughta lay a cowwhip cross your backside fer not minding. You stack that stovewood on the back porch like I told you?"

"Yessir," Chance says, sucking up sobs. "Momma says I have to stay in my room studying and I have to help her in the kitchen. I got to write an English composition—"

"You mind her, you heah me? Her tryin to raise you without a real pa round. And you, youngun, tend to yore schoolin. It's the only way a smart young feller like you ever gonna make it outta this heathen country."

"Yessir. Grandpa, I sure learned my lesson, you betcha I did." Then, drawing a sleeve across his tear-wet face, Chance brightens, his eyes clearing of despair. He touches the Old Man's hand. "Grandpa, Roscoe Ransum—shoulda seen him. He went across the highway and into that old pool room like he'd kill them—"

"Seed nough that, youngun. You keep way from Hasty Ponds' place. Nothun but a cesspool for heathen huntin trouble. Hasty likes to pistol-whip folks or swing that old baseball bat—"

"Aw, Grandpa, we were just sitting on the post office porch, like Roscoe told us to. Roscoe called the sheriff, too."

"Right to do so. Roscoe showed good sense. If I'd caught em they'd been damn glad the law come to save em. Never shoulda come to this—"

"They locked up, Grandpa. Deputy had them handcuffed, heading for the county jail. He said I might have to testify before the judge. Roscoe said he'd take care of it."

"Just tell the truth. No need lyin."

The Old Man turns silent, rolls the tobacco wad and spits off the porch, spraying a yaupon bush. "Chance, it all goes back to when them younguns cross the river walked up on Whiskey George Gillwater dead on the river bank, his head busted wide open."

Chance drops to his knees at the Old Man's broganed feet. "Yessir, they sure do still talk about that."

The Old Man hesitates, clearing his throat. "They said buzzards were already pecking at his head. Sheriff said somebody musta used a two-by-four or maybe a piece of metal. He had us searchin them river woods, lookin for a murder weapon. Roscoe Ransum was no more'n a yearlin boy, but already strong as an ox. He knew that river like the back of his hand. Always divin and bringin up ol Indian flints. Sheriff had him divin above the shoal. He come up out of that water with an old lead well point. Somebody membered Lige diggin a water well bout the time of the killin." The Old Man trails his hoarse words into muttering, as if remembrance was trapped behind his brown-stained lips. "That Reddoake youngun back then no more'n six year old the day they sent his daddy to the gang for cold-blooded murder."

"Rooster's eighteen now," Chance says.

"Eaten up with hate. His momma let him run wild, what with no daddy round. Burnin a helpless boy— meanest heathen thang I ever heared of. Oughta put both of em on a chain gang and sweat the pure hell outta em—"

"Grandpa, I just thought Rooster was teasing," Chance says, eyes again glassy with tears. "Him pestering Willy Buck like everybody does, saying he'd might hang him from a tree like they did his cousin Buck Santee—

"*Buck Santee?* That youngun don't know nothun bout that killin. That was Lige Reddoake talking. His pa always bragged bout being the one who put the rope roun Buck's neck when they strung him up on the courthouse square. Sheriff shoulda shot Lige then. Saved lotta misery and torment."

"Yessir, Rooster said show you this little brand on my hand like it was payment for his hatred. Rooster called you a bad name and said he wished he could have cut off your head like you did Whiskey George Gillwater—"

"Whiskey George?"

"Yessir, then ol crazy Hunky Hoggen grabbed me. Held a knife blade to my face. Said he'd cut my throat—"

"Damn sneakin bully, sorry as his ol whorehoppin pa!"

"And Rooster, drunk as a skunk, pulled that old piece of red-hot haywire from the fire, waving it in my face, giggling like an idiot, talking about how folks brand a cow. Then he plunged that old twisted piece of wire into my hand like a crazy man—"

"They after me, boy. Took it out on you."

Chance rushes his words, sucking up sobs. "Crazy old Rooster said tell you, Grandpa, that he could have cut off my head." The boy turns away, looking at the bandaged hand. "Grandpa, hope Roscoe Ransum put a brand on him."

The Old Man nods, closing his eyes. "That boy's branded awright—branded a goddam coward."

The Old Man is silent again. Then, lips quivering, Sol Cahoon says, "Chance, gonna tell you. Listen, heah?"

"Yessir, Grandpa."

"Chance—"

But he stops. He reaches across the space between them, laying his ruddy hand on the boy's shoulder and moving it lightly over his soft cheek; then he squeezes his shoulder before dropping his hand back to the curved bow of the cane. Hoarsely, slowly he speaks as if forced from a long deep chamber. "Never intended to use my knife agin. Ever time I look at that old blade these days I see another nightmare rushin back up mah spine. But back then—" His lips move in silence, his eyes watery. "—back then when Sheriff Cicero Turnbull come up heah and ast me to dig up the body of Whiskey George Gillwater...." He's suddenly mute, lips drawn tightly.

"Grandpa!"

The Old Man rasps a cough; specks of brown tobacco darken his moist pale trembling lips. "My duty, son. Hit had to be done, an awful thang it was. The sheriff had a court order. Them lawyers were tryin to convict Lige Reddoake for the murder of Whiskey George. Toughest work I ever done, cuttin the head off a man once my friend. Me and Whiskey George and Lige worked tuppentine woods long time ago. Hell, they were friends—Whiskey George even lived with Lige and his wife Floride down yonder on the river at Bullet Bend. They fished the river and cooked likker together down yonder in Buzzard Bay Swamp.

"Then somethin happen. Bad blood between them, Whiskey George accusin Lige of messin with his wife Corrina and that old high-yaller washerwoman—folks called her Buttercup. Claimed she was a Creole—a grass widder living down yonder by Mulehead Pond. Everybody knew George was seeing that washerwoman, and one time he came up to cut her some stovewood and

looked in the window where Lige was lying in bed with
that colored woman in broad daylight. He ran through
in the door swinging his lighterd axe like a crazy man
and Lige and Buttercup scampered out the back door and
hid in the woods. George just stood there, cussin—said
he'd kill em both."

The Old Man pauses, smiles, hastily turns his quid
and draws a hand across his browned lips. He laughs as
if memory had a sensual moment. "Buttercup knew
George wouldn't shoot her—too many men roun heah
would have skint his head.

"Then when George told Lige's wife, Lige tracked him
down in a peanut patch near the river with a double-
barreled shotgun. When Lige lifted the gun to fire,
George grabbed the barrel and the gun went off. Buckshot
shattered George's left leg bove the knee.

"Now Whiskey George could never pass up a drank—
that's how he got his name.

"Not even that afternoon Doc Nodd cut off his shot-
splintered leg. Folks say George Gillwater just laid back
on that old oak kitchen table, swigging on a pint of
bootleg whiskey, with a mattress and a chair across his
legs and four men holding him down, and him cussing a
blue streak and singing like a drunk sailor and his wife
and younguns running out back into the pinewoods,
running from the cries and screams and fearing the worst.

"Worse still, Whiskey George got it in his mind he'd
have a funeral for his leg."

Chance laughs. "Funeral for a leg?"

"He shorely done it. Moses Trottah built that
pinewood coffin and ol Charley Crowe dug the grave.
Buried that leg in Chipola Cemetery. A holiness preacher
conducted the prayer service. Some women from the
Pentecostal Church sang. Folks even sent flowers. Ol
Charley Crowe said it was the damnest thing he evah saw
in all his years workin in Ring Jaw Cemetery. Ol Charley

would dig a grave and cover it up, but he didn't like dead folks—even parts of um.

"Folks talked about that for years roun heah. Moses Trottah—the blacksmith who used to be the town marshal—built him a cypress-wood leg and attached harness leather. As he walked, hikin his bulky hip, the thump of Moses' hand-carved leg rose from the floor or the ground and thumped again. Each thump reminded Whiskey George, owner of the wooden leg, of the dreary day he was finally able to ride to the cemetery in a goat cart that Moses Trottah built for him. Doc Nodd told him not to get out of bed—that stump hadn't fully healed—but his wife steadied him on a pair of crutches and he stood before that open grave, tears in his eyes, sayin goodbye to his own real flesh and blood left leg.

"He said he could still hear the cock of the shotgun hammer and the explosion and feel the buckshot tearin flesh and bone."

"Ever thump. Ever day til they found him with the buzzards at Look'n Tremble.

"Some folks started callin him Pegleg George after that, but not to his face.

"But pegleg or not, he shorely warnt finished with ol Red Reddoake.

"Then one night down yonder at Frozen Bluff fish camp on the Dead Lake, while we were playin poker and drankin, Whiskey George got up thumpin that old wooden leg across the floor to take a leak from the porch when Lige come up on him in the dark. You could have heared em cussin clean cross that old cypress lake. Then we heard a scream, like a panther; there was Whiskey George standin over Lige with a bloody Barlow knife. He'd cut Lige's belly clear cross and deep as if he would have opened a shoat carcass at a hogkillin. His entrails spilled out in his hands, and he shoved em back in and stumbled back inside the camp and lay down on the bed and

212 / EARLE BOWDEN

screamed like he was gonna die. Doc Nodd come down there and sewed him up and took him to the hospital in Dothan. I thought Lige was gonna die but, hell, he overed it. After that, I figgered the only way this would end would be a mankillin.

"Everybody roun Ring Jaw runnin their gossipy tongues about how Whiskey George wound up with a cracked skull. Bunch of boys bout your age found him sprawled beside a log up the bank at Look'n Tremble. Buzzards walkin bout, feastin on his face.

"Some folks took Lige's side, sayin he didn't do it. Doc Dowling told me he coulda been struck with lightnin. Looked like the shoe of his one good leg been knocked off his foot. The wooden leg was somewhar off in the woods broken in two, like somebody had slung it agin a pine tree.

"But Sheriff Turnbull suspected Lige, cause he had motive. But he had to put the old lead pumppoint in the hands of the killer.

"Chance, I sho didn't see all this comin—that Reddoake boy growed up hatin you for somethin happen long time ago. I member the day I's gruntin fer worms down yonder in the River Styx woods like it was yesterday—"

Sol Cahoon pushes the flat iron from a Model-T Ford body spring over the wood stob, the steady shrill groaning of metal on wood breaking the pineywoods morning silence. Around him the wet weeded ground vibrates. Then, with metal snoring across the quivering wood, worms ooze slowly from the dark wet earth, curling in the grass about his soggy broganed feet, like miniature snakes. He quickly gathers clumps of earth alive with crawlers and drops them in the moist earth bed of a syrup bucket.

He wipes beads of sweat off his brow, turns, looking

up under the brim of a sweated-stained felt hat through the slender pines toward the tire-rutted lane trailing from the Estiffanulga highway. The steady click of the engine reaches his ear; he sees a muddy black Ford automobile turn off the highway onto the string of two sand ruts. He turns, stands. Then, before him, he feels the engine's heat and hears the crunch of the tires of the Ford sedan with a Fayette County Sheriff's star on the front door.

"Hidy, Sol. Hidy!" says Sheriff Turnbull. The portly man suited in black with a small badge in the coat lapel slides from behind the steering wheel and drops his booted feet in weeds edging the sandbed road. A deputy—younger, with a forty-five Colt revolver sagging from his right hip—slams the other door, his face shadowed by the tan brim of his hat. He walks to the hood of the car, silent. From the back seat Charley Crowe grins and lifts a hand. "Mistah Sol, how do you do, suh?"

Sol nods, grins. "Howdy. Sheriff, looks like you finally caught up with ol Charley, huh?"

"Nawsir, Mistah Sol," Charley says. "Just helpin the sheriff."

Sol Cahoon looks at Charley, framed in the car window, his bronze crown covered with tight wooly dark ringlets. He turns to the sheriff. "Yessir, Cicero, shorely hot day for you to be prowlin these backwoods. You already got my vote—"

"Need your help, Sol," Sheriff Turnbull says, removing his tan Stetson hat and rolling beads of sweat from his forehead. "Need it today."

"Yessir, if I kin."

"Want you and Charley to dig up the body of Whiskey George Gillwater."

"What fer?"

"Got a court order from Judge Hannah Hawke. The state attorney's convinced he can prove Lige Reddoake cracked his skull."

"How so?"

"Removing the head."

"Cut off his head? Damn, Cicero! Aint never heared sech a thang—"

"Yeah, Sol. I know—sounds mean and bad ugly. Unchristian. But, dammit, Judge Hawke done ordered me to have that head removed."

"Tough, mean ugly work, Sheriff, and it hotter hell hitself. What'll folks say? Don't rightly know bout that—"

"County will pay you and Charley twenty dollars apiece, Sol. More'n you'll make grunting fishbait in this heat. Besides, I got you a gallon of the best likker you'll ever taste."

"Sheriff, now, don't know. Cuttin the head off a man who's already had a leg shot off—"

"My deputy here will help y'all. Under court order to bring that head back to Estiffanulga this afternoon. Charley, heah, he'll do most the digging. Will you oblige the county?"

"Got shovels, sheriff?"

"Under the cooterhull."

"Something to cut with?"

"Sol, never knew you far from that ol Barlow."

Sol Cahoon lowers his head, and pulls the hat from his moist gray hair, sweat glistening on matted tufts falling over his brows. He draws a wet denim shirtsleeve across his sweat-beaded face and looks across the flat pineywoods. "Well, Sheriff"—he slows his words—"reckon me and ol Charley might oughta do it. Be our citizen duty. Charley, you willin?"

"Yassuh," Charley says, "twenty dollar shorely look might good right bout now. Aint had a grave to dig in quite a spell. Twenty'll put groceries on the table."

Sheriff Turnbull laughs, wrapping an arm around Sol Cahoon's sweat-soaked shoulder. "It would be right, Sol.

I gotta get it done today. Why don't you just get'n the car, Sol. Let's go back up yonder, have a snort. We brung long a coupla ice-cold chasers."

Sol Cahoon grins, turns over his tobacco cud and moves toward the sedan. "Cicero, you know I'd never pass up a drank from the sheriff of Fayette County."

Sheriff Turnbull steers the Ford sedan by the Chipola Primitive Baptist Church slowly, following a narrow sand trail edged by stone and wooden grave markers, and slopes down into a dark weeded fence corner of Ring Jaw Cemetery edging Mulejaw Creek. He parks under a flowering magnolia tree shadowing the clay mound. Sol Cahoon and Charley step from the back seat. "There's the grave Charley dug," Sol says.

"Only in the ground three months," Charley mutters. "Comin up agin—"

"Aint no marker," the deputy says. "Y'all sure this that man's grave?"

"I's at the funeral," Sol Cahoon says. "Stood right heah, talking with Charley in that slow drizzlin rain the mornin he dug the hole."

"Yessir, I shorely dug it, capm," Charley says, already pushing a shovel into the soft crusted clay. "Dug that little grave yonder thar beside Mistah George—fer his left leg, long time ago. You know, Mistah George wuz a determined man. He had a funeral fer that leg. Yassuh shorely did. Me and Mistah Sol standing right heah, listenin to that preacherman pray that leg into Heaven and those women singing bout the Lord takin us home." Charley lifts the shovel, pouring clods of clay beside the fresh grave. "Lordee, lordee me, Mistah Sol, no rest for the weary. Now, gonna dig agin."

Sol Cahoon stands before the two graves. "I saw his leg go in the ground—"

"Gotta do it, Sol," Sheriff Turnbull says, removing his

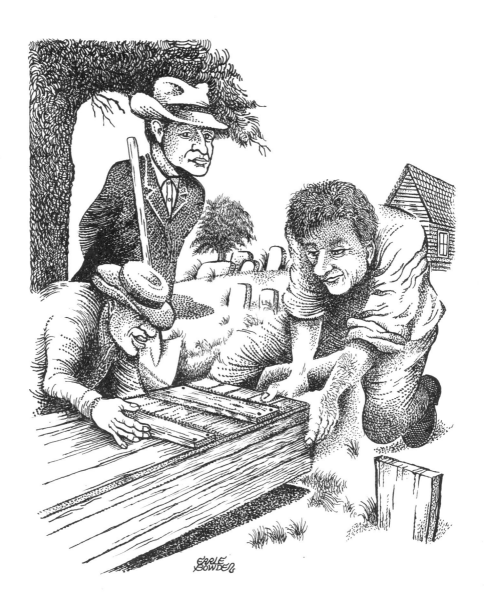

hat, exposing a thick thatch of iron-gray hair. "Deputy, let's go get that half-pint of that likker outta the cooterhull and open one them cool sodiewatahs."

Sol Cahoon walks to the rear of the car. "Sho gonna need a drank, Cicero. Charley, wanna snort?"

"Yessuh. Got kinda thirst, thankee, suh."

Sol Cahoon hands the half-pint bottle to the man grinning and leaning on the shovel. "Hell, Charley, you always thirsty. You know, Cicero, way back yonder, ol Charley Crowe heah could cook likker in the moonlight so smooth it would go down without cutting it with sodiewatah."

"Yassuh, Mistah Sol," Charley says, shaking the bottle, inspecting the white whiskey beads. "Now you talkin. Drankin always better'n cookin, specially if them revenue men sneakin up on you. Sheriff, I quit makin likker long long time ago. Life's too short to run for your life cross a plowed field fearing buckshot in your back. Thank God the law never caught up with me like they done pore ol Willy Santee. Never did know who shot Willy. Him bleedin like a stuck hog, tryin to wade outta Bearthick Swamp. Lord took him, Lord let me live. *Praise the Lord!* May he wrap ol Willy in his arms. Yessuh, Mistah Sheriff, makin likker shorely can be mean business. Drankin hit lot more pleasin."

Sheriff Turnbull laughs, watching Sol and Charley drain the bottle. He hands the Nehi chaser to Sol. "Whiskey's yours, Sol. And a brand new twenty-dollar greenback for you and for Charley."

Charley grins, emptying the sodawater bottle. "Yassuh! Lordy me, me and Mistah Sol heah having a snort in broad daylight with the high sheriff. Let's turn a shovel."

"Chance," the Old Man says, his jaws moving with each tumble of the tobacco wad, "the deputy helped, but had to give up and find a shade. Bear got him in that heat. Charley done most the digging. Finally pulled the pine box out of the ground, broke open the lid. Smelt worse than a buzzard's beak. Nearly puked, pullin up that ol pine coffin and draggin it in the shade of the magnolia tree. Wouldn't have known it was Whiskey George. Face sunk in, flesh pullin way from the skull. That black suit they put on him already rottin away. But he had a wooden leg strapped on him—Moses Trottah had made another one. Had nasty gash cross his head."

The Old Man turns in the sunlight, as if the words choked his throat.

"Grandpa"—the boy looks into the Old man's eyes—"what happened?"

"Charley wouldn't look, said he'd just sit in the car til I got through. He said, 'I dug the hole for Mistah George's leg and then another for the rest of him. Aint gonna go messin with no dead man's head.'

"Sheriff kept saying, 'Sol, don't quit on me—you gotta remove that head.' Sho didn't wanna do that.

"Then he sat another half-pint of that likker side me—purtiest bead ever saw. Me and the sheriff had a stiff drink, chasin with a Nehi sodiewatah. Sheriff told me 'Take another,' and I did—heavy belt, tryin to gentle my nerves.

"Opened my Barlow. Awful strange feelin come over me as I worked. I looked up and saw two buzzards over yonder on a dead pine limb in Mulejaw Creek. Sheriff had the deputy fire a coupla shots, scarin em off. Drank right smart of that likker by the time we wrapped the head in a newspaper and put it on the backseat of the Ford. Me and Charley soaked with sweat and smelled like two polecats time we shoved that coffin back in the hole and shoveled the clay back over the grave.

"Then Sheriff Turnbull drove like hell to Estiffanulga, me and Charley there on the back seat with Whiskey

George's head. Warn't pleasant, sittin there, the head of a man I'd knowed all my life wrapped in a soggy newspaper. I'd seen that man's left leg buried, him standing there on crutches for that strange kind of funeral service, hatred for Lige Reddoake written on his long solemn face, cussin under his breath as tears spilled from his pained eyes. Now his head was on the seat beside me. Damn miserable trip, them eleven miles, Charley and me quiet as a stump, and the sheriff talkin bout trying to convict Lige of murder.

"The sheriff drove into the jailhouse yard. Said he'd get witnesses from the courthouse. Nobody said much. Few minutes he come back with of bunch of county officers, grumblin under their breath bout how hot is was and havin to see sech a horrible thing. They stood and hunkered round that jailyard. The deputy struck a match to them pine knots, and suddenly the dry creaking fire leaped round that old smutty lard can full of water. Sheriff Turnbull dropped Whiskey George's head into the steamin water.

"Stunk so bad some witnesses puked. Folks said they could smell the stench all over Estiffanulga. We stood there, watchin the water boil, steam rise, eyes burnin from smoke of the fatlightered fire. And Whiskey George's head bobbed up and down in the gurglin water til tatters of flesh boiled off, and the skull chalky white as cow milk in a saucer.

"Could see the jagged crack in the skull when the sheriff fished it out with a shovel. Deputy wrapped the skull in another newspaper. Sheriff kept the skull on his roll-top desk til trial started. Me and Charley never talked bout it much after that, exceptin he said, 'Mistah Sol, hope we aint gonna ever have to do that agin. Buryin folks has to be, but diggin em up and cuttin up corpses in the graveyard bad trouble when you think bout hit.'

"Sho didn't like to, but Judge Hawke had me testify

how the sheriff had hired me and ol Charley to do the nasty work.

"Shoulda seen eyes light up in that packed courtroom when the sheriff unwrapped the newspaper and set the skull on the evidence table. Folks standin, crowdin the hallways, sittin in the open windows, swattin flies, fannin to beat summer heat.

"Lige's lawyer—a small, cigar-chewing baldheaded man from Pensacola, name of Rhett Crockett Hood—told how Whiskey George had cut open Lige's stomach and he almost bled to death, causing him and his wife and small son great pain. And State Attorney J. Frank Ashburn bemoaned the fact that George Gillwater had suffered greatly from the evil of Lige Reddoake—first firing the shotgun that severed his leg, nearly ending his life and causing him a great loss and pain the rest of his days that ended in a horrible death; now in death, the family must endure the horror and the humiliation of having his head severed to prove for a fact that Lige Reddoake was guilty of coldblooded, premeditated murder.

"Hardware feller from Estiffanulga testified that Lige had bought a well point in his store a few days before the killin. And when the state's attorney laid Lige Reddoake's lead waterpump point across the crack in the skull and it fit like a glove a loud rumble went over the courtroom. Judge Hawke banged the gavel. Threatened to empty the room. Jury out no more'n an hour.

"Helluva way to put a man sweatin twenty years on the hard road. One man loses his life messin round with another man's wife and a colored woman. Yeah, fools they were. Killin bout women—one unfaithful married woman with a small son; the other a high yaller gal who washed folks clothes for a dollar a week.

"Then the law takes away his head and puts it before the frightened eyes of everyone who knowed him. And his widow weepin and that youngun Rufus squallin like a stuck hog.

"Lige Reddoake turned white as the cracked skull. The bony emptiness is examined and tossed hand to hand by smart-talkin lawyers. Then the skull sits there on the evidence table with yeller rotten teeth like dried corn on a cob, and holes for eyes and nose.

"When the jury returned, the judge banged the gavel like she was killin a snake, screamin for quiet.

"That widderwoman and her youngun bawled loud, and Lige Reddoake stood starin at the oak floor, wipin tears. And the searchin eyes of everyone moved from Whiskey George's skull back to Lige Reddoake, him alone, cryin—staring at nothing, knowin his life would be shovelin on the hard road and he must pay the law for one blow that killed an old friend that cold black night at Look'n Tremble.

"Chance, I tell you this story cause folks round heah tell lies about a headless pegleg man comin out at night moanin for his head at Look'n Tremble. Call it the ghost, a haint, just scarin younguns. Damn pack'un lies—"

"Grandpa," Chance says, "I knew it was untrue. I thought I could convince Willy Buck, R.C., and Ben Henry."

The Old Man again bangs the cane against the planked porch. "Tryin to prove the truth, and you ran into your own ghost."

The boy jumps to his feet. "Grandpa, maybe I can make up my own ghost story. My English teacher, Miss Marianna Murphee, likes the stories I write in my Big Chief notebook. And the principal, Mistah Musing, he's always telling us about books he's reading. I wish I could write a book and tell stories like you do—"

"Moss Musing's a fine feller," the Old Man says. "Educated man. Knows all bout this river meanness. He wrote up the Look'n Tremble murder case for a detective

222 / EARLE BOWDEN

magazine and he told the truth. Just be honest, son, when you tell stories. You don't have to make em up."

The Old Man pauses, chewing his tobacco quid, staring into the sunlight. "I'd rather you member the shoal as a purty place where the rivah turns white and dances—where your great-great grandpa Shawn Solomon Cahoon first saw the pretty Creek Indian woman that became yore flesh and blood.

"If there be ghosts, they are the heathen your Grandma spoke of—maybe livin ghosts of the sins of damn fools frightened by the truth of their own meanness and selfish pride.

"I kin still see Whiskey George's skull, in that little wooden coffin lined with white satin that the sheriff got from the funeral home. Me and Charley dug a new grave behind Whiskey George's in the shadow of the pineboard marker for the severed leg. It was nearly twilight when Charley finished shoveling the clay and smoothing out the small mound.

"Charley said, grinning, 'Well, Mistah Sol, old Whiskey George's back together, even if he's kinda scattered about.'

"None of us was in any mood to see the humor in it, but Sheriff Turnbull said, 'Charley I'm with you. I don't wanna do this agin.'

"Sheriff give me and Charley another twenty dollars apiece. But no likker.

"Charley even says he can still see Whiskey George's head in the night and him cold sober as a judge.

"Even now, sometimes, fightin for sleep, I see it. And the leg, the real one and the wooden one, thumpin cross the floor. Maybe that's the ghost they tell lies bout. Them liars will never know the real haints boogering folks in my day.

"Chance, like Momma used to say, you make your own memories. I made mine nothun but misery hangin on me like beggar's lice and old age."

"Grandpa, you did right, helping the sheriff—"

"Hope the Lord—if I see Him—will understand. I've spent nough time in hell. Boy, I tell you agin, a warnin. Don't you ever, *ever* run with heathen—*heah?*"

"Yessir," Chance says softly, looking in the dark, watering eyes of the Old Man sitting in the shadows of morning falling across the porch. "I'll never again go looking for the ghost of Look and Tremble."

The Old Man leans back, his jaws moving hastily over the tobacco wad. "Like yore great-grandmomma Savannah used to say, 'Why do the heathen rage? Declare his glory among the heathen; his marvelous works among nations ... thus saith the Lord, learn not the ways of the heathen.' "

Chance stands before his grandfather, tears watering his eyes; pain fevering his burned left hand where the jagged S brand festers and sears his soul. The Old Man turns his head against the chair, suddenly asleep, morning sun falling over the long knife-scar that violated his jaw years before the boy was born.

13

The Funeral

Lil Sol and his barefoot brigade play out their summer fantasies: stalking imaginary Yankees, Germans, Japanese, New York gangsters and Wild West cattle rustlers along Mulejaw Creek and through the tall timber of the Pine Thicket.

Some days they gather in the gnawed-out cave at Chalkhead, where Ring Jaw Branch oozes from the wooded red ridge and flows toward the Chipola River; they cook potatoes in a syrup can over a fire of twigs and decayed pine limbs. Some days they splash buck-naked in Ring Jaw Branch washhole. They often whirl in the hot still afternoon air on the pine-log Flying Jenny in the Pine Thicket. Some days they play choose-up baseball with a broken town-team bat and a hideless ball covered with black friction tape on a vacant lot near the Holiness Tabernacle. They often gather in the calaboose, telling and retelling the stories, enlarging each episode into Ring Jaw legend during the last hot summer days into the autumnal leaf-turn.

Lil Sol's burned hand heals, but the flesh is scarred, the S brand etched like a browned hardened crust that won't go away. The boys of summer barely notice any more as they freely make up their own imaginary world.

Some days Lil Sol helps his grandfather along the pigtrail from the squatting Cracker house to the mercantile

store bench. Increasingly feeble, Sol Cahoon now depends on the strength of his grandson.

"Steady me, boy," he'll say, gripping Chance's arm, and stepping off the porch from his ladder-back chair. "Can't see much no more. But seed a lot in my time, Chance."

One day, as the Old Man sits on the loafer's bench, Lil Sol quietly enters the Old Man's room and shows Ben Henry, R.C. and Willy Buck the long whiskers and dark stern eyes of Jeremiah Cahoon in a sepia portrait hanging on the wall behind the bed.

"Just think, fightin Yankees just up the road yonder," says Ben Henry. "Mean looking old scudder. Bet he killed some Yankees at Chipola Springs."

Chance points to a larger portrait. "And, look here, this is Major Malcolm Grant MacNab in his Confederate uniform—"

"Look at that beard, R.C.," says Ben Henry. "Bet he'd shoot a Yankee quicker a rattler could strike."

"Grandpa says he was in Nathan Bedford Forrest's cavalry til a Yankee chopped off his arm somewhere up in Alabama. He led the troops at the Battle of Chipola Springs. And ol Jeremiah shot that Yankee General Asboth in the jaw—"

"Boy," says R.C., "if them old soldiers could talk, they'd tell some good stories."

"Let me show y'all somethng else," Chance says.

Then from a dark corner, he opens a hand-hammered wooden box and withdraws Jeremiah's frayed Confederate jacket and the broken Federal saber blade.

"Look at that blade!" says R.C. "Reckon it's got any blood on it?"

"Don't be silly," Lil Sol says.

"Too bad we can't use it for our cavalry charges," says Ben Henry. "I'm tired on makin old stick swords."

Lil Sol returns the artifacts to the closet. "It's not to play with, Ben Henry—these are historic relics. Grandpa says these will be mine someday after he's gone."

Willy Buck looks at the blade. "Shoot, Uncle Sol's gone live forever."

Icy November wind chills Becky Cahoon, cradling a hoe as she walks through the silence of the gray stones and wooden markers of Chipola Cemetery toward the family plot. She works among the many others, hoeing and hauling leaves to the burning fire just outside the wire fence.

The cemetery cleaning is an annual ritual, drawing voluntary workers from Ring Jaw and Chipola Country. They spend most of a Saturday clearing summer weeds from the graves.

Becky gathers fallen leaves, twigs and limbs in a crokersack. She hacks the brown grass from the graves of her mother Sarah Rachel and the slain brother Adam. She clears the space for the Old Man between her mother and Adam. In late afternoon, her legs benumbed, the work complete, she hurries back through the stones to the highway. Walking home, she thinks of the Old Man sitting by the fireplace, surrounded by the pungent aromas from her Thanksgiving cooking.

Three days before Thanksgiving, the Old Man rises from his rocking chair by the fireplace. "Becky, I'm going to the store for chewing tobacco."

"Chance's not here. You can't go alone."

"I was goin to that ol store long time, daughter, before you were born. Reckon I can make it one more time."

"You hurry back now. Don't be late for supper. Be careful."

"I reckon can feel my way long that ol pigtrail one more time."

"I'll send Chance for you."

"I know the way home, daughter."

In the twilight, Rebecca looks up from the hot kitchen stove, a frown tightening her face as Chance races across the yard and opens the back screen door. "Chance, where were you?

"Playing down at the calaboose. Where's grandpa?"

"He insisted on going to the store. Run up there and bring your grandfather home. Supper's about ready."

"Yessum. Telling them old stories again, I betcha."

"That's about all he's got, son—the past more alive than anything else. I'm worried about him. He's getting feeble and he can't see well. You hurry, now."

Chance walks briskly along the old foot-worn path, thinking about Christmas coming. He reaches the shadow of the store; there before him, in the dimming twilight, he sees a mass of old age sprawling across the pigtrail only a few steps from the store porch. Blood oozes from Sol Cahoon's twisted mouth, his knotted hands still gripping the walking cane.

The boy freezes. "Grandpa! Grandpa! Speak to me, *Grandpa!*"

"Your grandpa's gone, son," says the storekeeper, standing as a shadow over the boy and the man stilled in death. "Uncle Sol was here, like always, sitting alone. Next thing I knew he was gone."

Rebecca expects the worst when, in gathering darkness, the storekeeper and Moses Trottah bring the bedsheet-covered corpse to the house in the back of a Ford pickup. They place the body on the bed.

"I'm sorry, Miss Becky," Moses says. "Sol, one minute he was talking; the next he was gone."

Tears fill her eyes; she embraces her son before the red coals of a dying fire in the silence of early evening. "Knew he didn't have long, Chance. Lived long time."

"Grandpa shouldn't gone by himself," Lil Sol says. "I should have been here, helping him—"

"It was his time, son," the storekeeper says. "We never know. As the Bible says, a time for all things; time to live, time to die."

"Your grandfather lived a long life, through all that hell and torment," Becky says.

Becky and Lil Sol sit by the bed. "Chance," Becky says slowly, "I've been thinking about moving away, once we have the funeral."

"Where?"

"Somewhere far away. Somewhere you can grow up and have a life."

Lil Sol sobs. "Ring Jaw won't be the same, with Grandpa gone."

"Yes, we have nothing here anymore. I can't spend my life cooking for Ruby Barefoot."

Soon the people of Ring Jaw come with covered dishes of food and soft words of sympathy; they crowd the house as night darkens. Becky sees Charley Crowe at the back door. He pulls his felt hat from the back of the head, and knocks on the screen door.

"Charley, come on in," Becky says.

"Sho sorry to hear bout Mistah Sol passin. He were bout the best friend Charley ever had, Miz Becky."

"I know, Charley. Thank you for coming. Will you have some supper?"

"No, thank you, ma'm. I'm just gone sit the night with Mistah Sol."

The sharp musty odor of the burning kerosene stings Lil Sol's nostrils as he slowly enters the room. Golden lamp flame shadows shift and dodge on the stained darkened pinewood walls. His eyes swerve over the body in the Oakwood casket by the window. Fluttering blobs of light spill onto the ashen face of Solomon Jackson Cahoon.

Turning, fearful of shadows, fearful of movement, Lil Sol sees the lamp light framing the stern, white-bearded face and the piercing eyes of Jeremiah Cahoon, frozen in a faded photographic portrait hanging on the wall behind Uncle Solomon's iron bedstead. Then the light catches the photographer's frozen face and dark gazing eyes of Major Malcolm Grant MacNab.

He sits on the edge of the quilt-covered feather mattress, looking at the photographs and the body of his grandfather. *Sourness of whiskey toddy on his breath; webbed brown tobacco stains on his lips; his robust, cackling laughter; his stories stitched in my soul; his strong quiet wisdom and stern warnings; Jeremiah, once the soldier in a bitter war long ago; Major MacNab, his iron-gray beard falling over his Confederate jacket and his ghostly eyes moving in the dancing lamplight—*

Stilled in death, erosions of the Old Man's tired face transmute as a mask of serenity as if suddenly tensions and burdens of time and years are brushed away. *Grandpa gone, now at peace, a hard death forever and ever.*

Tears well in Lil Sol's eyes as he finds courage, kissing the Old Man's forehead. The cold lifelessness chill his lips. Icy wind from a broken window pane bathes his face. Instantly his blood runs smoothly again, his heart beating steadily before the fixed countenance frozen in lamplight: There is nothing to fear.

"Lil Sol, yo grandpa's gone home to Jesus."

Chance whirls, the gravelly voice from the man sitting in shadows startling him. "This is Uncle Charley heah, young man."

"Oh, Uncle Charley, I didn't see you—"

"Just sittin heah with my ol friend, son," Charley says,

sitting in a straight-back chair, partially buried in shadow. "We spent lotta years together, young feller. Somebody's gotta sit with him. Most of em up yonder by the fireplace, jawing. I don't mind atall. Sho do hate to put him in that grave I dug this morning."

Then Chance turns toward the doorway, hearing the soft hushed voice of his mother. "Son, time for bed. We have a long day ahead of us in the morning."

"Yessum."

"You rest good now, Mistah Chance," Charley says. "I'll be right heah with your grandpa."

Falling across his bed, Lil Sol hears the din of voices by the fireplace.

Out of the distant darkness, the slow thunder roll builds and sharply cracking lightning zigzags fingers of whiteness across the night. With the slow drumming splatter of rain wetting the tin roof, Lil Sol is sound asleep.

In the other room, Charley Crowe hears the heavenly rumbling and fights sleep, a steady ache running up his tired back muscles.

They stand and sit, some silent, some talking, drinking coffee and crowding plates with food on the oak dining table, watching the fire chase the November chill.

"Sure thought ol Uncle Solomon would live forever," says Big Bone Stakewood. "Most of his bunch about gone now."

"Never saw the likes of his kind before," says Moses Trottah. "Never see it agin neither."

"Much of a man in his prime," says Sheriff Cicero Turnbull, sipping coffee.

"Cicero, he was a helluva man in a fight," Moses says. "Ever see him crack a bullwhip? Or handle a knife? No sir, didn't know the meaning of being scared."

"Mostly he did the scaring," Big Bone says." Now, ol Jeremiah, there was a hellraiser."

"Yeah, and Solomon Cahoon was a spitting image." Moses says. "Rebecca's boy just like Uncle Solomon."

"Yes sir, but he'll never ever know all the meanness. Not in his whole lifetime," Big Bone says.

"Well, Solomon Cahoon tried to teach that boy right," Moses says. "Taught him about life and surviving in the woods. Made him study his schooling. Taught him how he loved that old six-fingered black moonshiner, Willy Santee, and how it was better to love your fellow man than to fight and hate.

"Sol said never bother nobody—and if they bother you, be prepared to protect yourself and your family. Meanness aint never gone get you nothing. Like he always said, a man's got to earn respect by being a man himself."

Cicero turns to the fire. "Sol's gone but we won't forget him. They'll be talking about the Old Man around here a long, long time...."

Cold rain drips from a murky sky as a small knot of mourners gather in the Chipola Primitive Baptist Church for the funeral. A young minister steps to the pulpit and reads scriptures and prays. He looks down on the oak coffin, speaking softly:

"His was a robust and full life, fourscore and seven years in a time when strong men were measured by their courage and their conviction—when they faced hard times and uncertainty and battled their fears with the only weapons they owned—their backbone and their determined will to stand up for surviving the worst of men and Satan's ways of the heathen...."

The brown blades of grass snap with frost-stiff cracking underfoot. The pallbearers trudge from the church to the center of the sloping graveyard where the earthen cavity had been readied for the lowering of the coffin.

Wet footsteps and cold pelting rain soaking the clothing of the sad-countenanced bearers interrupt the haunting quiet of the brooding earth.

Up past the magnolias, on a slope dropping into a creek bed of titi, hickory, sweet gum and pine, amid gray stones and rotted plank markers of generations, between the earthly beds of Sarah Rachel and Adam, near Old Jeremiah and Savannah, they bury Solomon Jackson Cahoon.

Ben Henry, R.C. and Willy Buck stand silently under the dripping magnolia limbs, watching rain-soaked Charley Crowe stand with a shovel. As mourners leave the cemetery amid the last echoes of the final grave-side prayer, Charley is pouring spadefuls of clay over the casket.

Now, in late afternoon, the sun will drop behind the tall tomb of Major Malcolm Grant MacNab, and throw a long shadow across the fresh grave of the Old Man of Ring Jaw.

Lil Sol turns from the grave and sees Willy Buck, Ben Henry and R.C. standing shivering under the umbrella of the magnolia. He breaks from his mother's embrace, and runs to join his friends.

"Grandpa gave me one last gift," Lil Sol says, sobbing.

"Let's see," says Ben Henry, his hair dripping wet.

Water gauzes Lil Sol's eyes as he pulls the Barlow knife from his pocket and holds it in the palm of his hand.

"Boy! If that knife could talk," says Willy Buck, all bright eyes and ivory buck teeth, nudging close but fearful to touch.

"Already has, Willy Buck," says R.C., slowly running his fingers across the brown bone handle. "Lordy mercy, Uncle Solomon talks from the grave!"

Lil Sol stares at the knife, words gushing through his sobbing:

"Grandpa always told me I could make my own memories. He said be a man—and not learn the ways of the heathen."

14

Walk to the Widderwoman

$\mathcal{U}$ncle Charley Crowe saunters along the narrow pebbled clay road. His body rigid, straining toward the destined distance, he hears the chatter of his teeth as the frigid November wind bathes his leathery brown face bronzed like dried clay and creviced by many summer suns. His dark, gray-sprigged ringlet mane curls about his ears. His broad nostrils turn his breath to smoky vapor.

A frayed blue denim jumper jacket covers his beer-barrel torso and sheathes his gangling arms. Scuffed brogans laced with baling wire on his size twelve feet pad the ice-spewed ground in a hypnotic rumble-crunch. And with a slow ambling gait his two hundred pounds of muscle and bone move with a determined bobbing rhythm of a man who knows where he's going.

With every steady stride of his stubby bowed legs and piston plunge of his stooped shoulders, he methodically tumbles a wad of Brown Mule chewing tobacco from jaw to jaw. Often he spews a rope of amber spittle, splattering in the tire-worn ruts before him. Behind him spidery patches mark his footpath. Fingers of his gloved right hand grip the bale of a gallon tin bucket of sugarcane syrup. His darting brown eyes are fixed on the lonesome road, bordered by old wire fences separating gray pastures of winter dotted with milkcows, hogs and cattle egrets.

The early Sunday sun pokes golden light through dishwater patches mucking leaden skies. Charley's always on the road north by first light, leaving behind his unpainted shotgun house squatting in the edge of a sloping sugarcane field spreading to a Bearthick Swamp cypresshead.

Every Sunday he walks the four miles north through Ring Jaw's morning sleepiness to spend the day with Aunt Hattie Santee, who washes and irons Ring Jaw folks' clothing for a dollar a week.

He walks the mile of claybed road leading to the slagged highway threading north through Ring Jaw. Charley talks to the coveys of cowbirds whitening the cold fields stubbed with brown cornstalks. "Lawse me, mighty pore pickins, you old birds," he mutters, his long, slow words flavored with self amusement. "Like ol Charley, heah, mighty pore pickins for Sunday breakfast, even if it's soppin this heah cane sweetenin with Miz Hattie's cornbread. Cold nough for a hog killin."

Even now, after all these years, all these years visiting Aunt Hattie, he carries hidden from all eyes a 1911 government-issue .45 caliber automatic pistol he has owned since American doughboys came home from the Great War in 1918. Even now he remembers how the doughboys said the U.S. Army weapon stopped the Germans in the blood-drenched trenches across the water.

The weapon is just a bulge behind his patched khaki shirt, always tight against his stomach when he walks on Sunday, winter and summer, rain or sunshine.

On the other six working days, when he sweats in the fields tending a herd of milkcows or feeds woodfires for the cane mill or cuts smokehouse pinetops for a hog-killing, the automatic he acquired in Georgia so many forgotten years ago is hidden away under the feather mattress that rests his bone-tired body.

But on Sunday the metallic bulge on his belly is a part of him.

Folks around Ring Jaw tell stories about the one they call Old Uncle Charley. They think of him when folks need a strong back for heavy lifting, grave-digging, cane-grinding or a hog-killing.

Some farmers and loafers sitting and jawing around the wood stove in Elleck Dunkane's grocery store like to tell how they believe Charley escaped from a Georgia chain gang, outrunning a pack of bloodhounds. They tell how they believe he got into a knife fight with a turpentine woods rider over the love of a mulatto woman and fled into the backwoods of West Florida long time ago, working in the logging camps.

Some are sure Charley once had been a fleet-footed whiskeymaker, back when Ring Jaw farmers and merchants financed the nocturnal enterprise and lived to tell another generation of paying off the sheriff and how rumstill operators like Charley Crowe and Sol Cahoon had evaded the revenue officers and bloodhounds in the river swamps.

But now they see Charley a relic of the timber and turpentine past. Folks say he's the last of the crew of mill hands who lived in the string of weathered shotgun houses at Mulehead Pond Plantation. Now with the other shacks crumbled to dust as if Shantytown never existed, his sagging house beside the dirt road survives, as does Charley, reminding Ring Jaw folks of the hardscrabble time when blacks and whites alike carved catfaces on pine to bleed the forests for the distillery that has been abandoned for years to rust and harbor woodrats along the railroad tracks in a tangle of weeds, vines and broken timbers.

Charley's all alone now, except for Aunt Hattie. She lives quietly smelling of lye soap and starch with her fireplace and lighterd-knot warmth, turnip and collard patch, smutted washpot and clothes-drying lines strung behind a rented house near Ring Jaw Branch on Doc Nodd's land north of Ring Jaw. Only four miles and the town separate them, except on Sunday. But between them is another world of which they are shadowy edges of antiquity.

"Gotta cut Miz Hattie some stovewood, old birds," he says, glancing up at their animated wings shadowed against the sweatshirt gray rags of sky. "You know how to tell a widderwoman's house? Aint no stovewood on the front porch. Nawsuh! *Hee hee!* But for the cuttin there might be a mess of greens and a lil pork in the pot. Maybe a warm toddy for the sitting. Maybe a little warm squeezin under the quilts. *Hee hee!*"

Charley reaches the slagged road and turns north, his crumple-toed brogans pounding the loose gravel as he passes a clump of pecan trees in the edge of Ring Jaw. "Birds gotta fly. Hogs gotta root. Ol Charley, he's gotta walk—walk a long way sure as Saturday night's rest brings Sunday mornin and a widderwoman with her washin and ironin done waits for a lil sweetening. *Hee hee!*"

Charley's humble, silent ways feed the mystery and the curiosity. Mostly they see Charley as a survivor on the edge of a white world, making his way virtually alone. Years ago Charley was tall and tightly muscular—straight as a West Florida pine and tough as the slobbering oxen he worked in the Chipola River logging camps. But to Ring Jaw youngsters, seeing him in old hand-me-down clothes walking the hard road or trading at Elleck Dunkane store, he's ageless—the one who feeds the fires as the sugarcane juice boils up in the hot pan for syrup makers, and always smells of smoke.

Except on Sundays.

Ring Jaw folks can count on his walk to the widderwoman.

Charley walks past the Sweet Bethel Methodist and Chipola Primitive Baptist churches, shrouded by pecan trees. "Folks gonna come and sing and shout, listenin to the preacherman like my Bible-hollerin Pa long time ago," he mutters to himself. "Yassuh, the Lord's Day when we gonna rest. He the Lord sholly put ol Jack Frost on the collards this mornin."

He stops, sits the bucket on the edge of the road and catches his breath within the shadow of the Baptist church. He's only a few steps from Chipola Cemetery sloping into the tree-clotted branchhead behind the church building. He spits tobacco juice onto the withered grass, and straightens his back in a slow creaking stretch. The ache in his back rushes hateful memories of other days when the Chipola Springs and Estiffanugla funeral homes hire him to carve out the red clay for many of the graves in the gray garden of stone.

"Over there, down the hill, they put ol Sol Cahoon to rest," he ponders, remembering the day he shoveled out the grave in a slow peppering rain. "Folks sholly miss Mistah Sol, sittin on that old loafers' bench at the mercantile store and fillin that old rockin chair in Mistah Elleck's grocery store, tellin stories bout heathenish mean ways. Specially ol Charley."

He lifts the syrup bucket and moves on into the brisk morning air, musing about Sol Cahoon. "Long time ago me and Willy Santee cooked the whiskey and Mistah Sol, why, he could drank more'n any grown white man I ever seed. *Hee hee!* But he was sholly good to ol Charley and Willy. Sitting there on the riverbank, with firelight in his eyes, talking about how we done outrun the law, and sharin a fruitjar of good beaded drankin whiskey. *Hee hee!* Lawse me, I member like it was yesterday—"

The swamp sleeps the night away, but Sol Cahoon and Charley listen to the moonlight rhythm of the river—

the swish of the current around the cypress roots and limestone rocks, the hum of insects, the low rumbling of bullfrogs. They sit before the lighterd-knot fire, eating canned sardines, pork and beans and soda crackers.

"Charley, gimme another shot of that rutgut," Sol says, fishing a sardine from the can with a cracker.

"Yassuh, Mistah Sol, you sholly put likker away."

"Damn right, Charley. Specially when you run it off. Gotta fine bead to it."

"Mistah Sol, you say that ever time we cook up a batch."

"There's somethin to makin good whiskey," Sol says. "Gotta have the touch with the sugar and chicken layin mash. Charley, you may be the best whiskeymaker in Fayette County."

"You used to say that to Willy, Mistah Sol. Dangerous work though—"

"Naw, now, Charley. That's the challenge—outfoxin the law. Remember that time we was totin them five-gallon demijohns cross that ol wet riverbank forty down by Ring Jaw Island?"

Charley pokes at the fire with a tree limb and with a grim face grunts and hesitates. "Yassuh, bad day that was. Law on us before we knew it. Almost caught you, Mistah Sol. And poor old Willy—"

"Hell, we had us one long hot foot race through the swamp. You and Willy, scampering like streaks of greased lightnin with that buckshot cuttin through them pine saplings like saws bitin cordwood."

Charley pauses, chewing on a sardine. "Ol Willy sholly did light out. Even after that buckshot tore open his backside he kept movin til I had to leave him deep in swampwater, bleedin like a stuck hog. I was one scared colored feller, tryin to drag him to high ground, and him chokin on his own blood, screamin for his woman, Hattie.

I finally waded out. Hid out all night in that corn crib, buryin myself under corn shucks."

"Ol Willy Santee, hell, I loved that old riverrat rummaker like he was my blood brother," Sol says. "He sho loved Hattie and them two boys."

"Yassuh, I miss him," Charley says. "Po Hattie, such a young widder, trying to feed them two younguns, Shawky and Willy Frank."

"A good lookin woman. You oughta take care of her."

"I looks in on her now and agin. Cut her some stovewood."

Sol laughs. "She'd make you a fine wife, Charley."

"Nawsuh, couldn't do that to Willy."

Sol looks into the night, sipping the whiskey. "Remember Willy had an extra lil thumb on his left hand. Sometimes in Elleck's store he'd stand there bout half lit, stinkin of rumstill smoke after a night in the swamp, wigglin it to for gigglin younguns. And them damn revenue officers who'd been lookin for us all night standin at the other end of the counter eating sardines, pork'n beans and sodiecrackers."

"Yeah, Mistah Sol, but most folks talk about how you went back and brought Willy outta the swamp—"

"Hell, right thing to do," Sol says. "I toted him nearly two miles to that sand ridge up from Ring Jaw Island. Dug a shallow grave and buried him best I could. Couldn't leave him to the law and gators or pineywoods rooters. Charley, you know, hightailin it through Bearthick Swamp all I could think of was them convict stripes and a year and a day on the hard road. But they didn't catch us. Pour us another drank."

"Mistah Sol, might not always be so lucky next time—"

"Hell, aint no sin runnin likker outta these woods. Most folks in this Chipola River country get into whiskey one way or nother to put pork'n gravy on the supper table.

Farmers and storekeepers—hell, churchgoin folks—make shine or hire it done. Even the sheriff's getting rich off bootleggers. And he dranks more'n both of us."

They laugh.

"Charley, you know what they say. Them folks that aint gruntin for fishbait, diggin stumps or pullin gophers or lyin out with dry cows or preaching the Holy Ghost are cookin sugar and mash in the moonlight."

Charley laughs. "Yassuh! You bout right."

"I know I'm right. Hell, you can buy rotgut everywhere in Ring Jaw but the Baptist Church and the post office, and I aint too sure about either one. Charley, old friend, let's have another snort."

Charley fills the Mason jar and hands the whiskey to Sol.

"You old rummaker, you take care of Hattie, you *hear?*"

Charley walks past the post office, Hasty Ponds' Pool Hall and Silas Haymoor's garage at the River Road crossing. The icy wind brushes his face as he strides forward along the empty road as the town sleeps. The lone figure reaches the old oak tree in the edge of the schoolyard. He rests, glancing into crooked limbs spreading a leafy green canopy over the edge of the roadway. *Never forget that night them two pesterin boys came after me, gonna try to cut mah head off, and then Mistah Roscoe, he come a-runnin.*

Charley quickens his stride, and crosses the road toward Elleck Dunkane's store, his nostrils filling with wood smoke snaking skyward from the brick chimney.

"Mawnin, mawnin, Mistah Elleck," Charley says, a grin splitting his face. He pushes through the screen door into the store, his brown eyes darting. The warmth of the wood stove fire embraces him momentarily, diminishing the chill holding him in its icy vice. He sits the bucket by the door and rubs his callused hands together. He turns to nod at Moses Trottah and Big Bone Stakewood sitting by the stove in the corner of the store. But they are too busy talking and laughing to notice.

Elleck Dunkane, stuffing foodstuff into a paper bag, looks up from the wooden counter. "Why, Charley, good morning! Sure a cold one for walking."

"Yassuh, sholly is, Mistah Elleck." Charley stands before the counter, feeling the red glow of the stove. In the corner, a rack of laughter animates the men. Moses turns, lifts his hand, nodding a grinned greeting.

"What'll it be?" Elleck says.

"Nothun much, Mistah Elleck. Quarter's worth of Rooster snuff. Half-pound of green coffee. Mistah Elleck, mind if I warm up in heah a lil while?"

"Why, sure, Charley. I'll tell you—none of us getting very far from the stove this morning. Say, I aint seen Aunt Hattie this week. She's not sick is she?"

"Nawsuh. Not as I knows of. She's mighty grieved these days—all these boys comin home from the war. She talks lot bout losing them two boys cross the water. Last time I come by she was sittin there readin the last letter Willy Frank wrote from somewhere in Germany."

Elleck stares at Charley. "Sure mighty sad, a widderwoman raisin Shawky and Willy Frank, then losing both of her sons in the war."

"Yassuh, sholly bad. Hattie don't stir much. Don't say much. But she grieves. Mistah Elleck, I brung this syrup heah—"

"Aw, Charley, take it on up to Aunt Hattie. She washes our clothes; we'll settle up. Don't worry bout it."

"Yassuh, thank you, Mistah Elleck, pleasesuh."

Charley turns, feeling the warmth of the store. He stuffs the brown paper bag into his jumper pocket and bends to lift the bucket. "Cold nough to butcher hogs, Mistah Elleck."

Elleck laughs. "Betcha glad it aint Monday morning."

"Yassuh, sholly is. The Lord must have his day."

"Yeah, Charley, you know what they say," Big Bone shouts. "It's pecker-shrinking weather!"

Charley nods, and a wide grin splits his face. "Yassuh. Yassuh. Ol Charley don't know much bout that."

Walking into the cold, icy air again bathes his face. He's only a mile from the old shotgun house where Aunt Hattie cooks biscuits. He thinks of the fume of smoke from her cookstove, curling through the naked gray skeletal fingers of pecan trees reaching skyward. He bends into the north wind.

"Ol Uncle Charley don't miss a Sunday, does he?" Moses says, turning to the window, watching Charley walking away. He snickers. "He sho does look after Aunt Hattie, toting that bucket all this way."

"Yeah, old Charley's something else," Big Bone says. "I once asked him how much time he'd served on the hard road. He said 'year and eighteen months.' And I said, 'you must mean two years and six months.' But he said, 'No sir, a year and eighteen months. Once for a year; the second time eighteen months.'"

They laugh.

"No wonder he ran," Moses says.

Big Bone turns, watching Charley walk toward the road. "Ran?"

Moses brings his hand to his chin. "Yeah, outran a pack of bloodhounds through a Georgia swamp. That's how he wound up heah, snakin logs and workin turpentine long time ago. He usta make whiskey with Uncle Sol Cahoon and Willy Santee. Hell, he flat out left them revenue officers and their hounds in Bearthick Swamp.—"

"Willy? He got killed, didn't he?" Big Bone says.

"Wad of buckshot in the back," Elleck says. "But they

never caught Charley. Quick on his feet in them days."

"He's slowing down a tad now," Big Bone says. "Gettin lil age on him."

Moses turns to the stove. "Hell, Charley aint as old as most folks think. He still outworks most white men I know, whether cutting cane stalks or grave digging. He aint walking to no widderwoman just to cut stovewood."

They laugh.

"Time was when Charley would have to fight his way through Ring Jaw. Specially after sundown," Moses says.

"Times change," Big Bone says. "Yeah, ol Charley and Aunt Hattie, they like family. Nobody's pestered colored folks roun heah in a coon's age."

Moses drops back into the creaking chair by the stove. "Not since that night Rooster Reddoake and that old Hoggen boy come out from behind that oak tree over yonder by the schoolhouse. They laid a Barlow knife agin Charley's throat. Hell, if it hadn't been for you, Elleck, and Roscoe Ransum, they'd cut Charley's head off."

"Mean as a snake, them boys," Elleck says. "But they run like hell when Roscoe pounced on em with both fists flying. Judge Hawke did us a favor, sending them boys to reform school."

"Kept em outta Korea, though," Big Bone says. "Hell, member ol redheaded Puddin Pooley? Shot off his left hand with a shotgun to keep outta the war. Claimed it got chewed off in a cane mill."

Moses chuckles. "Ol Puddin with that nub. Hell, he'd rather run likker to Georgia and chase poontang."

They laugh.

"Well, ol Charley's lot smarter you think," Moses says. "You know what they say. Black stuff at night makes the morning smile."

They laugh.

"One thing's for sure," Elleck says. "Charley didn't

run that night. Nobody's messed with Charley Crowe since that night. *Nobody*."

"Lawse me, Charley, thought it might be too cold for you," Hattie Santee says, pushing open the front door.

Charley climbs the wooden steps. "Mighty cold. But I got heah somehow."

"Always do. Come on in. Warm up by the fire. I know you must be chilled. I got biscuits on the stove."

Charley puts the bucket on the kitchen table and turns, warming his back before the fire. "Well, they buried ol Uncle Sol Cahoon the other day. Thought he'd live forever. His grave mount be the last one I dig. I's tired of buryin all my friends."

Hattie turns from the fire, looking through the window at the gray flatness of her garden where in summer she grows corn, butterbeans and okra. She hesitates, nervously fishing a folded paper from her apron pocket. "Got this letter from the Army bout my boy Willy Frank."

"What the letter say?"

Hattie is silent, chin shaking, eyes swimming in tears. "Tells bout him dying over yonder in the last days of the war."

"Oh, my God, Hattie—"

"You raise em, two boys. All alone, with my Willy gone all these long years. Like their Pa, they go into the woods and fields working land they don't own. They go away to war. Then all's left is bad news wrote on a piece of paper."

"Hattie, sorry you have to live it all agin. Lord amighty, times don't get no better."

"They say neither of my boys can be brung home. Buried where they fell across the water."

"Just as well, Hattie. Aint no burying ground for us roun heah nohow."

Hattie sobs. "The letter says Willy Frank won some kinda medal for bravery. They sendin it to me in the mail. Said it was the Silver Star."

"He deserves it, Hattie. Willy Frank was a good soldier. I member him and Roscoe Ransum goin off to the Army together."

"But Roscoe, he come home. Lotta these men roun heah comin home now."

They sit in silence before Hattie moves her lips, searching for words. "Reckon what's gonna happen to us all alone heah. We aint spring chickens no more—"

"The Lord shows the way," Charley says, wrapping his arm around the slender aproned woman. "We do what's we gotta do, Hattie. Like my old Pa back'n Georgia used to say, someday it's gonna be a great gettin-up mornin with them coffins popping and everybody happy and free. Yo two sons gonna be with us, too. And Willy."

Out across the fields, beyond Ring Jaw Creek, in the river valley, Old Sol Cahoon buried Willy Santee.

Hattie stares into the fire. "Suppose so. But I grieves, Charley. Getting them telegrams during the war were the worse two days of life. My chilrun was all I had— long way from home, not comin back. One blown up at Pearl Harbor. Now my baby buried yonder cross the water, gone forever."

"Hattie, don't you fret," Charley says. "Them fine young boys with the Lord. Besides, you got your grand baby, Willy Buck."

Hattie nods, smiling. "I try to raise that boy, what with his momma done married again and moved uppen Redlands County. She didn't wait long, runnin off with that Baptist preacher, leavin Willy Buck heah. But he's been a good boy. I worries bout them mean white boys always pesterin him."

"That boy gonna needs some raisin. I'll try to keep him straight. Where's Willy Buck, anyhow?"

"He's gone down yonder, looking for that white boy, Mistah Sol's grandson. Said he wanted to say goodbye afore they left—"

"Miz Becky did say she was movin away somers."

"Willy Buck's sho tore up bout that boy leavin. Said he was losin his best friend. And him white."

"That boy jest lak Mister Sol. Miz Becky told me at the funeral she had nothun left heah. Said she wanted to get as far from Ring Jaw as she could. Start a new life."

"At least she's got her son with her."

Hattie moves to the table. "Charley you must be tuckered, toting that syrup bucket all the way."

"Naw, I'm awright. Lil stiff from the cold."

"Want some biscuits and coffee?"

"Hot biscuits and coffee beats a long lonesome road and cold cornbread anytime," Charley says, laughing.

They sit at the kitchen table, quietly staring at the snapping red flames in the fireplace. "Don't you worry none now, Hattie," Charley says, gnawing on a biscuit. "Every Sunday ol Charley's gonna be right heah, putting stovewood on your porch. Just as sholly as Saturday night brings the morning."

Before it's pitch-dark, and shadows rushing night cold, Charley's on the road again, the smell of woodsmoke in his nostrils. Slowly walking through the Ring Jaw quietness, seeing lamplight blobs in houses and shadows streaking across the slagged road, he feels the weight of the pistol under his shirt. He wonders now why he still carries the gun that he has not fired in so many years he cannot remember, and only then while chasing rabbits from a collard patch. "Guns are for killing," he mutters to himself. "Old Charley never meant no harm to a living soul. No one bothers old Charley no more. Not since that night they came out of darkness like ghosts so many years ago I can't rightly recollect." *Never was a knife blade so cold as that summer night when out of the darkness I felt the sharp steel stingin my throat. Them two boys like wildcats leapin from behind that old oak tree, breathin hot stinkin wind in my face and clawin and slobberin cusswords like maddogs, sayin they'd send Old Charley to the hereafter. But ol Roscoe Ransum done come a-runnin and yellin from the store across the road with Mistah Elleck at his heels. Then Mistah Roscoe hit em with his fists like they was kicked by a mule and them boys lit out.*

Old Charley run many a time and hid in the swamp, water up to my waist, fearin cottonmouths and the law, hearing yelpin hounddogs, waitin for daylight and the warmth of my feather bed that's too long a-comin.

But that night by the old oak, as I stood in the shadows, feeling the trickle of blood from the gash on my neck, shiverin as if it was a cold winter night, I vowed to myself: never agin. Never agin. Folks don't know about it, but this ol pistol from the war been agin my belly as I walk ever since. But them boys who always said what many folks said in those days— "don't let the sun go down on your black ass in Ring Jaw"— never crossed old Charley's path again. And many a Sunday I pass this way hopin they weren't somewhere in the dark like them Germans with their bayonets who kilt Willy Frank Santee cross the water. Them two boys done a mean evil thang, burnin Mistah Sol's grand youngun, and they oughta keep em locked up in the jailhouse an throw way the key.

Charley goes south into the quiet darkness, his brogans padding the slagged road. He turns over his chew of tobacco, and spits as he reaches the old oak tree with the gnarled limbs canopying the highway. In the far distance he hears a yelping yarddog in the hollow cold silence. And above him, clouds like torn bedsheets partially smother the ghostly oval as splinters of moonglow weave shadows of the naked limbs.

Charley moves on in twilight, the ache of shoveling clay in Chipola Cemetery upon him in the cold. He longs for his feather-mattress bed and the warmth of the quilts Hattie made for him, miles ahead into the gathering night. Sleep will bring rest before another workday feeding the woodfires of the cane mill. Sunup and another gettin-up time for the long six days, waiting for Sunday and the long, lonely walk to the widderwoman. Now, in the cold brooding night, there's only the beat of the brogans, his step steady on a road that had been drawn on the map so long ago he cannot remember.

Part Three
Remember a River

15

Ghosts

The morning sun slants down upon the waters, and a whisper of cooling wind bathes the tree canopy up from the Chipola. Chance Cahoon, standing by the live oak with a moss-bearded limb jutting over the river edge, his face salved with sweat, squints searchingly into the blinding sunlight striking the roiling, shoal-splattering white water of Look and Tremble. He stands alone, all alone, seeing in the shoal a time within him that is timeless.

The aloneness sharpens inward images of Chipola Country's ancestral flow, now flooding and cascading through his mind. Scenes snap into view and reshape other episodes, as if plucked from old grayed newsreel film of the Forties, unspooling jerkily. Two currents flow: one away from the river; the other back to the river again—threading a continuity of blood and soul—as does the ageless, restless river before him, gushing moodily through swamp and darkwater sloughs toward the Gulf.

The water swirls lyrical turbulence, plunging swiftly and deeply through the rocky curvature, sculpted by unrelenting timeless pressure. He hears the frantic white water boom and burble against webbed, pocked river trough sinks. A cool wind brushes his face, and combs the pine needles. He sees oak leaves cascading into the eddying pools.

Yet, transfixed, he sees beyond the river.

His mind speeds through corridors of time: a spectator; sometimes an actor center stage, with ghosts transcending the years. *Seeing, feeling, sharing, crying, laughing, knowing, wondering, yearning.*

He sees his past.

Chance Cahoon, no longer a stranger, now searching his soul, stands there in the fresh river morning a long time.

Rooster Reddoake turns the chewed cheroot cigar a full circle with his yellowed teeth. He drives the dusty black pickup truck along the River Road, approaching Willis Bridge. Hunky sits beside him silently, filling the hot cab with cigarette smoke, and aimlessly pushing the buttons of the cassette tape player.

"Don't mess with the tape deck, Hunky!" Rooster barks.

Hunky pushes "Eject" and out pops "Folsom Prison Blues." "Old Johnny Cash," Hunky says, "stuck in Folsom and time keep draggin—"

"Dammit, I said quit, you heah?"

"I thought you liked this album. Johnny speaks up for you jailbirds."

"Heared enough. Don't start none that racket."

"Pardon me, Mistah Nub Reddoake! You didn't shoot a man just to watch—"

"Dammit, shet up!"

Hunky giggles.

Rooster mashes the brake pedal, slowing the pickup to a crawl on the bridge. His eyes search the wooded banks and finally fall on the tannic blackwater gleaming with sunspurs below.

"River's low. Damned low." Rooster pulls the moist

cigar stub from his teeth and skeets a rope of brown spittle out the window. "Hell, Hunky, that feller's gotta be down yonder at the shoal."

Hunky coughs, spewing dregs of tobacco smoke. "Follow them tire tracks yonder—"

"Hell, I know the way, you pissant!"

"Don't snap at me. You drug me off down heah, lookin fer a feller we aint seen in thirty years. What's he gone think? You gone shoot him?"

"We'll give him plenty to think bout, Hunky."

Hunky glances at the Colt .45 revolver in a cowhide holster in the seat. "You better hide that gun, Rooster."

"Hell, it's always on the seat, everywhere I go. Belonged to my daddy. He made that cowhide scabbard. Ever tell you how my Pa won the Colt pistol in a poker game?—"

"Yeah, you might not be so damn lucky. Might find yourself on the road back to Atlanta."

"Never. Never goin back to prison. My po ol Pa died in that Raiford cesspool, and Momma grieved herself to death. Never, even if I have to get lost in these river swamps. *Never! Dammit!*"

"Rooster's stuck in Hotlanta prison," Hunky sings gravelly, unevenly, his bony fingers thumping the dashboard, "and he aint comin back!"

Rooster draws his face hard, and sweat beads freckle his brow. "Damn you!—stick that gas nozzle up yo ass!"

Hunky giggles.

Beyond the bridge, Rooster quickly turns the pickup onto the river trail, and drives slowly by vine-tangled trees and bushes fencing the tire-wallowed sand ruts. Tire treads crunch the soft white sand and fallen leaves; the engine sings a steady cadence as spurs of sunlight slice through treetops and slide across the windshield.

"Well, ol Hunky, I suppose that feller must be still

searching for the many ghosts of Look'n Tremble," Rooster says, laughing. The cold nicotine taste suddenly sours; he flings the moist cigar stub out the window.

Hunky nods, grins and coughs jerkily. "We may run into another ghost. Willy Buck's somers roun heah."

"Hell with him," Rooster says, dropping his eyes to the revolver on the seat. "Besides, we just lookin for an ol friend from long ago. Gonna see what he's made of, *right?*"

Hunky laughs, fragments of smoke worming through his teeth. He slaps a buzzing fly. "If Willy Buck spots you with that gun, you may go back to Atlanta."

"Naw, nobody will ever know. Hell, I aint going back to the pen."

Through sunlight stabbing the forest, Rooster sees the shoal. He brakes the truck, listening to the steady roar and smelling the river freshness.

"He's our man," Hunky whispers, seeing the man with a shock of red hair and a spray of freckles. "That's the Louisiana Ford I gassed up."

Rooster jerks his shirt loose, shoves the .45 snug behind his cowhide belt, pulls down his shirt over the weapon and steps from the cab, fanning a swarm of gnats. He hears footsteps, turns quickly. Willy Buck Santee steps out of the forest. "Mawnin, Willy Buck," Rooster says, grinning.

Willy Buck walks toward the truck, the sun striking his bronze face. "Morning. Hunky, the truck fixed yet?"

"Ol Hickernut's still working on the engine."

"I need that truck today." Willy Buck says. "Say, why y'all down here? Hunky aren't you supposed to be pumping gas?"

Hunky coughs. "Rooster heah, he asked me to come with him—"

"Hell," Rooster yells, giggling, "Hunky saw a ghost!"

"Ghost?" Willy Buck says. "Likely it came out of a liquor bottle. Hunky, I can smell you."

"Nawsuh, this is real," Hunky says.

"We aint sure, Willy Buck, but Hunky thinks that feller yonder's someone we know—"

"Yeah," Hunky blurts, "remember Lil Sol? Look up yonder."

Willy Buck turns, seeing the figure in the shadow of the live oak. "Chance?"

"Yeah, Solomon Chance Cahoon," Hunky says. "He bought gas and asked about the river. I saw him write his name; he's got a bad scar on his left hand."

Startled, Willy Buck tightens his eyes, still looking toward the man framed in tree shadows. "Looks like he's got red hair—"

"Sorta like his daddy." Hunky snickers.

Willy Buck stares, then lowers his head. "Talk about ghosts! No wonder you're carrying that .45, Rooster. Hell, maybe you could build a fire. Heat up a branding iron." He turns, his eyes falling on the brown revolver handle bulging from the unbuttoned shirt. "Rooster, I'm going to tell you again. You're not supposed to have a gun. Want to go back to Atlanta?"

"Hell, Willy Buck, a man needs a gun in these woods. Cottonmouths, rattlers, varmints. You've got a rifle in your truck."

"Not for stalking people. Since when you ever go snake hunting so early in the morning? Don't you do it, Rooster."

"Don't do what? What the hell you mean?"

"That man yonder. He may have come back for Rattler's funeral. Can't you ever think about anything but aggravating folks who don't bother you?"

"Aw, just having a little friendly fun," Hunky says, giggling. "Hell, Rooster, he couldn't hit the broad side of a barn with that ol Colt."

Rooster pivots and spits, looking toward the man through the trees. "Aw, I just thought we might stir a memory or two—"

"You thought he'd be easy prey again, Rooster." Willy Buck snaps, lifting his voice. "And after all your troubles. You never learn. Put the damn gun away. You'd never use it, except to scare someone—if you've got the advantage."

"You're boss," Rooster says. "You buy the groceries. Driving one of your trucks helluva lot better'n doing hard time." He slowly pulls the revolver from his belt. "But he might remember us from that night—"

"Sure, he remembers," Willy Buck says. "So do I. So does Hunky. Hell, y'all pestered me, a black boy scared when I saw you coming. But a lotta water gone over the shoal. A boy is expected to become a man if he discovers the steel of his humanity. You were wrong then, burning an old man's innocent grandson. You ought to be begging for forgiveness."

Rooster grins, placing the gun back in the holster. "You're talking like a holiness preacher."

"No. Rooster, no. I'm talking about boys who never grow up—boys who never see beyond foolish heathen ways. Besides, I went to a helluva lotta trouble helping your mother get you released from Atlanta. I thought it was the right thing to do, her all alone and sickly and didn't have any income. Any more meanness and, dammit, you're behind bars again. *You understand?*"

"All right! I know," Rooster says, his voice lowering to a hushed whisper. "You stood for me when I needed it, Willy Buck, and, dammit, I owe you my freedom. I don't wanna lose it agin."

"Okay, okay," Willy Buck says. "Now get in the truck and we'll go meet that feller. Like old friends."

"Like ol buddies," Rooster says, grinning.

"Yeah," Hunky says, giggling, thumping cigarette ash

in the sand. "He's sholly gonna faint dead to the world when he sees these old ghosts—old Rooster Nub coming outta the woods with his ol buddy, Willy Buck Santee."

Chance turns from the river, hearing the crunch of tires and hum of the engine. Suddenly the pickup truck stops within thirty feet of him, and a deep bass voice comes from the cab.

"*Howdy!*" Rivah's sho purty heah, aint it?"

Chance hesitates. "Why, hello there. Yes, this is a beautiful place."

Rooster steps from the cab. "Always been my favorite stretch of the Chipola."

Chance hears the truck door slam behind the rotund, paunchy driver with one arm, a straw cattleman's hat brim shadowing his face.

"Coolest place I know on a hot July day," Rooster says. "Mind if some ol friends join you?"

"By no means, do." Chance holds his eyes on the two other men suddenly out of the cab and standing by the truck hood. He closes the blade, concealing the Barlow in his left hand.

By the hood, he recognizes the reed-thin, grinning man in the Rebel Oil cap with tattooed arms. The sun strikes Hunky's yellow teeth as he comes out of a fog of cigarette smoke. Behind him, a tall, lean black man cracks a twisted smile with pearly teeth splitting a bony bronze face beneath a smoky ringlet mane.

Chance thrusts out his right hand to Rooster, seeing brown-gray sideburns, tight hazel eyes and thin pale lips flecked with tobacco brown. "I'm Chance Cahoon. Happy to meet you fellers."

"Pleased to know you," Rooster says, spitting a saliva slug in the sand. "Gonna be nother scorcher."

"Do the river look like you remember, Mistah Cahoon," Hunky says. He giggles, pulls the cigarette from his lips and pumps Chance's hand.

"Why, yes—it does." Chance again sees the red-veined eyes and smells the sour whiskey breath. "Brings back memories of a time that will not come again."

"Yeah, lotta white water flowed over them rocks," Rooster says. "Some folks say this place is haunted—"

"Yeah," Hunky says, "that old ghost story, member? Hell, hit won't never die."

Chance looks at the one-armed man, then turns to Hunky, a chuckle in his throat. "Ghosts? They prowl mostly at night, don't they?"

"Hell, they're here, I can tell you," Rooster says, kicking a road-flattened rusted tin can loose from the sand. He picks up the can and tosses it in the river, watching the metal wedge floating on curls of white foam. "Woods roun heah still full of em."

Hunky snickers. "Yeah, some still cook likker by moonlight, some just chase poontang ... some just stompdown mean."

"Shut up, Hunky," Rooster says.

Chance glances at the large-girded man in frayed denim pants and a unbuttoned shirt falling over a protruding stomach like a parted window curtain. "May I ask your name, sir?" Chance says.

Rooster chuckles, and with a twisted grin, turns his eyes from the shoal to the freckled man in a blue chambray shirt and chukka boots. "You oughta know me, Mistah Cahoon."

"Maybe. I used to live here."

Rooster pauses, bringing his fingers to the folded sleeve. "We met one time, right here. Long time ago. Back when we were no more'n shirttail younguns." Rooster tightens his mouth. "I remember you from that scar on your hand—"

"Hell, Mistah Cahoon, I'm Hunky Hoggen and this here's Rooster Reddoake—"

Chance tightens his fingers gripping the knife. His eyes fall on the scar; he quickly slides his other hand over the reddish disfigurement.

—"And betcha recognize this heah feller, Willy Buck—"

"Oh, my God, talk about ghosts!" Chance says, his voice charged with emotion. "I can't believe this!" Chance looks at the slender man standing near the truck cab with a widening bronze toothy smile: *Willy Buck*. Then he hears voices as if echoes spewing up from the burbling white water: *Hunky* and *Rooster*. He stands silent, stunned, snapped back across time, thirteen again—his burned hand fevered pain; two dark snarling figures stomping around a lightered-knot fire, loosening the fires of hell ...and there again, on the chilled edge of summer night, the barefooted black boy they insult as Dink and Nig, grinning into fire flames lighting the cold gray ashes of time.

"Talk about ghosts!" Chance says. "I can't believe it. What sweet irony—after all these years...."

Willy Buck grins widely, the sun striking his ivory white teeth. "Yessuh, friendly ghosts. Who would have thought, seeing you here again. Not in a million years."

"Willy Buck, you're not going to believe this, but I've been standing here—thinking about when we were boys, boiling peanuts. Now—it's uncanny—you're *here!*"

"So are *we*," Rooster says, glancing at Hunky. "But this time we come as friends. All that boyhood foolishness—hell, can't even member very much of it— washed down the river long time ago."

Fayette County Deputy Wiley Widderson drives slowly across the Willis Bridge, searching the river foliage.

"Wiley, the Mobile County sheriff told me a one-armed man about Rooster's age had been in the jook the night

Rattler Ransum was killed," says Sheriff Ben Henry Swinnard. "Turn yonder on that sand road. Keep alert—"

"Why'd he call you?" Wiley says.

"Sheriff said a man in the Blue Bay Bar west of Mobile remembered a feller talking about a place called Ring Jaw. Said he tried to start a fight with a Mobile shipyard worker over a big blonde woman waiting tables, pulling a switchblade. The bartender threatened to call the police and he left in a hurry in a Ford pickup. He wrote down a Florida license plate number. The bartender told him that Roscoe was an elderly feller, with a frozen arthritic shoulder—he'd been shot in the war— who came in some nights, mostly just sitting alone, drinking a beer. Never any trouble. Said folks there called him the old goat farmer. He mostly raised goats, kept to himself."

"Yeah, could've been Reddoake. He's been kinda quiet lately—"

"Rooster carries his hate long time—way back to when we were younguns. And he was about eighteen. Hell, we were no more than thirteen. I'll never forget that night long as I live—"

"The night he burned the boy?"

"Yeah, Chance Cahoon. We called him Lil Sol. He moved away with his mother after old man Sol Cahoon passed on. Helluva scary night for four barefooted younguns boiling peanuts at the shoal yonder."

Wiley turns to the sheriff, smiling. "Y'all looking for the ghost?"

Ben Henry laughs. "Yeah, Lil Sol wanted to show us there was no ghost." The sheriff pulls away his sunglasses; his jaws tighten in somber reflection. "They come out of the woods drunk and mean, pretending they were the ghost hunting his head. Hunky Hoggen grabbed that boy kicking and screaming, laid a knife blade against his throat and scared us half to death. Hell, I didn't wanna be there after sundown, anyway. Lil Sol thought them rowdies were just bluffing, just teasing.

"Then Rooster branded a S-mark on his hand with a piece of baling wire. But Chance Cahoon never backed up. Wonder what ever became of Lil Sol? Imagine, damn piece of haywire—scarring that boy for life."

"Helluva mean thing—"

"Next day Roscoe called the law, and Rooster came on him with an ice pick in the pool hall—but he ran into the toughest man in Fayette County, just back from the war, not scared of anything. Judge Hawke put both boys in the state reform school. Rooster's momma pleaded with the judge, said with Lige Reddoake off in prison she needed the boy to be home. After a few months, he was released and, hell, he just went on hunting and finding meanness. Hunky, though, served his time, finally clearing his record. He enlisted in the Navy and became a cook, over yonder in Pensacola.

"Then Rooster began stalking Roscoe Ransum—shot at him with his daddy's Colt .45 at that old jook Buttermilk Hill, and ol Rattler hacked off his arm with a machete. After that, he went crazy. Robbed the Scotts Ferry Post Office, shooting up the place with a shotgun, fled into the Dead Lake swamp. Hell, we tracked him with bloodhounds for nearly a week. He spent a couple of years in Atlanta til his momma pleaded with Willy Buck to help get him paroled. Po old lady nearly starved to death.

"Willy Buck even helped Rooster get his momma in the county nursing home, where she died. Willy sees goodness in everyone, even a snake like Rooster. He's sort of a preacher, in a way, a godly man. We enlisted in the Army together. I ran into him once in Korea. He won a Silver Star but you'll never hear him mention it. He came back, went to Chipola Springs College; next thing I knew he was in business, cutting and hauling pulpwood for the mill at Port St. Joe.

"Rooster's been working for Willy Buck ever since. I can't believe he'd sneak off, driving all the way to Mobile looking for Rattler after all these years."

"That's lot of hate, Sheriff," Wiley says.

"Yeah, hate—and he winds up hating himself. Drive slow now. Rooster might run if he sees us."

Wiley steers the cruiser along the sand trail near the river's edge, the morning sun slanting through the hardwoods and vine-tangled foliage. Somewhere a mockingbird throats a long cadenza. Then Wiley hears the river roar. "Look, up yonder. Two vehicles, one a pickup."

Ben Henry jerks off his sun shades. "That's one of Willy Buck's trucks. Stop. I'll just walk up there. Wiley, you take the shotgun and flank around through the woods. If you see a one-armed man, keep your eyes and your sight on him. Hope you don't have to use the buckshot."

"Yessir. You do be careful, Sheriff."

"I'm always careful with ol Nub Reddoake."

Hunky Hoggen stands smoking, listening as Willy Buck and Chance talk. Rooster drifts away, soured by all the sweet reminiscent stories going back thirty years and then spinning forward, layering the unknown years with surprising twists and turns. But Hunky stands childlike, amused, sometimes cackling. Then Hunky looks up, waves away a cloudlet of cigarette smoke, seeing the silver badge and black gunbelt of the lawman, walking slowly with a slight stiff-knee limp, emerging from the woods, his eyes covered with dark sunglasses. Hunky coughs, clearing his tobacco throat. "I'll be damned if it aint our own high sheriff, Ben Henry Swinnard. Howdy, sheriff!"

Chance turns, with the others, seeing the sheriff, his

face shadowed by the broad hat brim, his chest badge gleaming in the sun.

"Morning," says Ben Henry, jerking away his glasses.

"Ben Henry, whatcha doin down heah in these river woods?" Hunky says. "Where's yer deputy?"

"Aw, I'm alone. Just parked back yonder a ways. I like to walk along the river, remembering the old days—"

"Sheriff, betcha don't know this redheaded feller," Willy Buck says, giggling.

"No, don't believe I recognize this gentleman," says Ben Henry, looking at Chance, offering a hand. "Sir, I'm Ben Henry Swinnard, sheriff of Fayette County."

"I'm Chance Cahoon—"

"Hell you say? Good Lord, it's been lotta years," Ben Henry says. "I'd never recognized you except for that red hair."

"Been thirty years."

"Yeah, now aint that strange—all of us meeting up here at Look 'n Tremble," the sheriff says, excitement in his voice. "Now, Chance, all we need is ol Hickernut Hickery—"

Hunky giggles. "Sheriff, R.C.'s working on Willy Buck's truck."

"Yeah, sorta strange, like a ghost," says Rooster sourly.

"Real flesh and blood ghost," says Hunky. "Sheriff, one uh yer old peanut-boiling buddies."

The sheriff pumps Chance's hand and grabs his arm. "Sure good to see you, Chance. *Lil Sol.* Good to see you! Where you living now?"

"New Orleans. I teach history at the university."

"*New Orleans!* Hell, that's not too far away."

"I just wanted to come back, Ben Henry."

"You know about Roscoe Ransum?"

"Yes, his death helped me decide to return."

Rooster suddenly turns toward the truck cab. "Want

a cigar, Sheriff?" says Rooster. "Gotta coupla stogies in the truck."

"No, thank you," Ben Henry says. "But I do need to talk with you, Rooster."

Willy Buck turns toward the truck. "Rooster!"

"C'mon, I'm just gettin a stogie. Hell, I need a smoke." Rooster opens the cab door. "What's all this about, Sheriff?"

"I got a call last night from the sheriff of Mobile County, Alabama."

Rooster slides under the steering wheel, grabs a cigar from the dashboard and plops the tobacco wrap between his teeth. "Mobile?"

"It's in connection with the stabbing death of Roscoe Ransum."

Quickly Rooster's hand's on the revolver; he quickly jams the gun into his belt and pulls the shirt over the Colt. He lights the cigar, drawing deeply, and steps back into the sand road. "Ben Henry, did the Mobile sheriff say who knifed ol Rattler?"

"No, but he asked if I knew a one-armed man from Ring Jaw."

Rooster pivots and pulls the .45 from his belt. Quickly he points the gun toward Ben Henry. "Now, I aint going back, Ben Henry."

"Put that gun down, *Rooster*!" Willy Buck yells. "I warned you—"

"Naw, I don't want to hurt anyone—I'm driving out of here."

"Rooster, you're making a mistake," Ben Henry says, slowly moving his hand toward his gun holster. "We gonna just go to Estiffanulga and we gonna clear up this matter."

"I aint goin. Hell, I aint never been to Mobile!"

"Now, could be mistaken identity, Rooster. I'm just following procedure."

"Just cause I got a prison record, you sonsabitches try to pin everythin on me."

"Give up the gun, Rooster," Willy Buck says. "You're gone get hurt, I'm tellin you!"

"I'm gettin in this truck and I'm driving outta here."

Ben Henry stands firm, his eyes on the revolver barrel, his fingers touching his own .45. "Don't you try it, Rooster."

Wiley Widderson crunches through the forest floor, seeing the four figures bunched on the riverbank. As he softly draws near, mashing the matted pine straw and brush under his police boots, crouching behind a pine tree, he sees the one-armed man backed against the truck cab, a glint of sun on the barrel of the black .45.

Wiley quickly lifts the shotgun to his shoulder, and sights along the valley of the two barrels, his right eye on the one-armed man. A drop of sweat rolls down the deputy's nose. He wraps his right finger around the trigger.

Rooster stands sweating by the cab, breathing heavily, his fingers firmly gripping the revolver. His darts his dark hazel eyes, shifting blankly from the sheriff to Willy Buck to Chance Cahoon.

"Man, you aint gonna shoot the sheriff!" Hunky bellows. "*Damn!* They'll fry yo red ass in the electric chair! I thought you just wanted to come down heah to see an ol friend and have a little fun—"

"Shut up, Hunky," Rooster says. "Or I'll put a slug in your rusty tail."

"Hell, you aint gone shoot nobody," Hunky growls. "Last time you tried you drew back a nub—"

"I said shut up, you damned pissant." Rooster fastens his eyes on Chance. "*You, you*—Chance Cahoon—*you* the redheaded basturd who started all this!"

Chance hesitates, his fingers tighten on the Barlow knife. "Rooster, now I don't really know you. I've just come back for the first time in thirty years. I came for a funeral—"

"You might have one yoself!"

—"I didn't come back to cause any trouble."

"I've got six slugs. You can have one."

"Rooster!" Ben Henry says, turning, his legs spread, firmly defying the Colt and the unknown nerve of its owner, "I'm telling you now—you try to pull that trigger and you gonna pick up your brains all over these woods."

"Hell, I aint gonna answer for the killing of Roscoe Ransum."

Ben Henry tightens his jaws, jerks away his dark glasses. "But you did kill him, didn't you? *Didn't you?*"

Rooster stands mute, his eyes drawn tightly, beads of sweat wetting his face and the darkened armpit circles of his open shirt. *Before me stands the mighty high sheriff, big badge and gun, thinking he's a Korean War hero, limping on that stiff knee, suckin up to the nigger vote to stay on the public tit all these years. He was scart to death, that night, whimperin like a snotnosed youngun . . .and that ol man's basturd grandson, standing yonder, thinkin he's a big shot from New Orleans, better'n everybody roun heah. Burnt hand, hell. Ah shoulda cut off his damn head.*

And the old dyin voice buzzes in my head: You gone pay for this. You gone pay....

Roscoe Ransum sits on the bar stool, draining the last foamy dregs of draft beer.

"Another suds, Mistah Ransum," the bartender says.

"Naw, one's enough. I'm heading on back up to the house."

"Home to your goats, huh?"

"Home to my family of billy goats!" he snaps, self-amused, grabbing his frozen shoulder.

"You don't barbecue em like you usta, Mistah Ransum."

"Naw, getting too old and ugly and feeble. This ol shoulder's kicking up agin. I mostly just feed my herd of goats. They aint like some folks—they don't bother you. Sho beats pulling gophers."

"You be careful," the bartender says, laughing.

"I'll try, Charley."

The stoop-shouldered man wearing a sweat-ringed khaki shirt slides off the stool and walks slowly toward the side screen door. He gazes into the early evening darkness. "I goin out this way—nearer to my old truck."

"Go head. Watch for all that pile of trash in the alley."

"Young feller, I been watching out for trash all my damn life. Goodnight, Charley."

"Be careful, Mistah Ransum."

He hears the dry, flat slam of the screen door and slowly feels his way along the dark, trash-strewn alley between the tin-roofed tavern and a windowless two-story brick building that once had been a hardware and feed store. His blue Chevrolet pickup with a chicken-wire cage for transporting goats sits parked in the unpaved lot behind the dimlit building with a broken neon sign flashing Blue Bay Bar.

"Hey, you, Rattler Ransum!"

"What?"

"You heard me, old man."

"Whatcha want? I'm goin home."

"Remember me?"

"Can't tell much in the dark. Eyes gone bad."

Suddenly flames of a Zippo lighter streak light across the man's face.

"Do I know you?"

"Ought to. You left me with an empty sleeve."

"You, you ... Rufus Reddoake?"

"You're looking at him. Minus a left arm."

"You're a little fur piece from home, aint you?—"

"Tracked you heah, oldtimer."

"*Yeah, I'm old. Too old and arthritic to fight any more. Go way. Don't want no trouble now, you hear?*"

"*Not too old to die.*"

Roscoe searches the darkness, facing the dark figure; he smells the sharp cigar aroma scenting the still night air. "Listen, we had lotta trouble back yonder in Ring Jaw. I left that Chipola Country cause I figgered either you or me would wind up in the pen or a pine box. Been living purty good these last years. No trouble atall. Just let a tired old man go on home—"

"*How bout sendin you to hell?*"

"*Likely I'm going there anyway—*"

"*You old sonofabitch, hell's too good for an ol drunk who'd hack off a feller's good arm with a machete.*"

"*Rooster, you know you come on me firing that pistol. I never bothered you til you come after me. That's when I up and left. I'm gone tell you somethin—meanest thing you ever done was burning my boy's hand, scarring him for life. He was flesh and blood. I just wish I could see him as a man—*"

"*Old man, you'll never see that redheaded basturd agin.*"

Rufus Reddoake presses the button and the blade leaps forth. Rattler detects the sharp snap of the switchblade, and backs away. "Leave me alone."

"*Goddamn you!" Rooster yells. And the man wrapped in dark shadows plunges the six-inch steel in Rattler's stomach, twisting the blade and quickly pulling back. The old man brings both hands gnawing at the wound, blood cascading over his fingers. He breathes deeply, pain stinging through his body. "You lowlife sonofabitch. I shoulda killed you long time ago."*

"*You gone die, old man," Rooster growls.*

Rattler coughs, stumbles, reels backward, then jerks erect, another cough caught in his throat, feeling the sting and the warm blood gushing over his fingers. "You miserable coward, taking advantage of an old man. Why?"

Rufus Reddoake lifts his left sleeve, now unrolled and empty. "See this nub, you basturd. Ever day of my life I feel the fingers on that hand. And ever day I promise myself I'm gone put you out of your misery. Sol Calhoun cut off a man's head, goddamn him, and ruined my daddy's life. My po momma didn't last long after Pa died in that damned ol prison. Now, you ol sonofabitch, I'm taking yuh life!"

Rattler stumbles, then pitches forward toward Rooster. Again he draws deeply from within, his slurred words mere whispers: "You'll pay for this, you'll pay for this, you sorry sonofabitch!"

The knife.

The knife cuts.

With one arm, Rufus Reddoake cuts and slashes and stabs and lacerates and drains blood trickling down Roscoe Ransum's neck and stomach and between his shoulder blades. Slowly, stiffly, then weakly, the victim of Rooster Reddoake's pearl-handled switchblade pitches forward, his face and bloody body thudding to the trash-littered earth.

Rooster stands, a dark alley shadow, looking down at his victim: the bloodied body quivers, then jerks rigidly still and stiff, legs spreadeagled over piles of cardboard boxes, beer and wine bottles, stained newspapers and maggot-infested fried-chicken cartons.

Rooster stays in the shadows, races to the pickup behind the empty brick building, and speeds away into the sultry Mobile night.

Pulse fluttering, rage subsiding, the one-armed man cruises over the Mobile Bay Causeway listening to "Folsom Prison Blues"—Johnny Cash, the man in black, singing his dark lyrics of the prisoner who shot a man in Reno just to watch him die and time just keep dragging on and he knows he can't be free. Free—freedom from the coffinlike suffocation of rottin and dyin in a piss-smelling metal cage like a wounded animal.

He snaps off the tape player angrily, and feels the cold sweating silence with Roscoe Ransum's blood dry-crusted on his five fingers and his blue denim shirt splotched with red droplets from the gouged-out wounds of a tired old man who's been hiding out on an Alabama creek with a herd of billy goats.

Now the chilling reality—cold, premeditated murder discoloring the sharp steel blade in his khaki pants pocket.

From the nocturnal silence, an echo from a pile of trash: "You'll pay for this. You'll pay for this...."

"Drop the gun, Rooster! Drop it *now!*"

Wiley Widderson's quick shrill command from the woods stuns Rooster, who turns, his darting frightened eyes searching the unknown. "What the hell—"

"Drop it, Rooster! *Now!* You're facing two barrels loaded with buckshot!"

Rooster swings back, pointing the old black Colt wobbly toward Chance Cahoon, who quickly moves away from the tree. "Sonofabitch, I'm taking you with me!" He jerks the trigger, the cracking explosion echoing through the woods, the wild shot spewing sand near Chance's chukka boots and thudding into the live oak trunk.

Chance jumps, squatting, colliding with the equally animated Willy Buck. From the tail of his eye, Chance sees Ben Henry drop to his knee, the silver of his revolver glinting in the sun.

Then, quickly, like a bolt of thunder, another echoing explosion.

Ben Henry's .45 bullet slams Rooster back against the truck cab; his gun slowly slips from his fingers and tumbles into the sand. Rooster reels, blood oozing over his shirt, the loose empty sleeve quivering, and plummets facedown in the sand road.

The sheriff rises stiffly from his pained war-wounded

knee, the .45 fixed on the one-armed man sprawled motionlessly before him. "You all right, Chance?"

"Yes, think so. Damn lucky."

"Good Lord amighty," Willy Buck yells. "I thought he'd kill us all! Thank you, Jesus!"

Wiley races out of the thicket, the shotgun barrel trained on Rooster's head.

Ben Henry bends slowly, cautiously, the gun barrel pointed at the head, touching Rooster's neck. "He's dead."

"Sheriff, I shoulda fired—"

"It's all right, Wiley. I wanted him alive. But we got him. What a wasted life. *Damn!*"

"I should have taken that gun when I first saw it in his belt up the road a while ago," says Willy Buck blankly, his shadow suddenly falling over the corpse.

Hunky slowly approaches the dead man, his nicotine fingers trembling, his eyes watery. "Sheriff, now I come down heah with him, but I aint no part of this. I knew he was always goin off somers, but I didn't know nothun bout him huntin down ol Rattler over'n Mobile."

"Hunky, Rooster killed Roscoe Ransum, no doubt about it," Ben Henry says. "The Alabama sheriff said a man leaving the bar saw a one-armed man running down the alley toward a pickup truck. Somebody found a bloody denim shirt over in Baldwin County. Rooster's name was on a W.B. Santee Wood Company credit-card receipt in the pocket." The sheriff turns to Wiley. "Go get on the horn and get us some help up here. Wiley, tell them to hurry. Buzzards be lighting in these trees before long."

"Yessir."

Ben Henry wipes a trickle of sweat from his cheek, and turns, facing Chance. "Sorry you had to come home to this, old friend. I didn't think he had the nerve. But when he turned, shooting, I had to stop him—"

"You saved my life," Chance says.

Ben Henry nods, returning the revolver to his holster. "And ended another." He hesitates nervously. "I've not had to fire a gun in the line of duty since I nearly froze to death in Korea and took a Red Chinese bullet in the knee." He stares down at the man he killed, a widening circle of blood from his chest seeping into the sand road. "Well, Rooster Reddoake's dead and gone. Folks in Ring Jaw will have another story to tell."

Sheriff Swinnard and Chance turn back toward the river, followed by Willy Buck. Hunky lingers, bending over the corpse, embracing Rooster's hat in his tattooed arms, smoke uncoiling from a dangling cigarette.

Willy Buck turns, looking sourly at the corpse. "Using my truck and my credit card to commit murder. My mistake, trying to help a man whose heart was so filled with hate, bent on vengeance. For no good reason. And Hunky, I just don't know about him."

Ben Henry looks back at the lean tattooed man. "Willy Buck, Hunky Hoggen's lost a friend. But Hunky's mostly harmless, mostly liquor talk."

"Not always," Chance says.

Ben Henry squints, glancing at Chance's hand. "Chance, the scar—"

"It's nothing. Not any more."

"Such cruelty, here, so long ago."

"Such a beautiful place, Look and Tremble," Chance says softly, his voice whispery, merging with the roar of the shoal.

Ben Henry smiles. "Yes, beautiful. If the ol *Chapully* could speak, what haunting stories the river would tell."

"The river *does* speak, Ben Henry. Don't you hear it?"

"I suppose."

"Remember what my grandfather told us long time ago?"

"I know he warned us about Look 'n Tremble."

"And he was always telling me, don't run with the heathen—you make your own memories."

"Chance, Uncle Sol Cahoon was a wise man, sort of country prophet. Rooster Reddoake, lying yonder in his own blood I spilled, may have been the last of the heathen. He mutilated and killed an American hero. Few people know Roscoe was highly decorated."

"I had to come back to know that," Chance says. "Such a tragedy, dying so horribly in a pile of trash. First time I remember seeing him, he was a soldier sleeping off a drunk in Hasty Ponds' trash pile."

"Yes, I remember thinking he was just another old sot, drunk when he left, drunk when he came home. Chance, your father deserves a monument in Chipola Cemetery."

"Yessir," says Willy Buck, "big one, like Major MacNab's stone."

"Willy Buck," Ben Henry says, hesitating, "I'm going to try to squeeze into my Army uniform for Roscoe Ransum's funeral."

"Me too," Willy Buck says. "In honor of two brave soldiers, Mistah Ransum and my dad, sleeping cross the water all these years. God bless their souls."

"I cannot believe all this," Chance Cahoon says, shaking his head, then looking warmly at the two men who—like Rooster Reddoake and Hunky Hoggen—had suddenly re-entered his life as if they were ghosts from old boyhood time that had come again. "I thought I'd never come back here. Then I got this strange feeling after Momma died. Suddenly, unexpectedly Mistah Musing telephoned, telling of his death—"

"Major Musing's giving a eulogy." Ben Henry says. "He called me about Uncle Charley Crowe digging the grave."

"Uncle Charley, bless his heart, he sure wanted to try," Willy Buck says. "But he gave up grave digging after putting your grandfather in the ground. Said he had already buried most of his friends. He was just too old. Two of my employees volunteered to prepare the grave. They are all gone now, except Charley Crowe ... a breed of hard men trapped in a time when violence was worn like a badge of honor."

Ben Henry glances through the thickness of riverbank trees—dark and evergreen—and on the water spurs of sun are silvering the rippling eddies. "And blood spilled, staining the sand and the soul, here at Look 'n Tremble. No wonder they say this place is haunted. I'm beginning to believe in ghosts."

Somewhere downriver, in the clear blue morning, two crows grumble and wing away, their animated ebony flaps shrinking to ink dots in the long distance. And the three men stand quietly in the cool tree shadows, the dry, hot unbreathing woods of July surrounding them. They look at the roiling water as if the Chipola River were a part of their being.

16

Taps for a Hero

The lone U.S. Army soldier grasping a silver trumpet at his side stands beneath the magnolia tree foliage, rigid as the fence posts enclosing Chipola Cemetery. The dark-green glossy canopy holds him in shadow. Sprigs of sun poke through the leaves, striking his white gloves, dark crimson Beret and high-gloss boots.

Fifty yards away, three soldiers—rifles canted at parade rest—stand like sentinels, sweat beading on their expressionless faces. Their shadows fall over grayed stones, and leaning broken-wood grave markers rising in wilted grass and briars. The Fort Rucker burial detachment—stern, mute—faces a small knot of people— some in military uniforms plucked from closets, brushed, and summoned to duty as a prideful honor for a fallen comrade. Mourners—men of the World War II generation, slightly stooped, in their seventies; white-crowned women with age-seamed faces—cluster in silence near the earthen cavity and a fresh reddish-yellow clay mound. Barefooted boys in cut-off denim overalls, thirteen and less, dart playfully among the stones, but draw near silently. Somewhere a mourning dove voices an anthem of loneliness in the sweltering July afternoon sun.

Sheriff Ben Henry Swinnard and Willy Buck Santee in U.S. Army uniforms with Korean War campaign ribbons and four others trudge from the ivory-white hearse parked on the sandy, red-pebble road up the slope from Mulejaw Creek. The pallbearers carry the flag-draped Oakwood casket containing the body of Private First Class William Roscoe Ransum, U.S. Army, 1941-1945. With shuffling cadences, their shoes pad through browned grass clumps and sand spurs.

An Army corporal with a lean lantern jaw and three other soldiers stand by the grave, rigidly waiting. The slender corporal snaps a long sharp white-gloved salute as the pallbearers place the casket on the steel frame over the grave. He pivots, quickly saluting lean, white-maned Finus Moss Musing in U.S. Army uniform festooned with gold oak leaves and World War II campaign ribbons, echoes of combat from a Normandy beach to the Rhine River.

Major Musing returns the salute and steps before the casket, his lips trembling while the hot July wind curls his jacket lapel and lifts the corners of the national banner spread over the casket. Smothering afternoon heat falls on his red-sunburnt neck.

He lifts his eyes, seeing Chance Cahoon standing between R.C. Hickery and Charley Crowe under the green funeral awning. The elderly gravedigger, his back slightly bent, holds a sweat-darkened felt hat over his denimed chest.

Beside them, Ben Henry and Willy Buck stand mute, soldierly, sweat beads shining on their faces. Major Musing squints into the cloudless sky, gathering thoughts of a battle-seasoned GI who once served his infantry command. Suddenly, overhead, a crow loops out of the blue afternoon, caw-cawing, and wings away.

Then Moss Musing speaks, his words firm, reverent, measured: "We bid farewell to Private First Class William

R. Ransum. He was a remarkably brave soldier, an unselfish man, a true American hero. His service in World War II brought proud and noble honor to our country. We honor him. We salute him—the best and the bravest soldier I knew in Europe.

"Roscoe was not a violent man implied by the name so familiar to many of you. Rather he was a kindly man—but violence shadowed him. And, in the end, on a dark night, Roscoe Ransum—crippled by life and pain of his war wound—surrendered his remaining years in a dastardly cruel, unspeakable act of violence. We may draw from the Old Testament Psalmist, chanting the unanswered question: Why do the heathen rage?"

Chance hears:

The Lord knoweth the way of the righeous, and by His way the ungodly shall perish.

He that sitteth in the heavens shall laugh.

The Lord shall have them in derision.

Then shall he speak unto them in his wrath.

And vex them in his sore displeasure.

"Yet we should not, my friends, dwell on his inglorious passing at the bloody hand of a vengeful murderer in a place far from Ring Jaw. Rather let us rejoice for his good nature and his unselfish allegiance to his friends. Indeed, let us honor and remember his heroic military service.

"Roscoe never really spoke of his war experiences, for in doing his duty, he asked no personal glory. He believed the real heroes did not come home, and indeed they did not. He preferred that they—the fallen—be remembered for their last full measure of devotion, giving all in honored sacrifice so we may live in freedom...."

Chance hears Major Musing's soft-spoken phrases, a eulogy from the heart of an Army infantry commander who scampered onto Omaha Beach with Private William R. Ransum on D-Day, enduring unmercifully the German machine-gun fire; then stood in a French field with him as General Omar Bradley read the citation for bravery.

Chance's eyes turn to the stones of his ancestors. *Now they rest, stilled in the quiet depths of death and now beneath the granite and marble standing against the sun and the hot blue sky. Ever more they are summoned here, their years gone in the haste of time—their lives so once vigorous, so animated in the bosom of family and friends, their laughter and their voices fused with the earthly sounds and the sweet lyrical rise of a morning birdsong. And now all that was has narrowed into the few sharp lines cut in cold stone to bleach and endure as silent remembrance.*

Whisks of hot July wind strike his freckled face, and softly stir the red clay at his feet. The breeze turns the leaves of the distant magnolia tree where the bugler stands, awaiting the moment that his breath will fill the trumpet with "Taps." Chance listens to Moss Musing's somber farewell, his eyes turning to old stones in the shadow of Major Malcolm Grant McNab's granite tower of remembrance. *And their voices are now mere echoes caught in the memory of the living who come here on missions of sorrow and remember and say goodbye and go away from the silence, knowing they too will someday know the stillness of the quiet depths of death.*

Major Musing pauses, hesitates, turning Biblical: "Yea, though I walk through the valley of the shadow of death, I will fear no evil, for thou art with me.... And may you dwell in the house of the Lord for ever ... from this time forth, and ever for evermore." Then the major raises his voice: "Farewell, noble soldier. Farewell, my good friend. *Farewell*. May God rest your soul."

Ashes to ashes, dust to dust.

Chance sees Moss Musing's age-lined face clenched with emotion as he snaps a salute as if he were still a soldier in a war now receding into history. And the riflemen bring their guns to their shoulders—quick loud volleys shatter the silence and roll across the cemetery, echoing explosions reverberating through the green-mass of trees fencing Mulejaw Creek. Bird wings flutter in treetops. Then the riflemen freeze again at parade dress.

Tears wet Chance's eyes as the Army corporal speaks of the nation's gratitude and presents him the flag, delicately squared and tightly folded by the gloved hands of the four young soldiers. He embraces the soft, sun-warmed fabric, thinking of his own Air Force service during the Korean War when the flag snapped in the wind and covered caskets and always was there, a comforting beacon for America.

Then his eyes turn to the distant soldier, a shadow under the mass of green leaves. The bugler brings the horn to his lips and the sound of Taps spills forth in lyrical, soldierly rhapsody over the hot smothery parching afternoon.

Private Ransum now rests alongside the others.

"I'm glad I called you," Moss Musing says, standing by the grave, his arm embracing Chance Cahoon's shoulder. "Your father would be proud of you—proud you came to be with him in this final hour."

Chance, holding the folded flag against his chest, nods, a slight smile parting his lips. "Major Musing, your words were most kind, from your heart. A soldier paying tribute to a comrade. I shall cherish your thoughtful remembrance."

Major Musing smiles. "I just wish I could have done more for a man I came to admire greatly. And, Chance, I regret you found yourself confronted with that horrific Look and Tremble tragedy. Looking down a loaded gun barrel is terrifying. I know."

"Ben Henry had no choice—"

"And that Reddoake feller's out of your life."

"Strange, bizarre, all this."

"Justice, maybe? Slaying Roscoe Ransum's killer after he takes a shot at his son. Him trying in his warped mind to inflict another—indeed, fatal—scar?"

"Yes, maybe justice. We have to believe that."

"Well, young man, you've got a book to write."

"Yes, should be easier now."

"Remember what I said? Your people here in Chipola Cemetery will write your book for you."

"Yes sir, I believe they have. I can see the story more clearly now."

"You must return, Chance. Your heart's here."

"I will, Mister Musing. I will."

Moss Musing extends his hand, firmly grasping Chance's. "Next time you come here Roscoe Ransum will have his own headstone."

"He already has a monument—you brought him into my heart."

"God bless you, Chance Cahoon, and I want to read the book." Moss Musing turns, then looks back into Chance's eyes. He waves a partial salute, smiles, and then walks slowly past the stones to his World War II Jeep parked on the red pebble road next to the Chipola Springs Funeral Home hearse. Pipe smoke trails into the air as he drives onto the highway.

"Mistah Cahoon, sir," Charley Crowe says, standing with Willy Buck, watching two men shoveling clay in the grave. "I want you to know your daddy—God rest his soul—once saved me from them fellers, Rooster and Hunky—"

"You, Charley?"

"Yessuh. Sholly did." Charley grins widely. "Rooster laid that knife agin my throat one night, and I thought ol Charley heah headed for the hereafter. But Mistah Roscoe, he come cross that highway from Mistah Elleck's store lak a wild yearlin, and them mean boys, they musta thought a mule kicked em. They run like scart rabbits. They sho lak to pester colored folks. You no mor'n a youngun back then, livin over on River Road with Mistah Sol—"

"You were a good friend to my grandfather."

"Mistah Sol?" Charley laughs. "Why, he was almost like kinfolks. Sad day that was, me digging his grave, right over yonder. Seems lak hit wuz yesterday. Mistah Sol, now he was good to ol Charley and ol Willy Santee way back yonder when we ran these woods and cooked likker herebouts."

"And you raised Willy Buck—"

"Mostly Aunt Hattie. After Willy Frank died yonder cross the water, Hattie done the best she could. You know, Hattie, she lost two her boys in the war. She's uppen age now. I looks in on her time to time."

"Willy Buck and I were friends—"

"I member you wuz no mor'n ah chile. Willy Buck, heah, now he sho was tore up, you up and leaving heah with yo momma after Mistah Sol passed on. He talked lot bout you."

"I thought I'd lost a friend, Uncle Charley," says Willy Buck, grinning. "But then, all of a sudden, he's back—the same Lil Sol!"

"Sho be. He's just like Mistah Sol Cahoon," Charley says, cracking a twisted smile. "Sho wish my ol friends wuz still heah. But me, I got my memories, and that's purty tolerable—not as bad as it could be. Mistah Cahoon, you made a fine lookin feller. Sholly glad you done come back to be with yo daddy."

Willy Buck pauses. "He's coming back again, aren't you, Chance?"

"Yes, I suppose."

"Hope so," Charley says. "I gotta get on to the house now. Willy Buck, you better look in on Aunt Hattie. Tell her I'll be up there Sunday, fer sho, if the Lord willin."

"Grandma surely looks forward to your Sunday visits," Willy Buck says.

"She ailing some, but I do the best I can for her," Charley says, turning back toward Chance. "You sho remind me of ol Mistah Sol Cahoon. And yer pa, God rest his soul, now there was a *man!* He'd be mount proud of you."

Charley Crowe turns back to the grave, watching the sweating two men shoveling red clay over the casket. Then the bent man places the felt hat on hair white as a bed sheet, and ambles toward the highway, his shadow falling on graves he dug so long ago he cannot remember.

"Chance," R.C. Hickery says, "they say you writing a book."

"Trying to. The idea has taken some unusual twists and turns since I returned here."

R.C. chuckles. "That sure was a good ending for you, down yonder at the river—"

"Aw, c'mon, Hickernut," says Ben Henry, "this man's had enough of Look 'n Tremble—"

"Sheriff, I know he's had a bad time, and thank God ol Rooster Reddoake missed—but look at it this way: our nightmare's over. Think about it."

"Yes, you could see it that way."

Chance pauses, looking across the cemetery. "I suppose Rufus Reddoake will be buried here."

"Yes," Ben Henry says, removing his U.S. Army cap and sweeping sweat from his brow. "Likely the county will have to bury him, over yonder beside his mother and father. He had no family left that I know of—"

"Shame, buried in the same place with the man he murdered," R.C. says dryly. "But this place is haunted with lots of them old heathen."

"Yeah," Willy Buck says, grinning, "like Look 'n Tremble."

Ben Henry turns away, then looks at Chance. "You're staying a while, I hope. We need to get together, talk."

"No, I need to get back to New Orleans. I have classes to teach and a book to write."

"Stay awhile," says R.C., laughing. "We could go boil some peanuts tonight—"

"Not me!" Willy Buck says, chuckling.

"Maybe another time, R.C," Chance says.

"Yeah, y'all let that old ghost rest," Ben Henry says. "Besides, it won't be long before these Ring Jaw boys will be scaring little younguns with another ghost story—"

"You mean *Rooster?*" says R.C.

"I sure wouldn't want to go looking for that ghost," Willy Buck says.

"Scary, huh?" says R.C. reflectively. "But give it time. *Another* killing at Look 'n Tremble? Why these old boys around heah will make up another ghost story and these younguns coming up will believe it. You mark my word. And ol Pigpen Swinnard heah, our high sheriff, he'll be legend, along with you, *Lil Sol!*"

Chance laughs, opening the car door. "One ghost of Look and Tremble is enough for this lifetime."

Driving away from the cemetery, Chance steers slowly beneath the traffic light, blinking a steady redundant yellow-red caution.

Hunky Hoggen stands in the gas station doorway, the Rebel Oil cap visor hiding his eyes, cigarette smoke curling from his nostrils. The tattooed man looks up, grins, stomps the moist butt on the concrete, and quickly lifts a hand in friendly gesture. And his lips move.

Chance Cahoon nods, returns the gesture, then mashes the accelerator. The Ford sedan gains speed. He passes Ring Jaw School and the ghostly boarded-shut building that once had been Elleck Dunkane's store. Chance glances in the rearview mirror: the town recedes rapidly from him, back yonder, beside the road, in the golden wash of a July afternoon.

Now Ring Jaw—and the river—again are another memory.

Epilogue

Now Ring Jaw's just a small old town with sleepy, unhurried streets. Salt-of-the-earth people rise in morning earliness, and in the cool of the evening they sit on front porches shelling butterbeans and listening to another day creeping into night's bosom.

It's just another town where two roads cross under the winking traffic caution light, a metaphor for the tick of time. And the people weather the years with back-fence and post office neighbors, and tend gardens growing blood-red tomatoes and yellow corn and Crowder peas and butterbean vines. Sometimes they walk quietly among the Chipola Cemetery gravestones, remembering.

The town shares the Florida Panhandle's redundance of many crossroads and smaller, obscure ink dots on state highway maps.

The place in the West Florida sun so much the center of my youth clings to comfortable smallness in the Twentieth century sunset years. I still go back, searching for friendly yet elusive ghosts.

The town I knew—village, hamlet, crossroads, flyspeck, dot on Florida highway maps; describe as we may in stories we tell—clings to the side of the road as if no one notices much anymore.

There are only tatters, remnants and fewer older faces from the Great Depression and World War II generation when Ring Jaw was mostly pinch-penny, patched-pants hardscrabble life of West Florida's pineywoods.

291

Yet memory can cast aside the old bleeding wounds and crystallize the Good Times of coming-of-age innocence and country road isolation. A Bigger World came narrowly through static-slurred radio, newspaper boxcar headlines and familiar faces in military uniform returning to tell war stories and others in flag-covered steel caskets.

Timbers creak and rot, time erodes, leaving only the wrinkled, wilted residue of a country town that was the place to be—as I was, a boy counting teens, brushed ever so gently by four war years on faraway fields of the 1940s.

Ring Jaw lingers as creaking antiquity, yet a friendly specter. The town smokes through memory with lyrical Glenn Miller's sweet moody swing and the Andrews Sisters' jumping GI jive, the funny papers' adventure of Terry and the Pirates and Joe Palooka and Little Orphan Annie and the patriotic Elton Britt singing "There's a star spangled banner waving somewhere" on the Wurlitzer jukebox in Ruby's Café.

I walk streets once rutted by farm wagons and Hoover carts and stained with horse and mule droppings and the spilled blood of hard, violent men the quiet civil folks then called "The Heathen."

I still search for whispers, remembering.

It may have come together in the crossroads: The place of hot biscuits and brown gravy and a jukebox and gossip gatherings in Ruby's Café, across the highway from the one-room wooden U.S. Post Office. And along the sandy River Road, with barefooted boys stomping around atop Tom-walkers and spinning tops and shooting marbles and growing up with the world at war; in the Tupelo Theatre with cowboy heroes Bob Steele and Charles Starrett riding across the silver screen; at the patent-medicine drugstore and Dixie Bus Stop with Roscoe Ransum home and war guns silent.

I may have found it in the sharp aromatic grocery and tobacco scents and the stories and the laughter in Elleck Dundane's store. Or in the wind in the tall trees of the Pine Thicket riding the Flying Jenny. Or on the porch of the Ring Jaw Mercantile Company where The Old Man told stories and shirttail boys embellished the tales into country-town legend.

And yet now—walking where once I ran and grew up barefooted, much too young for the draft and Army olive drab and sailor blue and the big war—the juiced-up war years sweep back the boyhood adventure everywhere on the sandspur-fringed sand trails of Ring Jaw.

I go back to Ring Jaw; I never really leave.

Sometimes now, in the night, as I write, finishing the last chapters of my book, I think of Ring Jaw and the river as if I'm there. I think of Look and Tremble, the stony shoal spitting white water; of my Grandpa and Rattler Ransum and my boyhood friends Willy Buck, Ben Henry and R.C. and others animating my dirt-poor boyhood remembrances.

They are characters of an unending dream, for imaginative writing must unfold an uninterrupted dream. And I now feel as if it all were a dream—part fantasy, part imagination, part nightmare, but the reality of my innocent time in a small place.

The stories I tell will not be believed—unless you were there.

Maybe the stories are really nonfiction-fiction or maybe the phrase reversed—the genre of facts woven in fictional narrative. These stories haunted me for thirty years.

Only the crude disfigurement on my left hand and Grandpa's old Barlow knife once were the only visible fragments of that old lost time, both painful, both scars.

Now too I see the old faded and frayed Red Goose shoe box, once shelved away and mostly forgotten, standing on my bookshelf with faded cherished relics and medals of the man who wrote of his love as my father. The World War II soldier—an unsung hero, really—wasted his life that ended in back-alley terror that cruel destiny wrought for William Roscoe Ransum.

I often look at portraits of Jeremiah Cahoon and Major MacNab, hanging on the wall in a cluster with the snapshots of my father in France and my mother at Look and Tremble with her son in her arms. And I treasure Jeremiah's frayed Confederate jacket and the broken Federal saber—relics boxed and behind glass, hanging among the books.

My bastardy origins once had been unassuageable emptiness, another scar on my innermost soul. Now my father—coming into my life after his death—lives fondly in my heart. And now Momma rests in a grave beside him. She once vowed she would never go back to Ring Jaw, not even in a pine box.

But she would be pleased, having her remains moved from the cemetery up the Memphis bluff from the wide brown Mississippi River draining a continent. She would like being back home with those she loved, especially the one she could not have in a life tormented.

Now flowers grow on the fresh grave as she sleeps beside Roscoe Ransum in the deep dark earth.

My wife Katherine Ann and my son Sol, walking among the weed-choked, briar-embraced stones, will never know the intricacies of my tortured heredity in a time and a small place—the past ever present, progenitors weathered by the changing seasons.

Winter merges into green and leafy, rain-washed spring, and spring ripens into another summer, dusty and hot and waxing hotter as July brings night as hot as day.

And yonder, still, a river, the cooling, soothing Chipola.

Now—the final strange, bizarre Look and Tremble homecoming; Rufus Reddoake's wasted life ended.

All of my known forebears now rest in the hard red clay in Chipola Cemetery. And down the slope, in a weedy corner, sleeps Rufus Reddoake, the grave unmarked except for a metallic plate placed by the funeral director.

My ancestors' only buzzing echoes are chiseled on stone markers. They bleach gray in shadows of the overpowering granite shaft with an eagle spreading its wings, heralding the memory of a family patriarch who once rode with Nathan Bedford Forrest. Their bones are dust, their stories muted—except for the living keeping them alive.

Yet now still, I hear whispers out of the dust—like ghosts, phantoms—speaking as a light cool summer wind brushes the canopying trees where a slow drifting peaceful river becomes, if only fleetingly, the turbulent white water, sculpting ageless seductive beauty and concealing dark haunting mystery.

And standing on the tree-rooted riverbank at Look and Tremble, as I often do now, with the seasons and the years coming and going, the ancient voices cry out from swift white roiling waters on an unending, serpentine wilderness journey to the eternal salt of the sea.